QUICKER THAN LIGHTNING

It was the moment when you had to jump or walk away. Hart saw it coming, smelled his own fear-sweat and hated Price for making him afraid.

Chad moved, but he was nowhere close to fast enough. Price cleared his holster in a blur. Hart fumbled with his own and waited for the shot, but what he heard instead was an explosive grunt from Chad, as Price clubbed him across the face and put him down. Chad's pistol clattered on the boards.

Hart froze, his guns still anchored in their holsters. Staring cross-eyed down the barrel of a six-inch Colt, he heard Price thumb the hammer back.

"What'll it be?" Price asked.

Please turn to the back of this book

for a special preview excerpt from Lyle Brandt's

JUSTICE GUN

Coming from Berkley Books in August 2003!

THE GUN

LYLE BRANDT

BERKLEY BOOKS, NEW YORK

THE GUN

A Berkley Book / published by arrangement with
the author

PRINTING HISTORY
Berkley edition / December 2002

Copyright © 2002 by Michael Newton.
Cover design by Jill Boltin.
Cover illustration by Bruce Emmett.
Interior text design by Julie Rogers.

Visit our website at
www.penguinputnam.com

ISBN: 0-425-18695-4

BERKLEY®
Berkley Books are published by The Berkley Publishing Group,
a division of Penguin Putnam Inc.,
375 Hudson Street, New York, New York 10014.
BERKLEY and the "B" design
are trademarks belonging to Penguin Putnam Inc.

PRINTED IN THE UNITED STATES OF AMERICA

10 9 8 7 6 5 4 3 2 1

For H.M.L.

Matt Price was stalling and he knew it. He had lingered over shaving, careful not to nick himself with the bone-handled straight razor, which had been handed down through generations of his forebears.

It was curious, what people valued. What they kept and passed along as small mementos of their fleeting lives. The razor meant no more to Price than wicked steel on skin, a close shave every time, but he most likely would have passed it on, had there been anyone in line to take delivery.

It ends with me, he thought. The glass in front of him reflected no emotion at the prospect of his family name's demise.

Small loss.

He was the son and grandson of beleaguered farmers, who had found his own way out of bondage to the unforgiving soil. The razor in Matt's hand was all his father left behind, and it was made in England, the inscription on its flat blade fading but still legible, a mute rebuke to those who gave their lives in the pursuit of some frontier. He had a sister, safely married somewhere in the East, but hadn't seen her for the better part of sixteen years. He wondered, sometimes, whether she would be ashamed of him, if she had known that he was still alive.

No matter. I'm it, for the name.

He didn't think the line would end today, but anything was possible. The young man Price would face at noon seemed capable enough, but he was cocky to a fault and noticeably damp behind the ears. Give him a couple notches on his Smith & Wesson, and he thought he knew it all.

The youngster's name was Billy Bannock, but he liked to call himself Kid Bannock, thinking it would breed respect. Never mind that Billy the Kid was seven years dead, across the line in New Mexico. Names were important, coming up.

On the way down, you couldn't shake them if you tried.

Price finished his shave with a long, last stroke and wiped the razor dry before he checked his pocket watch. More than two hours left, with ample time for breakfast. It had been years since he had suffered any loss of appetite before a contest. Growling guts were a distraction when he needed focus, and the nervous feeling that preceded murder had deserted him so long ago that Price barely remembered how it felt.

It would be Tuesday all day long, but Price put on his Sunday-best regardless. His opponent would be dressed to the nines—they almost always were, except the suicidal drunks—and there were spectators to think about. Some would have come in early from outlying spreads to make a day of it. Price didn't care if they were entertained, but part of him *did* care how they remembered him.

And if he lost the draw this time, the undertaker

wouldn't have to rummage through his things, looking for casket rags.

Price buckled his gun belt last and tied down the holster. The Colt was loose enough beneath the hammer thong. He didn't need to check it to be sure. The piece had never failed him, and it wouldn't fail today. As for his part of the arrangement, Price would know how that worked out a little after noon.

Downstairs, he had the hotel restaurant all to himself. Price ordered steak and eggs, pan-fried potatoes, and a quarter-loaf of fresh-baked bread with marmalade. His sole surviving trait from childhood was a sweet tooth he could never shake, and Price indulged it when he had the chance. A dentist in El Paso once had warned him not to overdo it, but the man was stumped for a reply when Price had asked him why it mattered.

The steak was cooked right through the way he liked it, dark and crisp around its fatty edges from the fire. Elzie Barter, a shooter he had known in Kansas, always dined on near-raw steak before a contest. He'd told Price the last time they sat down together that the blood gave him a taste for what was coming; gave him confidence that he could eat his adversary up alive, if that was what it took.

It hadn't helped that afternoon, of course. The last blood Elzie Barter tasted was his own, after a gunslick half his age surprised him with the second-fastest draw Matt Price had ever seen. The kid had tried to fill his straight a few weeks later when he called Price out in Wichita, but Price had left him in the street.

It wasn't payback. It was simply getting by.

Price wondered sometimes if he had survived this long because he really didn't care who won the draw. It should have been a troubling thought, but nothing seemed to trouble him these days.

Or so he thought, at least, before the boy showed up.

Price reckoned he was ten or twelve years old. His pants were shiny at the knees and held up by green sus-

penders, and the Western Union cap he wore was big
enough to hide his eyebrows and rested on a pair of ears
that brought to mind the bat-wing doors of a saloon. The
kid had sandy-colored freckles and a gap dead-center in
his smile.

"Would you be Mr. Price, sir?" the boy asked as he approached the table.

"It's a possibility."

"You have a telegram, sir."

Price sat waiting. Sipped his coffee, strong and black.
"I get to read it?"

"Sir, it's waiting for you at the railroad office."

"They just send you out to tell me that?"

"Yes, sir."

"We're finished, then." Price passed the boy a nickel
and received another gap-toothed smile in parting.

He was mildly curious about the telegram, less for the
contents than the means by which its unknown sender
had discovered where he was. Price traveled widely and
had no address, per se. A measure of determination
would've been required to learn that he was still in
Arizona Territory, much less in a played-out mining
town called Purgatory, a day's ride north of the Mexican
line.

Price went back to work on his breakfast, eating with
determination now. The telegram intrigued him. It had
been nearly two years since he'd received his last one,
from a sometime friend in Colorado Springs, informing
him the charges had been dropped over some trouble
there. It seemed that no one missed the Skerritt brothers
after all.

The thing about a telegram was that it almost guaran-
teed bad news. Price had no wealthy kinfolk to surprise
him with remembrance in their wills. In fact, he had no
kin at all on speaking terms. The men he trusted well
enough to label friends had mostly fallen by the way. Of
the three or four who still hung on, one had a seven spot
to pull at Yuma, while the rest were scattered far and

wide, from Deadwood to Sonora. Any one of them would spring for drinks if he met Price by chance, but none would write him if their lives depended on it.

So, a mystery.

He finished mopping up his plate with bread and drank down his coffee. Breakfast had taken forty minutes, stretched out thin, and he had time to spare for the short walk to fetch his telegram.

There wasn't much to Purgatory now that all but one small silver mine had been tapped out. Prospectors didn't line up at the general store. The assay office had a sad, neglected look. The younger whores were gone, and even the saloon had fallen on lean times. Price hadn't had to ask if there was room for him at the hotel.

It was a fluke that Billy Bannock had discovered him in Purgatory. Price hadn't been hiding, but he hadn't advertised his presence, either. After Albuquerque and the Harding County war, he had been looking for a place to rest, but trouble found him anyway.

It was the way of life.

Outside, the day was clear and fine. By noon it would be hot enough that Purgatory's name made sense. Price guessed that for the settlers who hung on after the larger mines went bust, it made sense other ways.

He gave no thought to Billy Bannock as he moved along the sidewalk, keeping to the shade. His challenger was full of pride, infatuated with formality and ritual. They had a date for straight-up noon, outside the Mother Lode Saloon, and Price knew Billy Bannock would be right on time. Early would give him time to fidget; late would start tongues wagging that he had a yellow streak, and maybe wet himself.

But he would be there. There was no escaping that.

The railroad office was located at the far south end of Purgatory's one and only street. The east-west tracks lay at right angles to the town, a demarcation line between tenuous civilization and wide-open desert, so disembarking passengers could see the whole of Purgatory—all two hundred yards of it—while they were picking up their bags.

It didn't look like much today, but twelve lean months made all the difference.

Price wondered if his business with Kid Bannock would do anything to help the fading town, or if a gunshot in the street would only be the echo of a hammer tapping on a coffin nail.

What did it matter, either way? Towns were like men: they lived and died. Some reached a ripe old age, while others choked to death in infancy or withered in their prime. It was a preacher's job to say if such things had been preordained.

Price didn't care.

The railroad office was a sweatbox, even with its door propped open. There was no sign of the freckled boy as Price went in and stood before the ticket agent's desk. The agent was a used-up man whose spectacles gave him an owlish look. He hadn't shaved that morning, but the shaky hands and smell of liquor on his breath told Price it had been a wise decision.

"I was told you have a telegram for me," he said.

"Hmm. You would be Matthew Price?"

"I would."

The shaky hands ducked out of sight beneath the counter and retrieved a flimsy yellow envelope. "You'll have to sign for it," the agent said.

Price signed the delivery roster, noting that his was the only wire received in nearly two weeks. It was another sign of Purgatory's failing health that no one cared enough to write. Nothing was urgent anymore.

Outside, he slit the envelope and took the message out. He read it twice, frowning, before he put the telegram back in its envelope and stashed it in the left-hand pocket of his frock coat. He was sweating underneath the coat already, but a sudden chill surprised him, wriggling down his spine.

Somebody's just walked across your grave.

He crossed the street, wide hat brim shading narrowed eyes, and walked north toward the Mother Lode. Price didn't normally indulge before a fight, but one drink wouldn't kill him.

That was Billy Bannock's job, if he was up to it.

The Mother Lode was cool and dark inside. Price was the only customer, except for one old-timer nursing a tequila at the far end of the bar. Price ordered whiskey, drank it down, and waited for the burn to loosen up an unaccustomed knot beneath his ribs.

He thought about the telegram but left it in his pocket. It was heavy—seemed to weigh more than his holstered Colt, in fact. Price thought it might unbalance him until he slipped the coat off, neatly folded it, and placed it on the bar.

He drank another whiskey, promising himself that it would be his last before the fight. Price knew his limits. Knew, also, that he was faster drunk than most men were cold sober, but today was not the time for negligence.

He had a telegram.

Consideration of an answer, if he should decide to offer one, consumed another twenty minutes, more or less. Price waved off the barkeep on his third pass, leaving the man to polish glasses.

Price wished briefly that he had refused to sign the railroad agent's log and take the telegram. There would've been no need to think about an answer then. He could have waited for Kid Bannock in the cool dark without thirsting for another whiskey. Liquor wouldn't help him solve the problem, though. Price had already tried that route, nine years ago, and it had nearly killed him.

No more.

He hadn't sworn off alcohol by any means, but drinking to forget was hopeless. It inevitably failed, and then he had a sick hangover to contend with the offensive memories. He might as well stay drunk, but if Price ever felt like dying there were cheaper, quicker ways to get it done.

Speaking of which . . .

It was 11:50 when he checked the time again. Price snapped his watch shut, stowed it in a pocket of his vest, and drew the Colt. He kept an empty chamber underneath the firing pin for safety's sake, but spun the cylinder and filled it now, taking a cartridge from his belt.

Six shots were more than he should need, but why take chances? Billy Bannock might surprise him after all.

The barkeep watched him put the Colt away, eyes tracking Price as he moved toward the swinging doors and sun-drenched street beyond. "Your coat, mister," the older man called after him.

"If I'm not back inside ten minutes, call it yours."

The telegram would make no difference then. Price wondered whether it would be his last thought or if something else would flash across the inside of his eyelids as he fell. Something to think about, but only for another beat, before he stepped into the brooding heat of Purgatory's noon.

Across the street, Price saw the town's fat marshal and the undertaker who did double duty as a barber, slouched together in the shade outside the dry goods store. He counted better than a dozen faces pressed to windows up and down the street. Those who couldn't resist the show were still leery of catching stray rounds when the guns went off. After some of the fiascos he had seen, Price couldn't blame them.

He waited on the sidewalk until he saw Billy Bannock coming from the general direction of the whorehouse, which some comedian had named the Purgatory Sporting Club. The kid was dressed up like a politician on the stump, the brim of his sombrero curled just so, a high gloss on his boots. Under a swallowtail coat, he wore his double-action Smith & Wesson in a custom holster, butt angled forward for a modified-twist draw. It looked impressive—to a novice, anyway—but Price knew from experience that fancy leather mattered less than steady nerves.

The kid was smiling, playing to his audience for all he was worth. "I wasn't sure you'd make it," he called out as Price stepped down into the street.

"I'm here."

"I see that, now."

"We still don't have to do this," Price reminded him.

The youngster blinked at him. "You think I'm scared of you?"

"I didn't say that."

"And you'd damn well better not. I say you're finished, *Mister* Price."

It was a waste of time to answer that. The kid was twenty feet away from him, the sun directly overhead—or close enough, at least—so neither of them had to squint. Price took the long view, watching Bannock's eyes and his right hand at the same time. The move would come from one place or the other, when it came.

At 12:02, it was the eyes.

They narrowed just a fraction, like a nervous tic, before the kid's gun hand went into action. Price's Colt was clear and locked on target, hammer drawn, as Bannock's fingers found the Smitty's butt. His first shot battered back and forth between the dusty shop fronts, echoing.

Kid Bannock blinked again. He tottered, dropping to his knees as crimson flowered on the left breast of his crisp white shirt. His lips moved, but no sound emerged. Slowly, with grim determination, he began to draw his pistol.

"Let it go," Price cautioned.

If the youngster heard or understood, he gave no sign. The Smith & Wesson wavered, muzzle inches from the dirt. Price let it rise to ankle height before he fired again, taking his time and aiming true to finish it.

Kid Bannock's head snapped back, his hat cartwheeling. He collapsed backward, legs folded under him, and spilled his final thoughts into the dust. Brute instinct let him squeeze the trigger once as he went down, the wild shot smashing glass somewhere behind Price.

A woman screamed back there, the sound cut off as if someone had clapped a hand across her mouth.

Price felt the marshal watching him. He sheathed his Colt and turned to face the fat man, while the undertaker scurried out to take stock of his customer. Another lawman might have challenged him, but Price had judged this one the day he'd ridden into Purgatory. There was less to him than met the eye. His pistol was for show, his job a sinecure, the badge a talisman he hid behind.

He was the ideal lawman for a dying town, which had nothing left to steal.

Price went back into the saloon, reclaimed his coat, leaving it draped across his left arm as he reemerged into the sunlight. Just in case. Sometimes a bit of gunsmoke made the natives restless, turned their thoughts toward hemp and hanging trees. Price didn't get that prickly feeling here, but vigilance was an established habit.

Walking back to the hotel, he passed the marshal.

"Um. Excuse me, Mr. Price—"

"I'm leaving. You can go back to your office now."

"Alright, then."

Packing was the easy part. He always traveled light: a change of clothes, spare cartridges, hardtack and jerky for the trail. He could replenish anything he needed at the dry goods store on his way out of town.

He would be riding eastward, damn it. Even if he chose another compass point to start, Price knew he would inevitably circle back. Despite his personal resolve, the draw was irresistible.

He had the Western Union message memorized. It would not be denied.

NEED HELP. PLEASE COME AT ONCE. REDEMPTION, TEXAS. BELLE.

2

Price made a late start out of Purgatory, east-bound on the Appaloosa gelding that had brought him into town ten days ago. The horse was tired of Purgatory and stamping in his livery stall. He didn't seem to care where Price was going, just as long as they were on the move.

A lot like me, Price thought.

He'd won the gelding in a San Diego poker game—three deuces beat two pair, even when it was aces over queens—and there had been a moment when Price thought the loser might turn froggy, but he had never jumped. Someone had whispered in his ear, perhaps, and told him he was better off afoot than having horses pull him in a box.

The Purgatory Western Union office had a big map on the wall. Price calculated it would take almost three weeks for him to reach his destination if he didn't push the horse too hard. Four hundred and fifty miles, much of it desert with a couple mountain ranges thrown across his path to make it interesting. Twenty-five miles a day might be wishful thinking, but he would do his best.

Need help.

Price knew what it had cost for Belle to send that telegram, but she was also smart enough to know he couldn't fly. Riding the horse to death would cost him time and maybe get him killed, so Price would hold a steady pace and hope that it was good enough.

Kid Bannock and the late start out of Purgatory cut his first day short. He made a forest camp at sundown, Ponderosa pine and quaking aspen all round him, sweet grass for the gelding and a stream nearby. Full dark brought wild eyes out to watch him, green and yellow pinpricks of reflected firelight, but the owners never got up nerve enough to show themselves.

He kept the Winchester nearby and watched his visitors, all the while thinking of Belle.

Her given name was Annabelle; the last name had been Ashton when they met. The first time Price had seen her she was sitting on a cowboy's lap, laughing at some offhand remark. Price had been three days on the road to Amarillo, grateful for the bright oasis of the Lucky Strike Saloon. Off-key piano music, smoky air, and whiskey that could put tears in a strong man's eyes.

Sharing the bar with drovers who had gone ripe on the trail, Price had watched Belle take the cowboy to her crib upstairs. He'd felt the pull of her like something tidal, but there'd been no jealousy—not then or later, even when he realized that she was more to him than just another working girl.

Price understood such things. People did what they had to do, got by the best they could. He couldn't offer any woman hearth and home, regardless. Promises were empty when a person lived from day to day on borrowed time.

The cowboy hadn't taken long. He came downstairs red-faced and sheepish-looking, as if he'd maybe been too quick on the draw. Price noted that his honey-haired companion didn't mock him like some working girls might do, for sport. She'd left him with a vestige of his dignity intact and moved along in search of someone else to help the night go by.

The moment that their eyes locked Price had felt a spark between them. When she stood beside him at the bar and asked him if he wanted company, he'd answered yes without a second thought. Later, upstairs, she'd ridden him as if he were a mustang primed for breaking. Afterward, exhausted as he was, Price wanted more.

He *needed* more.

That's how it had started, with the need. It was a new sensation for him. Wanting had been all he'd known before Belle, coming off a dry spell with an itch that anyone could scratch. Need left him with an empty spot inside that wanted filling—and an ache that came from knowing it could never be.

He hadn't planned on staying more than two, three days in Amarillo but it had stretched into a week, then two. He spent each night with Belle, monopolizing her time until the Lucky Strike's proprietor complained. Price paid him off and someone else had clued him in, and the little man returned Price's money with apologies for interest. Price had let him keep it, tossing in some free advice. If there were any repercussions after Price left town, he'd hear of it and see the barkeep later, in an unforgiving mood.

There'd been no question of him settling down in Amarillo—settling anywhere, in fact. A shooter travels. If he isn't chasing trigger work he's ducking men who want to lay him out. A stationary target doesn't last.

Sleeping among the pine trees that night he dreamed of Belle, the first time in a year or more, but lost the details of it as he woke to early sunlight streaming into the clearing. Breakfast was the past night's sour coffee and a strip of jerky that would last him well into the morning. Price was on his way before the sun burned off a layer of ground mist, riding easy through a forest that reminded him of something from a children's fairy tale.

He found the desert where he'd left it, stretching fifty brutal miles across the line into New Mexico and washing up against the foothills of the Cedar Mountains like a windswept sea of rock and sand.

Price knew this land from grim experience. It didn't frighten him, but it held no implicit welcome for him either. He was packing extra water bags against the heat and stopped at intervals to let the Appaloosa drink out of his hat.

The dead land gave him time to think. There was no place for an ambush, when he could see a rider's dust an hour before he saw the man. Night was the time to worry, when he couldn't see and might not hear a stealthy tracker closing in. Trail markers on the journey were an axle-busted wagon and the bleached bones of a mule scattered by scavengers. Price wondered briefly where the mule's owner had gone, then put it out of mind.

Please come at once.

Ten years, two months and seven days had passed since Price last heard Belle Ashton's voice. She had been telling him to get out of her life and stay out, take the stink of gun smoke with him. There had been no point in arguing. Next morning, riding out of Amarillo bright and early, Price imagined he had glimpsed her watching from an upstairs window at the Lucky Strike, but by the time he turned his head the curtain had dropped back in place and she was gone.

If she was ever there at all.

It was a killing that had pushed her over. No surprise in that, though she had known his line of work from the beginning. Knowing it was one thing, Price supposed, but seeing it up close was something else.

For years he'd blamed the Farrell brothers, Ike and Jubal, putting it on them until he'd finally admitted to himself that it had been his own fault, just as much as theirs. It was inevitable, probably, that Belle would see the dark heart of his world one day and turn away from him in loathing.

Just thinking about those brothers made him simmer, even now.

Price had killed the elder Farrell, wall-eyed Micah, in the last week of October 1878. It was business—a range war in Grant County, Kansas—but the family took it hard and let it fester. Ike and Jubal caught his scent and rode it all the way to Texas for the sake of blood and honor. They had time to think about it riding south, though, and decided that a sneak attack was safer than a stand-up fight.

So much for strategy.

They'd spent a quiet day in Amarillo, sniffing after Price and working out his moves. Their second night in town they took a pair of Lucky Strike girls up to bed, then coldcocked them and rushed along to Belle's crib in their stocking feet. Ike cracked his shinbone when he kicked the door and he was hobbling when they broke it open on the second try, Price standing naked to one side and blazing with his Colt as they came through.

It took five shots to put them down and Belle was screaming at the sight of all that blood. Her voice was hoarse and ragged when she told him to get out and not come back.

Price went along with it because he had no choice. He couldn't make Belle want him, any more than she could hide the loathing in her eyes. Renting her body by the hour held no appeal for him after the spark was gone. Some things, when lost, can never be regained.

He hadn't known that at the start, of course. From Amarillo he had ridden north, done some business in the Oklahoma panhandle before circling back two months later. Price reckoned Belle would've had time to put her mind at ease, forgive and forget.

Instead he'd found her gone.

The way they told it at the Lucky Strike, a peddler had stopped in a few days after Price left town. One look at

Belle and he was lost, head over heels. She must've felt
the same or near enough, because she'd married him the
fourth or fifth time he proposed, after he settled up her
debts in town and bought out her contract. They were out
of Amarillo, headed south. Nobody seemed to know exactly where they'd gone.

Redemption, Texas.

Price had nosed around some more until he got the
peddler's last name—Mercer—and thought about pursu-
ing Belle but finally gave it up. He had nothing but grief
to offer any woman who cared for him and Belle had
forcefully removed herself from that sorority.

If she could move on, so could he.

But sometimes, deep down, it still hurt.

His fourth night on the road, Price camped out in the
Cedar Mountains and refilled his water bags the next
morning before riding on. More desert after that, and
dusk on day five found Price in Columbus, kissing close
to the Mexican border. He found a room, stabled his
mount, and settled in to pass the night.

Columbus was a rowdy place, like most border towns.
Farmers scratched the dry soil for a living or turned their
long-horned cattle out to graze at will on brittle grass.
The Indian problem was more or less settled, but rustlers
and sundry border trash still worked both sides of the
line, swinging a wide loop from Las Cruces down into
Chihuahua. Rangers and *federales* chased them back and
forth, killing more harmless peons than outlaws, solving
little or nothing.

It kept the town's blood up, the locals constantly defensive, either spoiling for a fight or dreading one.

There had been trouble last time Price passed through
Columbus, sixteen months ago. The sheriff's drunken
nephew had a need to prove himself the better man,
egged on by so-called friends who wanted blood no matter whose it was. Price hadn't killed him, but stomach
wounds were slow to heal and sometimes interfered with
control of bodily functions. A posse dogged Price for

three days after that, and he'd stayed clear of Columbus ever since, despite reports that the sheriff had been fired and slapped in jail for looting county funds.

Now he was back and all he wanted was a good night's sleep. Price gave the hotel clerk a made-up name and wedged his room's one chair under the doorknob on his way to bed. He left the window shut and latched, so anyone who wanted in that way would have to break the glass.

As Price lay down to sleep, his Colt beneath the pillow and his Winchester beside the sagging bed, he steeled himself against the rush of dreams that had pursued him every night since he received Belle's telegram. He woke near sunrise with the half-remembered feel of her beside him, snuggled close, and took his sour mood downstairs to breakfast in the hotel restaurant. The mood burned off only later, after he had been some hours on the trail.

More desert, pancake flat until he skirted the Potrillo Mountains. Twice he reined in the Appaloosa and watched the dust of riders passing to the south, too far away for him to see the men themselves. Five years ago he would've had to think about Apaches, but the government had penned them up in Lincoln County, chasing the ragtag survivors into Mexico. Today he thought about rustlers and regulators, either one of which might shoot first and forget to ask the questions later.

He passed a homestead in late afternoon, remaining well out from the house, beyond Winchester range. Price counted half a dozen horses in a pen behind the squat adobe house, all standing listlessly in the sun. If there was any green to speak of on the place he couldn't see it, nothing in the way of crops or shade trees. This was life pared to the bone, his father's way.

Price wouldn't wish it on an enemy, but there was something to be said for planting roots, even in barren soil.

He was well past the spread before a lanky figure stepped out of the house to follow him with shaded eyes, a rifle glinting sunlight at his side. Price spurred the Appaloosa to a trot and left the squatter staring after him, watching his dust to see if Price turned back.

You're safe from me, Price thought. *I'm not your enemy.*

He slept out that night and the next, reaching El Paso on his eighth day out of Purgatory. Huddled on the border opposite the sprawl of Ciudad Juarez, El Paso was the largest town he'd seen since Phoenix, two months earlier. Its bustling streets felt cramped after the open desert, but it cut both ways.

The crowd that jostled Price would hide him, too.

He had no reason to believe that anyone was looking for him in El Paso, but it never hurt to keep a low profile.

He was in Texas now and that much closer to Redemption.

That much closer to Belle.

Price tried to imagine what sort of trouble would make her reach out to him across the years. Something her husband couldn't handle, anyway. Something that made her swallow the disgust he'd seen in her eyes the last time they'd spoken, with Belle doing most of the talking.

He hadn't yet decided whether he would take the job, spite telling him it would be worth the long ride just to see her face when he refused. He could remind her that she'd picked a man to do for her and she was stuck with him. If Mercer couldn't cut the mustard that was too damn bad.

It came to Price then, for the first time—consciously, at least; he couldn't vouch for those forgotten dreams— that Belle might now be free. Maybe it didn't work out with the peddler or his horse had stepped into a gopher hole and dropped him on his head. Such things were known to happen in the Lone Star State, and worse besides.

If Belle was free—

Price caught himself before the mustang thought could gallop out of lasso range. It made no sense for Belle to speak of trouble—which to Price meant *danger*—if she'd simply left her husband or the man had died. That kind of trouble she could handle on her own, though it might set her thinking back to what she'd given up.

No good, he thought. Whatever else Belle did, she wasn't fool enough to try rekindling what they'd had between them with a lie. She knew Price well enough to understand that it would be the kiss of death.

He was a shooter but he still had certain standards, even now.

The telegram meant trigger work then, or at least the risk of it. Killing was all Price really knew, the only image that a mention of his name inspired.

Killing for Belle, to keep her safe from harm, would've been automatic in the old days—a reflex Price didn't even have to think about.

Today, ten years after she'd cut him loose and sent him on his way, Price knew he'd have to think about it long and hard.

He had enough blood on his hands already, much of it from total strangers, without riding three weeks through the desert to find more.

It's Belle, the small voice in his head reminded him.

And Price had no reply to that.

He bought a bath for fifty cents and soaked the trail dust off in water nearly hot enough to scald him. Supper was a steak charred black, with beans and cabbage on the side. His hotel room was overpriced but only two blocks from the livery stable and his mount. Price slept that night between starched sheets and woke next morning ready for the trail.

Desert and grassland alternated for the next ten days, Price riding southeast on the last leg of his journey, sleeping rough at night under the Texas sky. He watched a quarter moon wax full and heard coyotes wail their serenades, but wild things mostly kept a distance from his fire and let Price sleep in peace.

With one hand on his Colt.

Along the road he passed more homesteads where the
squatters cultivated rocks and weeds; skirted a giant
spread with several hundred cattle on the move; and met
a family of Navajo. Recognizing them by the beadwork
on their buckskins, Price reached up to touch his hat brim
as he passed. They watched him go with eyes set deep in
narrow faces weathered dark. The only man among them
kept an old Sharp's rifle handy but made no move to ex-
tract it from its saddle sheath.

Price wondered whether they were headed toward
some reservation or away from one and how long they
would last in white man's country. There were settlers
hereabouts—and lawmen, too—who would be pleased to
slaughter half a dozen Indians and brag about it over
whiskey someone else had paid for, to congratulate the
heroes.

Price considered warning them but let it go. A waste of
breath, assuming they spoke English. Any Indian alive in
Texas knew the risk better than Price himself.

Red skin or white, the hunted always know.

Mid-morning on the nineteenth day Price sat atop a
grassy knoll and saw Redemption in the distance. It was
just a smudge on the horizon; too drab for a mirage. Price
let the Appaloosa set its own pace on the flats, no hurry
now that he had the settlement in sight.

Belle had waited this long, if a few more hours made
the difference he was already too late.

There was a time that afternoon when Price's goal appeared to be retreating from him, moving faster when he
spurred his mount, then slowing when the Appaloosa
slowed. It was a trick of light and distance, nothing su-
pernatural, but Price was tempted to turn back.

There's no Redemption here, the skull voice whispered
to him. *You've come full-circle. It's Purgatory all over
again.*

"So what?" he said aloud, pricking the Appaloosa's
ears. "It's not like I have somewhere else to go."

Dusk trailed Price into town as if he'd hitched the purple shadows to his mount and dragged them after him across the flats. He rode past shops already closed and found Redemption's one hotel dead-center on the north side of Main Street. It was an optimistic four-story box planted between a lawyer's office, closed, and barber shop, still open if the lights inside meant anything.

Price hitched his mount and entered the hotel. The lobby had a pair of easy chairs set far enough apart that conversation would've been a strain and far from private, but it didn't matter since both chairs were empty. Price's entry rang a little fairy-bell above the street door, summoning a gray man from his office to the registration desk.

It wasn't just the clerk's sparse hair and frock coat that were gray. His skin had taken on a grayish tinge as well, reminding Price of certain deep-pit miners he had known. The clerk's soft hands belied that imagery and left Price wondering if some men took on color in accordance with their lives.

Price had a sudden urge to check his hands for crimson stains but squelched it.

"May I help you, sir?"

"How much the night?" Price asked.

"Two dollars by the night, sir. If you're staying longer in Redemption there's a weekly rate of twelve."

"Two nights for now," Price said, counting the cash out in his hand. He paid the clerk and signed the bulky register. "I'll let you know about the week."

"Of course, sir. If you'd prefer a certain floor—?"

"Two bucks a night, I may as well be up on top."

The clerk managed a constipated smile and handed Price a key labeled 4-D. "We recommend O'Malley's restaurant," he said. "Across the street and two doors east."

"The livery stable?"

"One block farther on."

Price climbed the stairs, paying attention to the view from each landing in turn. It was an ingrained habit, checking visibility and lines of fire. Halfway along to Room 4-D a floorboard groaned beneath his heel and Price made mental note of it.

Most likely he would have no need of early-warning systems. If it went the other way, though, ten seconds made all the difference in the world.

The room was simple but immaculate. Price left his saddlebags, canteen and Winchester behind and locked it up. The hotel clerk was missing when he passed the registration desk again; Price mounted by the time the fairy bell could beckon him again.

He found the livery stable adequate and struck a bargain with the old man who appeared to be in charge of half a dozen mounts and one fat mule. That done, Price walked back to the barber shop, paid six bits for a bath and shave that left him feeling almost born-again.

It was remarkable what soap and steel could do.

O'Malley's restaurant was homey almost to a fault, the chubby waitress looking like she took her salary in trade and wolfed it down. She had a smile ready for Price and recommended the beef stew, which proved to be delicious. Price stopped short of feeling stuffed, passed on the dessert and stepped into a night that had begun to chill off from the scorching day.

He didn't feel like sleeping and his ears picked up the jingle of piano music mixed with boozy laughter, drifting toward him from the east end of the street. Price moved in that direction, studying the citizens who passed him on the wooden sidewalk. They were few and far between at that hour, all moving in the opposite direction, giving Price the illusion of swimming against a mild current.

He knew the wrong side of the tracks when he saw it, even when there were no literal tracks to draw the line. Redemption's red-light district boasted two saloons, facing each other with the dusty street between them, and a drab two-story structure that could only be a cathouse. Price had one foot on the wrong side of the line when something snagged the corner of his eye.

He turned and faced a darkened shop across the street.

The painted sign told him that it was Mercer's Dry Goods, Founded 1881.

Eight years.

He wrestled down an urge to cross the street and instead turned back toward the nearer of the two saloons. It had been christened Trail's End, while its competition on the south side of the street was called The Nugget. Batwing doors spilled smoky light and tinny music out of both to make the street a temperance worker's fair idea of Hell.

Price entered the saloon and wound his way past poker tables to the bar. He ordered beer and was relieved to find it served below room temperature.

"I know you."

Price half-turned to face the woman who had spoken. She had cherry-colored hair in ringlets falling to bare shoulders and breasts that challenged the bodice of a low-cut scquined dress.

"That right?" Price asked.

She nodded, smiling coyly. "You're Matthew Price."

"You have me at a disadvantage, ma'am."

"I'd say it was the other way around in Wichita, two years ago this June."

"I do hate to insult a lady."

"But you don't remember me?" She kept the smile, twirled ringlets with a finger.

"My mind isn't what it used to be," he said.

"Too much trail dust," she said. "Too much gun smoke."

"I wouldn't argue that."

"Man needs to rest from time to time," she told him, moving close enough to let one breast graze Price's arm. "You want to rest with me tonight? Be like old times."

"I'm flattered, Miss . . ."

"Rowena."

"I'm afraid I wouldn't do you any good tonight, Rowena. I've been ridden hard and put up wet."

"Sounds good to me."

Something was coming back to him from Wichita, a sweaty image fogged by alcohol and lust. There was a heart-shaped birthmark, just above—

"Maybe another time."

She had a way of smiling, even when she pouted. "If you're sure?"

"I'll kick myself tomorrow, I've no doubt."

"Come back around, I'll kick you too, if that's what it takes."

Price tipped his hat and left his beer half-finished on the bar. Leaving, he checked the place for any more familiar faces that he might've missed and spotted none.

It seemed like a long walk back to the hotel, but it was barely nine o'clock when Price finished securing his door against the night.

Habits die hard.

Some men, likewise.

But not tonight, Price thought, slipping the Colt beneath his pillow.

Not tonight.

3

"I could do without that moon," Lee Fowler said.

"More light to work by," Perry Hart replied, his harelip getting in the way a bit.

Fowler was not appeased. "More light for them to see us by, you mean."

"Won't matter," Chad Saxon reminded him. "Nobody's running to the marshal when we're done."

"Marshal." Joe Orland's laughter could've been mistaken for a snort from his roan gelding.

Fowler shifted in his saddle, spat tobacco juice into the night and cut a sidelong glance at Saxon on his left. "It's not the law I had in mind."

They were already five miles north of town and nearly halfway to their destination. It was coming up on ten o'-clock. They had the road all to themselves, riding four abreast.

"You're thinking about Kelsey's Winchester," Hart said. His smile was crooked from the scar that marked his upper lip.

"It crossed my mind," Fowler admitted.

"For a man who rode with Quantrill's Raiders," Saxon said, "you've got a funny nervous streak."

Fowler knew better than to take offense. "Twenty-five years ago, that was. I learnt a thing or two since then."

"Like how to fret," Hart goaded him.

The weight of Fowler's big Colt Navy pistol on his hip reminded him that he could blast Hart from the saddle for his sass, but that meant killing Saxon too, and maybe Orland. Fowler wasn't sure he could take two of them, much less all three—and if he did, what then?

Where could he hide in Texas if Sedge Rankin put a bounty on his head?

"They ain't expecting us," Saxon reminded him. "They're prob'ly all asleep by now."

Fowler had six or seven years on Saxon but he couldn't match the younger man's enthusiasm for a killing. He was not afraid of bloodshed—never had been—but sometime within the past ten years or so he'd lost the craving for it. Killing was a job like any other, cut and dried, but there were always risks involved.

It helped that Rankin owned the local law, but that was only part of it. Lee Fowler didn't want to die tonight.

"One man," Hart said. "That's nothing."

"Four of them, all told," Fowler replied.

"Two women and a brat." There was a sneer in Saxon's tone. "I understand you've done that kinda work before."

Fowler couldn't deny it. Quantrill's rule had been no prisoners and chivalry be damned. They'd taken what they wanted as they found it, in the old days. Frank and Jesse had been famous for it, old Arch Clements and the Youngers.

Dead or doing time now, all of them.

Fowler expelled another stream of juice, blood-black by moonlight. "Let's just get it done," he said.

Hart's wheeze of laughter made his hand twitch on the smooth butt of the Navy Colt.

Another time, he thought and let the sorrel carry him along.

Fowler's companions made an odd assortment. Perry Hart, the youngest of the four at twenty-three, had short red hair and freckles underneath a wide-brimmed hat. He'd given up on growing whiskers to conceal the hare-lip, but a matched set of Schofield break-top .45's drew attention from his narrow face. He'd grown up fighting over childhood insults, quick to rile and often short on common sense.

Joe Orland was the next youngest, at thirty-two. He had brown hair and muddy eyes that lost their focus when he started swilling whiskey. Rumor had it that he'd done a couple years for rustling in New Mexico, but Fowler couldn't swear to it. Orland wore a Remington Model 75 Army revolver on his left hip, reversed for a cross-hand draw, but he preferred a Greener double-barreled shotgun if he had a choice. He was a back-shooter who drowned his ghosts in alcohol.

Chad Saxon was the ramrod, Rankin's favorite. That didn't make them friends or equals, but it gave Saxon an arrogance that worked on Fowler's nerves. Saxon had dark wiry hair and a thick mustache screening teeth like chips of yellowed ivory. Between his rancid breath and body odor Saxon had a rough time with the ladies, but he bought or took by force that which would not be freely given. He had killed nine men that Fowler knew of and was prone to boast of more.

Fowler, for his part, had done more killing than the rest of them combined but he'd grown out of any need to brag about it. He appreciated steady pay, and if that meant he had to pull a trigger now and then, so be it. When it came to shooting, he remembered one verse from his mother's Bible:

It is more blessed to give than to receive.

Amen.

Wishing a cloud would mask the moon's skull face, he rode on with the others, keeping one hand on his gun.

• • •

Light sleeping is a farmer's curse. He needs to hear a fox among the chickens, creaky hinges on a barn door that was latched at sundown, or the restless lowing of his cattle when they ought to be asleep.

A farmer keeps his weapon close at hand, where he can find it in the dark.

Arthur Kelsey was wide awake before the scattered fragments of his dream had time to fade. Uncertain what had roused him, he lay still and listened to the prairie night. There was no wind to speak of and the house was silent. Rachel lay beside him with her back turned, knees drawn up and favoring her belly even now, before the baby had a chance to show. Young Thomas was dead quiet in the loft and Rachel's mother wasn't snoring for a change.

Something . . .

He lay still, closed his eyes against the darkness, listening. Another moment and he knew his pulse would start to echo in his head like marching drums.

A muffled sound brought Kelsey bolt upright in bed. His sudden movement startled Rachel. Dreamily, she muttered something Kelsey couldn't understand.

He pressed a hand over her mouth and felt her stiffen, wide awake and trembling. He whispered to her in the dark, lips close beside her ear.

"Be quiet. We've got company outside."

Kelsey rolled out of bed, barefoot on smooth timber, hefting the weight of his Winchester '73. He worked the lever action, chambering a cartridge. It was almost loud enough to cover Rachel's stifled sob.

He knew the layout of the house by heart, had built it from the dirt up with his own two hands and Rachel's help. Moving around the kitchen table and its straight-backed chairs, he found the bed where Mrs. Chalmers slept. Kelsey bent down, covered her mouth as he had done his wife's and said, "Wake up. There's someone in the yard."

The older woman nodded once, lips tight against his palm.

They all knew what it meant when uninvited company showed up at night.

I've maybe got an edge, thought Kelsey, *if the bastards think I'm sleeping.*

Maybe had an edge, and maybe not.

It would depend on numbers, what they wanted, whether they were careless or alert—so many different things, in fact, that Kelsey gave up counting variables.

He had twelve shots with the Winchester without reloading. If he made the first one count he just might have a chance.

Kelsey had never killed a man or truly wanted to, but there were limits to his easygoing nature. Even peaceful, law-abiding men will snap if pushed too far. This, now—

Turning, Kelsey almost collided with his wife.

"Christ, woman!"

"Arthur—"

He shushed her. "Wake Thomas and keep him quiet."

"But—"

"Go on!"

The darkness wasn't perfect now that Kelsey's eyes had started to adjust. There was a razor line of moonlight down the center of each window, where the shutters met and latched. Same thing around the door, but nothing wide enough for him to scan the outer yard. Crossing the room, he made a point of stepping wide across a noisy floorboard halfway to the door.

Fix that sometime, he thought, hoping he'd have the chance.

A shuffling sound of horses in the yard made Kelsey's hard hands tighten on the rifle. He couldn't count the riders without seeing them, could not repel them without making himself a target.

The night would help him there. It cut both ways.

Moonlight outside to make his targets visible, but he would also be exposed.

Kelsey considered getting dressed but knew he didn't have the time. Whatever the nightriders wanted, he was bound to resist them with everything he had.

Get on with it!

Kelsey unlatched the door and turned to Mrs. Chalmers. "Bar this after me," he said, "as soon as I'm outside."

He saw her nod, pinch-faced, holding the kitchen cleaver in one hand.

The door's hinges were silent, lately oiled. Kelsey slipped out and shut the door behind him, waiting for the wooden beam that was his backup lock to make its telltale sound. A long two seconds passed before he heard it fall in place.

By that time Kelsey had them spotted. Three men near the barn, two of them already afoot. The third man sat astride a sorrel mare and held the other reins, watching his friends.

He should've paid attention to the house.

Kelsey shouldered his Winchester, aiming at a point midway between the mounted stranger and the two on foot. One of them fiddled with the barn door's latch and cursed the other man for standing in his light.

"That's far enough!" Kelsey called out to them. "Throw up your hands!"

Kelsey hadn't considered what to do with them if they obeyed. As it turned out, he didn't need to think about it.

"Squatter!"

Kelsey flinched. The voice came from behind him.

And he knew that he was dead.

The farmer could've done most anything, but he surprised Joe Orland when he fired the Winchester. It was hellacious loud, a sharp *crack* that rebounded from the barn to slap at Orland's ears.

His roan shied from the noise and did a little dance

that threw his aim off. Orland cursed and yanked the
reins, dropping the Greener's muzzle for a body shot.

It should've been an easy kill, but once again the
farmer managed to surprise him. Pivoting on bare feet in
the dust, he jacked another round into the rifle's breech
and blazed away at Orland from a range of twenty feet or
less.

Joe felt the bullet sizzle past his face and jerked the
Greener's forward trigger, letting go the right barrel. In-
credibly, he missed, blasting a spray of dust and shavings
from the wall beside his target.

Blam!

This time the bullet plucked at Orland's jacket, snip-
ping fabric. Orland lunged across his saddle with the
Greener thrust ahead of him and fired his second buckshot charge.

The spray of mist was crimson, Orland's target sprawling backward with his arms outflung like Jesus on the
cross. Dead center that was, with the emphasis on *dead*.
The farmer's feet thrashed dust awhile, before his life ran
out.

A woman screamed inside the house.

Lee Fowler spurred his sorrel mare across the yard and
reined in smartly next to Orland's roan. "What's wrong
with you?" he snapped. "That bastard nearly took my
head off!"

Orland might've sassed him if he hadn't fired both barrels on the Greener, but his hands were full and Fowler
was a pure-dee pistol fighter from the old school.

"Sorry," Orland said. "I didn't think he'd fire."

"Don't think next time. Just shoot."

"I will."

"See that you do."

Orland could feel his hackles rise. "I said—"

"You ladies 'bout done there?" Saxon called out to
them across the yard. "We still got work to do."

"Mind what I said and watch the house."

Fowler turned back to join the others. Orland made a

face at his retreating back and broke the Greener open,
dumped the empties and reloaded with another pair of fat
red cartridges.

The house was dark and silent now, after the scream.
No way out through the back, as Orland knew from
scouting it last week. He watched the front and let the
others do their work.

Saxon and Hart had disappeared inside the barn.
Lamplight spilled out the open door a moment later, troubled horses jostling in their stalls. Whooping and pistol
shots drowned out the other noise.

Fowler reined back before the first horse cleared the
barn, running flat-out across the yard and out of sight.
Three more followed, hammering past Orland neck-and-
neck. Their dust hung in the yard behind them, ghostlike.

Saxon left the barn a moment later, carrying a double-
bladed axe across his shoulder. Hart was close behind
him with the lamp. He hesitated on the threshold, turned
and pitched the lamp into the barn. There came a *whoosh*
and flare of firelight as the flames caught on and spread.

Smoke had begun to show around the barn's eaves,
leaking from the hay loft by the time they gathered in the
yard. Orland ignored the farmer's corpse. That part of it
was done. The man had tried to kill him. Anything that
happened after that was self-defense in Orland's mind.

He thought about the rifle, wondered if it had a mate
inside the house, and kept his shotgun leveled at the nearest window just in case. Saxon approached the door as if
he didn't have a care and knocked with the flat of the axe
blade.

"Miz Kelsey? I believe your man could use some help
out here. He's had hisself an accident."

Long silence from the house before a woman's voice
came back at him. "You go to hell!"

It was an older voice than Orland had imagined—older
than the screamer, certainly. Must be the mother, then.
Two women and a pup remaining in the house after he
took the squatter down.

"You hadn't oughta talk that way, ma'am," Saxon told the house. "Some folks might take offense. Last chance now, if you want to help your man."

Whatever the old lady had in mind to say, she kept it to herself this time.

"Awright, then," Saxon said, "we'll do this thing the hard way."

Drawing back the axe, he swung it hard against the door.

The first blow made the door jump in its frame. The impact startled Justine Chalmers but the older woman stood her ground, the cleaver heavy in her hand. She wished herself a better weapon but the Winchester was Arthur's only gun, and it was lost to them.

At least the men outside weren't shooting yet. That would come later, if they found the axe too slow.

Or maybe they'd just set the house afire.

That would deprive them of their sport, though. She imagined they were working up an appetite.

She heard her daughter weeping, muttering her husband's name.

"Hush, child," she said. "Arthur can't hear you now. We're on our own."

"Where's Daddy?" little Thomas asked.

"Gone on ahead," Justine replied. "You be the man now."

On the fourth or fifth stroke of the axe a long crack opened in the door, spanning a quarter of its length down from the top. Arthur had built a solid house, Justine would give him that.

It was a shame he'd never see his second child.

A shame that child would never see the light of day.

Justine stepped closer to the door, although it frightened her to do so. She'd survived her share of frights in fifty-seven years—Apaches, cholera, rustlers and floods—but this bid fair to be the last. She thought about her husband, fifteen years gone, and wondered if he would be waiting for her at the pearly gates.

It would be disappointing if he wasn't, worse if it turned out there were no pearly gates at all.

Have faith.

The crack was widening, a wedge of axe blade catching on the downstroke, so they had to tug it clear. The bar across the door still held, but it was only timber. They could hack through it or cut an opening and reach inside to lift it clear.

But not for free.

Justine turned to her weeping daughter in the dark and said, "You need to arm yourself."

"Mama, we don't have—"

"Kitchen knives will do if that's the best we have."

Rachel was winding up to start another crying jag when Justine slapped her full across the face. The impact sounded gunshot loud. It numbed her hand and pained her heart.

Thomas was back before Justine knew he had left them, holding up a knife in each small hand. Justine relieved him of a butcher knife and pressed it into Rachel's fist, wrapping her clammy fingers tight around the grip.

"You *will* do what you have to do," she hissed at Rachel. "For yourself and for the boy."

Snuffling, her daughter nodded.

"We can stick 'em, Grammy," Thomas said.

"I wouldn't be surprised."

She calculated there were three or four of them, at least. The different voices told her that, although her hearing wasn't what it used to be and it was possible some of the men knew how to keep their mouths shut.

Stepping into darkness through the door they would be vulnerable—or the first one, anyway. If she could slice him good and proper with the cleaver there would be no stopping all the blood. Might even kill him outright with a fair swing at the head or neck.

The rest won't be so easy, Justine thought.

Even dumb animals learned from mistakes, and once the first man fell the others would be wary. They would use their guns or fire the house, unless they had another pressing need too urgent to ignore.

That need could be their one last chance.

If nothing else, it might allow the boy to slip away.

She thought about her son-in-law, dead in the yard. Justine had seen her husband buried, and her older child, a boy. Neither had lived to reach the fullness of his years. If she could save her grandson now, at least, it would've been a good night's work.

A mangled strip of wood three inches wide and two feet long fell to the floor. By firelight from the barn Justine could see a dark face pressed against the opening.

"You ladies open this here door," the axe man said, "it might improve my mood some."

"Damn your mood," Justine replied.

"Wallflowers, eh?" The stranger giggled. "That's alright, then. I don't mind 'em shy."

He stepped back from the door and showered blows upon it with renewed ferocity. In nothing flat he had a porthole six or seven inches wide.

An arm snaked through, its pale hand groping for the board that barred the door. Justine leapt forward to the sound of Rachel's scream and swung the cleaver. She was aiming for the wrist but haste makes waste. Her blade came down across the forearm in an awkward glancing blow.

"God *damn* it!"

She retreated from the sounds of pain and fury, pleased to know she'd marked one of the raiders, anyway.

And seconds later, when a shotgun blast ripped through the door, she knew it wasn't good enough.

"Still bleeding?"

"Hell yes!" Perry Hart was messing with the red bandana tied around his arm. It had been blue that morning, when he put it on.

"When we get back," Saxon told him, "you best have the sawbones stitch that up."

"Or wait until tomorrow maybe," Fowler said, "so he don't think about it twice."

"And bleed all night, you mean? To hell with that."

"Why don't we cauterize it?"

That from Orland, coming back with makeshift torches from the barn.

"To hell with *you*!" Hart snapped. "Nobody's setting me on fire."

"It's just like brandin' stock," said Orland. "Nothin' to it."

"Nothin's right," the redhead told him. "You just stay the hell away from me."

Saxon took one of Orland's torches. "Best be quiet then," he told Hart. "Let us finish up so you can get them stitches in."

"I can't believe she cut me, damn it!"

Fowler spat a brown stream toward the silent house. "Lucky that's all she did. Cleaver used right can take your arm off."

"Anyway, it's settled now," said Orland, torchlight burnishing his sweaty face.

"Hell, let's roast 'em then."

They'd left the door open, a lamp burning inside. Saxon had wanted light while they were at it with the squatter's wife, but he could do without it now. He tipped the lamp's glass chimney off and let it shatter on the floor, turned down the wick and blew it out. There was a second lamp they hadn't bothered with, above the stove.

"Take that," Saxon told Fowler, pointing with his smoky torch, "and spread the kerosene around. Joe, you and Perry lend a hand. Drag Old McDonald in here by the bed."

"My arm—"

"Just *do* it!"

The squatter's wife might've been sleeping, if he closed one eye and squinted in the darkness with the other one. Maybe she'd had a nightmare that made her thrash the bedding off and tear her nightdress all to pieces.

Sleeping Beauty, Saxon thought, as he began to dribble kerosene across her still form. He made a trail back to the center of the room, detouring once to douse the boy's small body.

Something fierce he'd been, with that big knife.

Not fierce enough, though.

"Say what?"

Saxon blinked back at Fowler, unaware that he had spoken. "Nothing. Let's get done with this."

"Suits me."

Saxon was looking forward to a few drinks at the Nugget, after they reported back. Another job well done. He wasn't worried about Hart. They would make up a story for the sawbones if he asked, tell him to take it up with Rankin if that wasn't good enough.

All the law there was in Redemption already belonged to Rankin, anyway. For all Chad knew, Rankin had a fix in with the Rangers, too.

"I'm dry," said Fowler as he pitched his empty lamp aside.

"Let's light her up."

Saxon retreated toward the open door, looking around the place once more to see if they'd forgotten anything. If so, he couldn't spot it and the fire would clean up after them, regardless.

Saxon lobbed his firebrand toward the squatter's bed, and was rewarded with a flash and gust of superheated wind that made him squint against the blaze. Fowler tossed his at the stove. Twin trails of fire raced toward the middle of the room, where the old lady lay sprawled in blood and kerosene.

Dry timber burns the best, and there had been no rain in Terrell County for a month of Sundays. By the time they'd mounted, Hart cursing a blue streak for his wounded arm, the house was totally engulfed by flame.

Its heat made Saxon's gray mare shy and snort in protest, anxious to be gone.

He clutched the reins more tightly, showing who was boss until the mare gave in and stood there, baking. Satisfied at last, he clucked his tongue and spurred her back toward town, the others falling into line behind him.

One more down, a handful left to go. Tonight's work would encourage some of them to leave; Saxon could take care of the rest.

It was his job and he was well worth every penny Rankin paid him—maybe more, in fact. It was a point to keep in mind next time they started talking figures.

Saxon didn't want the world, but he would settle for his portion and a little more besides.

Why not?

The fastest gun in Terrell County had it coming to him.

He was well and truly on his way.

4

Price woke at five o'clock from force of habit. He had never been much of a sleeper, even as a child. There had been chores to do around the farm and later, when he made his own way on the road, it always seemed to Price that every hour he wasted sleeping was a giveaway, diminishing his time on earth.

He wondered sometimes if the dead could dream.

Price could've skipped the razor after last night's shave, but he was in a mood to look his best for Belle. He hadn't quite decided why—whether he wanted to impress her or remind her of what she had given up.

She already knows that. It wasn't much.

Price didn't feel at home with mirrors. He was not impressed by what they showed him, but he searched the hotel's glass for anything that could've made Belle change her mind.

His eyes were brown with flecks of green and gold. Someone had called them "hazel" once, but Price was never one to put on airs. He checked the eyes and tried to find a hint of warmth but only saw the flat, unflinching stare that some men glimpsed before they died.

His face would never pass for anything but average. Price owed the scar above his left eye to a beating he'd received at age thirteen—the last time he'd fought anyone with empty hands. He had a weathered look beneath a full head of dark hair. The tiny wrinkles etched around his eyes were not from laughter.

If his face was relatively plain, the shooter's body told a different story in the looking glass. He had been shot five times in twenty years, stabbed once—a careless moment that had nearly put him off of whiskey altogether— and had snapped his right leg in two places when a rifle shot took down his pony, back in '81.

The men who'd given him those scars were all dead now, but Price was still alive.

"You call this living?"

He received no answer from his image in the glass. Those flat eyes watched him lather up and raise the English razor to his face.

Last night had been the worst so far, for dreams. Price had expected nothing less, sleeping within a hundred yards of where Belle and her storekeeper had put down roots, but it disturbed him that he couldn't hold the images in mind. He saw her face but couldn't read the eyes, and when she spoke to him her lips moved silently, as if Price had been stricken deaf.

Talking had never been their strong point, anyway.

Belle wasn't one of those women who sought Price out because he had a pistol and a reputation to go with it. Price had known his share of them, although they weren't as common as the young men looking for a chance to take him down. Both shared a trait in common though— that willingness to give up everything they had and flirt with death.

Belle hadn't cared about his reputation or his work until the night it kicked in her door at the Lucky Strike. Their time before that had been something else. Price couldn't pin it down, but he had almost felt as if it was a second chance—an opportunity to stand outside himself and choose another road.

So much for dreams.

They were for children and old maids, in Price's view. Sweet dreams showed off a world that never was and never would be. Nightmares, on the other hand, too often told the truth.

Price didn't know he'd cut himself until he saw the blood spill down his lathered neck. The pain came afterward, a tribute to the razor's edge. Price let it bleed until he finished up, then bloodied two of the hotel's white towels before he got it stopped.

There was an old black woman in Fort Worth—or had been, anyway, the last time Price rode through there—who believed such things were signs and omens. Price had paid her fifty cents to read his future in the cards once, but she gave the money back after she'd drawn the death card four times in a row.

At least it hadn't been the hanged man or the fool.

Four years and counting since the old woman had read his fate, and Price was still above ground. He had dealt the death card out to others in the meantime but it never turned his way.

Not yet.

The suit he'd worn in Purgatory could've used a pressing, but at least it wasn't dirty from the trail. Price wore his last clean shirt and made a note to find out if there was a washer woman in town to handle laundry. By the time he finished polishing his boots and strapped on the Colt it was time for breakfast.

Price was pleased to find that troubled sleep and his proximity to Belle had done no damage to his appetite.

A plain young woman had replaced the gray man who had checked Price in the night before. He touched his hat brim, noting how her eyes dipped toward the pistol on his hip before they found his face.

"Morning," she said, unwilling to commit on whether it was good or bad.

It was already warm out, with a dry feel to the air that would've made a farmer wince. No rain today, or anything resembling clouds. The vast sky had a washed-out look, as if the Texas sun had faded it somehow.

Price hoped Belle and her merchant had a place in town. He didn't feel like riding out to look for them today.

He was halfway across the street and angling toward O'Malley's with the smell of bacon in his nostrils, when a man's voice called him out by name.

Price turned, his right hand drifting toward the Colt instinctively, stopping when he saw the glint of sunlight from the stranger's badge.

The shooter had a wary look about him, which was only natural. He wasn't twitchy, like a mean drunk or a nervous kid, but there was something in his eyes and how he held himself that radiated menace. It was sometimes possible to talk a boozer or a greenhorn into giving up his gun. This one would use his pistol and to hell with consequences.

Gil Gresham knew a thing or three about killers. He'd been one himself, back in the day, and he was still a fair hand with the odds stacked just right, but he had never been in this one's league.

The marshal couldn't fool himself.

He didn't think Matt Price would give a damn about his tin badge either, if the play got rough.

He would've recognized the shooter even if Jerome at the hotel hadn't reported his arrival in Redemption. Gresham didn't need a WANTED poster to identify a stone-cold killer at first glance. The name and reputation simply nailed it down, confirming what his head and gut already knew.

Matt Price was trouble, the explosive kind.

Handling him carelessly could get a fellow killed.

Despite a sudden case of nerves, Gresham decided he could push his luck a little for the sake of pride. He had a badge and witnesses. For all the stories that surrounded him, Price hadn't been accused of shooting lawmen on a whim—or anyone, in fact—unless they threatened him somehow.

That's it, then. Hide behind the badge.

His call stopped Price halfway across the street, angling in the direction of O'Malley's restaurant. Turning to face him, Price gave up nothing through his expression or his attitude.

You've still got leeway, Gresham told himself. *Be careful, though.*

"Your name *is* Matthew Price?"

Price thought about it for a second, then nodded once without speaking.

"Like to have a word with you if that's alright." Showing some manners, even as he held his ground. Gresham would make the shooter come to him, a small concession in the circumstances, but it set a certain mood.

Price glanced off toward the restaurant as if his breakfast were already waiting, then closed the twenty feet between them with slow, easy strides. Mounting the wooden sidewalk, he topped Gresham's six feet by at least two inches. He had dead eyes in a perfect poker face.

"Gil Gresham. I'm the law here in Redemption."

"Saw the badge right off," Price said. "What can I do for you?"

"A quick word, like I said. You're new in town."

The shooter waited for a question.

"We're a small town here," Gresham pressed on, "but that don't mean we're out of touch. Word gets around."

"What word is that?"

"You've made a reputation for yourself," the marshal said and cut a glance toward Price's Colt, "with that."

"Not everything you hear is true," Price said.

"Enough to make folks nervous, though."

"Who's nervous, Marshal?"

Gresham tried to find a sneer behind his title but it wasn't there. "Nobody yet," he said. "That's how I like it."

"So we've got no problem, then."

"Depends on you, I'd say. Whether you're passing through or you've got business hereabouts."

"Business?"

"The kind you're known for, that would be."

Gresham felt people watching him, the upright citizens who paid his salary. Well, part of it. He kept his shoulders squared and blinked as seldom as his fifty-year-old eyes could manage.

"I was on my way to breakfast when you stopped me," Price replied, sidestepping Gresham's question.

"Everybody needs to eat. And after that?"

"Haven't decided yet."

Gresham was patient, speaking as he might to an old woman or a child. "We have a nice town here," he said.

"Looks like."

"You may not see it, but we're on the go. Good things are happening around Redemption."

"Glad to hear it."

Gresham hated being interrupted, trying not to let it break his train of thought. "We're not some hick town where anything goes."

"They know that up the street?" Price cocked his head toward the east end of town without moving his eyes.

"Free enterprise," the marshal said. "We have a lot of working men in town. They need to let the steam off now and then."

"Makes sense."

"But you're not working here."

"Nobody's hired me yet," Price said.

"So you're just passing through. Nothing to keep you."

"Are you telling me to leave, Marshal?" There was a

token of amusement in the shooter's tone that rankled Gresham.

"I've no cause to do that," he replied. "You haven't broken any laws I know about."

Price glanced off toward the restaurant again and held his peace.

"My point is, we're a peaceful and law-abiding town. Nothing much to interest you at all."

"I might know someone here," Price said.

"And that would be . . . ?"

"My business."

Gresham felt the color rising up his neck, flushing his cheeks. He hoped it wouldn't show beneath his tan. Anger could be a weakness.

It could get him killed.

"I'll ask it this way, then. You *might* know someone, or you *do*?"

"Have to get back to you on that."

"It's not clear in your mind?"

"A name's one thing. You put it with a face, that's something else."

"Your lucky day. I know most everyone in town."

"That keeps you busy, I expect."

"You play it close."

"I never learned the other way," Price said.

"Then let me tell you plain, I'd hate for any of our upright citizens to have this fine day ruined. Someone shows up dead or missing in Redemption while you're here, I know who to come looking for."

Price showed a smile at that, not much of one but near enough. "If it's my work you won't have to come looking, Marshal."

"I'm just saying."

"Can I have my breakfast now?"

"Free country, Mr. Price."

The shooter turned away from him and went along the sidewalk toward O'Malley's. Gresham felt the trembling start behind his belt buckle and spread out to his limbs.

The only antidote he knew was motion, but he stood there for another moment, watching Price before he turned away.

The Nugget wasn't open yet, but he would roust somebody out.

Bad news was best delivered fresh.

Sedge Rankin always had a good time counting money. He began each day with coins and greenbacks, checking the accounts from both of his saloons and Molly Deegan's cathouse, where he also held controlling interest in the property and girls. Counting the money never failed to whet his appetite for breakfast.

Only one thing better in the world was finding out that someone at the Nugget or the Trail's End had been fiddling with the books to sell him short.

There had been none of that for months, though, since he'd turned the boys loose on the Nugget's last bartender. Saxon and the rest had worked him over for the best part of a day, then sent him marching off toward Lubbock barefoot, in his union suit.

Sometimes his children needed an example, just to set them straight.

And they were all his children, every mother's son or daughter in Redemption or within a three-day ride. The land he didn't own already would be his by autumn at the latest—starting with the Kelsey spread. He considered them squatters. They were not encouraged to remain on land Rankin wanted for himself. Holdouts who spurned his generous first offer rarely got a second.

They were prone to accidents that made the plagues of Job seem like a picnic in the park.

Receipts were down a fraction at the Nugget, but they had increased at the Trail's End. Rankin enjoyed competing with himself, knowing before he counted each morning that he'd raked in every dollar spent an alcohol or poontang in the whole damned town.

He had begun as a saloonkeeper and never strayed far from his roots. No matter how much he expanded into ranching, real estate, or oil, Rankin maintained his link to pleasures of the flesh.

It kept him human, which would never be confused with humble.

Rankin was starting on the cathouse cash, deciding whether he should order ham or steak with his four eggs and fried potatoes, when the Nugget's daytime bar man stuck his head in.

"Marshal here to see you, Mr. Rankin."

"Send him back and bring us in some coffee, will you, Skeeter?"

"Yessir."

Gresham had his hat on when he walked into the office, but he noticed Rankin's frown and doffed it, smoothing down his salt-and-pepper hair with his free hand.

"Good morning, Mr. Rankin."

"Take a load off, Gil. There's coffee coming."

Gresham took the only chair available. It was a wooden straight-back facing Rankin's desk, constructed by an artisan who gave no thought to comfort. Rankin didn't like his business visitors relaxing too much in his presence. If he wanted them to feel good, he could always book them into Molly Deegan's for a poke.

"I saw that shooter like we talked about," said Gresham.

Like I told you to, thought Rankin, but he let it go. It was a small slip of the tongue. Gresham would never make the fatal error of believing they were equals.

"Is it Price?"

"Yes, sir. It's him, alright."

"What brings him to Redemption?"

Gresham delayed his answer while the coffee was served and the bar man took himself away. He tried a sip and set the mug back down before he said, "I think he's passing through."

"You think."

The marshal frowned. "Yes, sir."

"Meaning he didn't tell you that himself."

"Well, not exactly. No."

"Alright, Gilmer." Rankin watched Gresham's color deepen at the use of his full given name. "What *did* he say, exactly?"

"Said he might know someone in Redemption."

It was Rankin's turn to frown. "I see. And did that strike you as a trifle vague?"

"Yes, sir."

It was like pulling teeth. Gresham had screwed the pooch but didn't want to take the heat.

"May I assume you asked him who that friend of his might be?"

"I did. He wouldn't say."

"You were polite, I take it?"

"Well . . ."

"Of course you were."

"You didn't say I ought to mess him up."

"That's absolutely right."

The best day Gilmer Gresham ever had, he would've had to backshoot Matthew Price—and even then Price might've killed him, with a little luck.

"I could go back and talk to him again," said Gresham, clearly not in love with the idea.

"No need for that just now," Rankin replied, watching the marshal sag a bit in his relief. "I would appreciate it if you'd keep an eye on Mr. Price, though. Maybe find out if he visits anybody in particular. Can I trust you to do that for me, Gil?"

"Yes, sir. You know I will."

"Good man. So, if there's nothing else . . . ?"

Gresham was reaching for his coffee but he drew his hand back, empty. "I'll just go look into that," he said.

"Discreetly."

"What?"

"Don't let him know you're dogging him. He might not like it."

"Right. Okay."

A little worry line appeared between the marshal's bushy eyebrows. Rankin guessed he would be wearing it as long as Matthew Price remained in town.

So much the better. It would keep Gil on his toes.

Rankin wasn't concerned about the shooter yet, in any major way. He made a point of checking new arrivals in Redemption, be they peddlers, cattle buyers, saddle tramps, or whores. A shooter passing through meant nothing much to him except more money spent on liquor or at Molly's cathouse.

But if the shooter stuck around for any reason . . .

Said he might know someone in Redemption.

Rankin took it as a challenge to discover who that someone was. His children needed guidance, after all.

It was a father's job.

Price walked into O'Malley's with his mind set on bacon and flapjacks drowned in maple syrup. The waitress who seated him and took his order was a polar opposite from the first one he'd met, lean and reserved, her smile more like a facial tic than a display of joviality.

Seated and waiting for his breakfast, Price replayed his confrontation with the marshal. Sizing up the man, he placed Gresham on the high side of fifty, once stocky but running to fat. Some men mistook bulk for strength, but Price knew the difference. When he looked at Gil Gresham he saw a hard man gone to seed.

That didn't make him harmless though.

Lawmen were dangerous by definition. Those who weren't much with a gun could always summon help, deputize a whole town if need be. If the badge was bought and paid for, as he guessed Gil Gresham's might be, the lawman became a front for someone else. Someone perhaps more dangerous and difficult to reach.

Who's that?

Price didn't know and wasn't sure he wanted to find out. He still hadn't made up his mind on helping Belle. He'd gone to sleep thinking he should, then woke up leaning back the other way. Until he found out what her problem was it would be foolish to decide.

Back to the marshal for another minute, then.

Someone had tipped him off that Price was in Redemption, probably the gray man on the hotel desk last night. The news had prompted a response, though not as harsh as some Price had endured. Gresham had cautioned him without insisting Price leave town. He would be happier if Price moved on but hadn't found the nerve to push it yet.

Price wondered if their little chat had been the marshal's own idea or someone else's. If the former, he would only have to watch Gresham, maybe a deputy or two. If someone else had called the tune, though, he would have to be on full alert.

What else is new?

The waitress brought his meal, topped off his coffee cup, and went away. Price took his time, no rush to finish, when he calculated that the shops in town wouldn't be open for at least an hour yet.

He had considered different ways to get in touch with Belle. It was a touchy thing on unfamiliar ground. He'd meant to ask at the hotel, but since the night clerk put the marshal on him that choice was out. Likewise the restaurant, although he might've risked a question to the waitress from last night.

Redemption was a relatively small town, even with the two saloons. Most of its citizens would know each other and he reckoned everyone would know the town's merchants. Not only by their stock, but where they lived, whether they went to church or not, how many kids they had and what they ate for supper. Price was confident he could locate Belle's residence by asking up and down Main Street, but at what cost?

One word in the wrong ear could easily put both of them at risk.

Gresham had made his mind up for him. Price would go to see Belle at the shop. He'd be another dry goods customer and nothing more. Maybe buy something to preserve appearances. It suddenly appealed to him, seeing her glance up from the counter as he came in through the door.

The first look on her face, beholding him, would tell Price something. She would be surprised of course, having received no answer to her telegram, but he needed to look for something else. A hint of yearning, maybe. Even sorrow would be good, if it derived from missing him.

If she was cool and distant to him Price could always turn around and ride back out the way he'd come, put Marshal Gresham's mind at ease that way.

What if she wasn't in the store?

Price thought about the husband he had never seen, coming around the counter with a big smile on his face and asking whether there was something he could help Price find. Price telling him, *Your wife, that's all.*

The peddler's smile would vanish in a heartbeat.

Or he didn't have to speak at all. He could produce the telegram and hand it over, let Belle's man see for himself who she ran crying to when there was trouble. Rub his nose in it and watch him squirm. Let him try something if he had the sand.

For what? Price asked himself. To hurt Belle through the man she'd chosen over him, seeking a decent life?

On second thought, it seemed a petty and destructive thing to do. Price let it go and bent to cleaning up his plate.

A new thought struck him on the last mouthful. What would he do if there was only hired help in the store this morning? Price would set tongues wagging if he walked in asking for the boss's home address, much less inquiring after Belle. A nervous clerk might put him off, then run to tip the marshal when Price left.

No harm in that, he thought. *It's not a crime to visit friends.*

Unless the marshal asked Belle's man and found out that he'd never heard of Matthew Price. Still nothing for the law to hold him on, but Gresham's interest made Price leery of alerting him.

Why chance it if there was another way to do this thing?

Just take it easy, one step at a time.

He didn't need to show his hand until somebody paid to see it, one way or another.

Finished with his meal, Price left a dollar on the table by his plate. He turned left coming out the door and started walking east, down toward the dry goods store. Before he traveled thirty feet another call arrested him.

"Matthew?"

Price stopped and turned. A dizzy rush swept over him. "Good morning, Belle."

5

Price couldn't say she looked the same, exactly, but he would've known her anywhere. Time's carving knife had been applied with care, no more wrinkles than the average thirty-two-year-old and less than some he'd known. Belle didn't paint her face these days, but she had never really needed to. Her blue eyes were as clear and sharp as Price remembered them.

He didn't want to think about her body underneath the high-necked gingham dress.

"I wasn't sure you'd come," she said.

"Me neither."

"But you're here."

"I am."

"It's good of you to come," she said, "after so long."

After you threw me out and married someone else, he thought. Instead he said, "Town called Redemption, I thought it was worth a look."

"Names are deceiving sometimes."

Faces, too. And hearts. Feelings.

"I've heard that."

"It's amazing, Matt. You've hardly changed at all."

She couldn't see the new scars he'd collected since the night he shot the Farrell brothers.

"You have."

"Ten years, Matthew."

Ten years, two months and twenty-seven days. But who's counting?

"You look better, maybe younger."

But not happier. That would be stretching it.

"You don't mean that," she said, blushing.

"I've never lied to you."

"No, you never did. We need to go somewhere and talk."

He half-turned from her, scanning up and down the street. None of the passersby said anything or stopped to gawk, but Price knew how it worked in towns below a certain size. Word got around, whether the word was true or not.

"You have someplace in mind?"

"Maybe your room at the hotel?"

"I don't know," Price replied. He thought about the gray man and the pinch-faced morning clerk. "A town like this, tongues wag."

"They're wagging now. It's ears that worry me."

"Your town, your call."

They crossed the street together, angling back toward the hotel. Price would've liked to rip the fairy-bell down from its place above the door. The day clerk poked her narrow head out of the office, blinked at them in rapid-fire, and drew back out of sight as if lassoed.

"Callie McGovern," Belle said. "Not the worst gossip in town, but a contender."

"We don't have to go upstairs," Price said.

Belle smiled at him, the first time since she'd called him on the street.

The first time in ten years.

"I used to care what people in Redemption thought about me," she replied. "Not anymore."

They met nobody on the stairs, saw no one as they passed each floor in turn to reach the fourth. It could've been a ghost hotel, for all the life it showed.

"Off-season now for visitors, I guess," Price said as they approached his fourth-floor room.

"Sightseers and the like don't stop much in Redemption," Belle replied. "There's nothing for them here."

"Fair land for farming, though."

"You'd think so."

Price unlocked the door and swung it wide for Belle to go ahead of him. When they were both inside he closed it without fastening the latch. It was a small nod to propriety, too little and too late.

"You want the chair or . . ." Price ran out of words and gestured vaguely toward the bed.

"The chair's fine. Thank you."

Belle sat down. Price eyed the bed, then half-sat on a corner of the vanity, dangling his right leg, left foot on the floor.

"Who's minding the store, Belle?"

"My husband. I'll join him as soon as we're done here."

"I see."

"Matthew—"

"What did you mean about the farming?"

Belle seemed disappointed by the interruption but she didn't push. "It's better if I start at the beginning."

"Good a place as any."

"I came here with Jared—that's my husband, Jared Mercer—in April of seventy-nine, to start the dry goods store."

"I saw it down the street."

"It's grown. Redemption was a small town then— smaller than now, I mean. It was a cow town in those days, mostly running herds to the railhead at Austin. Sedge Rankin owned the stockyard and the entertainment east of town—still does, in fact, but he's grown with the town. They hit oil on his land in eighty-three and he's been buying up the county ever since. He owns three-quarters of the town, including this hotel and both saloons, along with Molly Deegan's."

"That's the—"

"Whorehouse? Yes." She didn't flinch or blush at all.

Still tough, the way Price had remembered her.

"I'm guessing part of the one-fourth he doesn't own belongs to you and . . . Jared, was it?"

"Yes—and you'd be right. Some others felt the same. Tom Mabry and his wife, Nadine, published a weekly newspaper, the *Times-Gazette*. They took a stand against land-grabbing in the county, but they never mentioned Rankin's name. It didn't save them from a fire one night last year. They're gone now."

"That was arson?"

"You could smell the kerosene a block away," Belle said. "Of course, our marshal saw it otherwise. He reckoned Tom or Nadine left a lamp lit when they closed up for the night and 'something' knocked it over. Like a ghost, maybe."

"I met the marshal on my way to breakfast."

"And?"

Price shrugged. "It wouldn't be a great surprise to find out someone bought his badge."

"That's Rankin. When you own the law it makes things easier."

"I've known a couple towns like that," Price said.

Almost stretched rope in one, before the careless jailer had an accident. Price let that slide.

"Uriah Giddings had a produce shop," Belle said. "He bought his goods from local farmers Rankin disapproved of. Claimed the lot of them were squatting on his range."

"Another fire?" Price asked her.

"Worse. One night last summer two men grabbed Uriah's daughter, Jasmine, off the street. They took her out behind the livery stable and . . . well, let's just say Uriah figured it was time to leave."

"Your marshal think that was another accident?"

"Gresham? No, he was Johnny-on-the-spot with a solution that time. He picked up two Mexicans and charged the pair of them. A few days later they were shot, supposedly while trying to escape."

"Saves rope," Price said. He had no sympathy for rapists.

"I'd agree with you, if they were guilty," Belle replied.

"But you don't think so?"

"Neither one of them spoke any English, Matthew. Jasmine said the two men who attacked her took their time explaining what would happen if her father didn't 'mind his manners' in Redemption. They were pigs, but neither one of them was Mexican."

"She told the marshal that, I guess."

"Of course. Before *and* after the arrests. Gresham decided she was too upset by the attack to think straight or remember small details like whether the two men were white or spoke Spanish."

"She didn't recognize them, though?"

Belle shook her head, swirling the honey-colored hair around her shoulders. "Rankin has his pick of border trash and guns for hire. They'd do a job like that for free and ride out happy."

"Some of them, maybe."

She cut her eyes away from his. "I didn't mean—"

"That's not the end of it, I guess."

"What? No. There've been some others. A lawyer, Emil Woolard, represented some of those on Rankin's list. He had in mind to ask the circuit court for an injunction, maybe sue Rankin for damages."

"What happened there?"

"Three riders called him out one night. They stripped him, beat him like an animal, then dragged him up and down the street behind a horse. He left the state as soon as he was fit to travel."

"No injunction, though."

"We haven't found another lawyer who would touch the case. Rankin gets bolder all the time. His guns have run at least four families off the land—the Stimsons, Oxendines, Freshours and Johnsons. All of them burned out or terrorized, their livestock killed, children threatened or worse."

"Your marshal blames the Mexicans for that?"

"Gil Gresham says his jurisdiction stops at the town limits. He has no authority to ride around the county solving crimes—as if he could."

"You have a county sheriff?"

"He 'confers' with Gresham and we hear no more about it. I think Rankin pays him off."

"There's more," Price said. "You didn't call me here for those already gone. This touches you."

"Jared, my husband—"

"I remember who he is."

She reddened, flustered. "Rankin wanted us to buy our stock through him, the way most other merchants in Redemption do. Of course his price was higher, so we'd have to mark things up or take a beating on the sales. Jared refused."

"And Rankin didn't like that, I suppose."

"First thing he did was ambush one of our deliveries, coming down from San Angelo. No one was hurt that time, but we had to pay twice for the goods."

"He hit the second shipment?"

"No. A Texas Ranger rode along with that one. Rankin's people wouldn't risk it."

"If you had a Ranger here—"

"We told him everything. He had a talk with Rankin—who of course denied it all. We had no proof of anything. Still don't, as far as any court would recognize. Dead Mexicans for Jasmine Giddings, and the rest of it comes down to gunmen no one can identify."

"You're still here, though."

"My— Jared wouldn't let it rest. He met with others

like himself who had it in for Rankin. They called themselves the Redemption Civic Betterment Society."

Belle's tone was bitter, but her eyes were sad.

"What happened then?" Price asked.

"They got up a petition to the sheriff, which he took under advisement."

"Meaning he did nothing."

"Same as always. Next, they wrote a letter to the governor. He sent back an expression of concern and sympathy."

"Hot air."

"Manure is what you meant to say. I don't know whether Rankin's paid *him* off or not, but that's the last we ever heard from Austin."

"But you heard from Rankin."

"Loud and clear," Belle said. "One night, about a week after he got that letter from the governor, Jared was closing up the shop alone. You've seen it?"

"Last night, passing by."

"A shooter in the alleyway across the street fired two shots from a Winchester. Gil Gresham found the cartridges. One shot missed clean and drilled a sack of pinto beans. The other one took Jared in the back."

Price was embarrassed and ashamed of the sensation tingling in his chest. It felt like hope.

"He's dead?"

Belle shook her head again. "I wouldn't be here if they'd killed him. Christ, sometimes I almost wish—"

She took a lacy handkerchief from hiding, up her sleeve, and dabbed her eyes. There was a tremor in her voice as she continued.

"Please forget I said that. It's a shameful thought."

"We're not responsible for what we think," he said. "It's what we do that matters."

"Jared's crippled, Matt. The bullet cut his spinal cord. He feels nothing below the waist. The doctors say he'll never walk again."

"Maybe an operation?"

"It's beyond them. Nothing they can do. We have a wheelchair. He—"

More tears. The handkerchief again.

"Why do you stay?" Price asked. "It can't be any kind of life."

"Jared's a stubborn man. He won't leave even now, for fear of what Jesse might think."

"And who might Jesse be?"

"Our son."

Price managed not to flinch. He hadn't counted on a child. The thought had never crossed his mind, in fact.

Why not?

"How old is he?"

"Nine and a half," Belle said.

She and the merchant hadn't wasted any time. It was a good thing too, now that a rifle slug had left Belle's husband half a man.

"Seems like the best thing for a boy that age would be to get him out of here while he's still got two parents breathing."

"Jared sees it differently. To him it's running, and that takes away whatever manhood he has left. He's told me that he'd rather die. Sometimes I think he's hoping Rankin's men will finish it."

"When was he shot?"

"November seventeenth. On Jesse's birthday."

"Jesus, Belle."

"I'd likely have been with him, otherwise. The birthday cake . . ."

Her voice trailed off to nothing. Price wanted to touch her, hold her, but he couldn't move. He couldn't close the space between them.

Six or seven feet and ten long years.

He had to break the silence. What to say?

"Have there been more threats since the shooting?"

"No." She plied her handkerchief. "The shot that crippled Jared killed the Civic Betterment Society. I'm told they held a meeting to dissolve the group. It took five minutes and they all went home. Can't say I blame them, really. They're afraid, that's all."

"And there's been no more trouble with the store?"

She laughed at that, if Price could call the sudden grating sound a laugh.

"Rankin sent flowers to the house. I threw them out and waited for his offer on the store, but there's been none. I think he likes it, having Jared and his wheelchair in Redemption. It reminds the other sheep of what could happen if they start to act like men."

Price steeled himself for what was coming next.

"So you wired me," he said.

"That's right."

"How did you find me, Belle?"

She smiled. "Do you remember Amy Watts?"

"Worked at the Lucky Strike?"

"The very same. We've kept in touch with letters two, three times a year. She's out in Albuquerque now, still working."

"I was through there, six or seven months ago."

"That's what she said."

"I didn't see her."

"She saw you. You leave a trail, Matt. Amy heard you were either in Benson or Purgatory. I sent wires to both."

"I never got to Benson."

"Purgatory, then. It fits."

"Redemption doesn't."

"I guess not. There was a time I thought it would."

"What do you want from me?" *As if I didn't know.*

"I didn't think it through before I sent the telegrams," she said. "I wasn't sure I'd reach you, much less that you'd come."

"What, Belle? Say it."

"I wanted *help,* Matthew, all right?"

"What kind of help? I can't give back your husband's legs or change his mind about this town."

"I know that."

"So it must be something else."

Price couldn't let it go. She had rejected him for killing and expelled him from her life. He had to know what was required to make her change her mind.

"If Jared stays," she said, "he'll find another way to rile Rankin. He can't just let it go. That's worse than running, in his mind. He wants to finish Rankin."

"From a wheelchair?"

"Did I say he had a chance in hell? It's pride, Matthew. His stupid pride. You know, the kind that won't let someone quit regardless of the cost?"

"You never asked me if I'd quit, Belle."

Blue eyes blinked at him, surprised.

"It's not about you, Matt. It's not about us."

"That's exactly right."

"I just thought—"

"That I'd ride in here and do your dirty work, then ride back out again."

"Matthew."

"You sent me down the road for dropping two gun-slicks who tried to kill me in our bed. They would've killed you too, without a second thought. Ten years without a word, and now you call me back to do your trigger work. Take out a man I've never met, who's done nothing to me."

"I didn't know who else—"

"You called it murder back in Amarillo, Belle. What's different now?"

"You're right," she said. "I never should have asked. If it helps, a part of me's regretted sending those telegrams out every day for the past three weeks."

Price watched her get up from the chair. He interlaced his fingers to disguise the tremor in his hands. Anger or fear?

He felt a last chance slipping through his grasp and couldn't bring himself to reel it back.

That stupid pride.

"I have no claim on you," Belle said. "I gave that up. I'll pay you for the wasted time."

Insulting him with money now. "Keep it," he said.

"I should've known better." Her hand was on the door-knob, turning it. "I should've told you."

"Told me what?"

"About Jesse."

"Your boy."

"Our boy," Belle said. "He's yours and mine."

6

Gil Gresham reckoned he had trouble when he saw Calliope McGovern waving at him from the sidewalk out in front of the hotel. She'd look both ways along the street, then fan the air with one pale hand for several seconds and repeat the peering ritual as if she were afraid of being noticed.

Gresham frowned and tried ignoring her, but she was having none of it. When waving at him failed, she raised her voice and called to him across the street.

"Oh, Marshal *Greeeesham*! Marshal *Greeeesham*!"

Everyone within two blocks was staring at her now and wondering what had her knickers in a twist.

So much for subtlety.

He raised a hand to silence her and crossed the street, not rushing it. She ducked back into the hotel when he was halfway there, then leaned out through the door to beckon him as if she was afraid he'd lose his way.

Fool woman had the fastest tongue in town. If backbiting was fatal, Gresham would've had to hang her years ago.

They had the hotel lobby to themselves.

"Miz Callie, how are you today?"

"Concerned is how I am," she said. "Our stranger had a visitor this morning—*in his room.*"

"That so?"

"It is!"

He could've asked her for the name but that would spoil the fun of watching as her face turned pink, then crimson from the strain of waiting.

"If you ask me, Marshal, it's improper for a lady to be calling on a stranger *in his room.*"

"My guess would be that if she called on him he must not be a stranger," Gresham answered, milking it.

"Indeed! And can you tell me how a gunfighter might know Mrs. Annabelle Mercer?"

There it was. Gil Gresham felt the day go sour on him, standing there.

"No ma'am," he said. "I surely can't."

Gresham was out the door and moving down the sidewalk when her peevish voice caught up with him.

"Is that all you can say?"

He waved her off, thinking, *That's all I'll say to you.*

But Gresham dreaded what might happen when he told Sedge Rankin.

Not my problem.

But the badge he wore might make it his, unless he found a way out of the box.

And that could get him killed.

The Nugget didn't really draw a crowd before sundown, but there were half a dozen early drinkers bellied up against the bar when Gresham entered. Two of them at least were Rankin's men—Chad Saxon and Perry Hart. They smirked at Gresham in the mirror. He pretended they were both invisible and flagged the barkeep off to one side for a private word.

"I need to see him. Is he in?"

"Reckon he is. I'll just make sure."

"Don't strain yourself."

Gresham brushed past him, moving toward the office Rankin kept in back. Two visits in one day would take a toll on anybody's nerves.

The door was open and Rankin was seated at his desk. He'd given up the money count and had a map spread out in front of him. Gresham waited on the threshold for a moment, then rapped knuckles on the doorframe.

"Gilmer. Back again?"

"I've got more news about the stranger."

"Meaning Price?"

"The one and only."

Rankin spent another moment on the map, his index finger following some line invisible to Gresham. *Plotting out the kingdom,* Gresham thought. He waited for an invitation to sit down but none was offered.

"Well?" A flick of Rankin's eyes stung Gresham like a quirt.

"Callie McGovern says Price had himself a visitor at the hotel."

"You want to play a guessing game?"

"No, sir. It was Annabelle Mercer, from the dry goods—"

"I know who she is, Gilmer."

You ought to, Gresham thought. But what he said was, "They went up to Price's room."

"I don't suppose fair Callie took a gander through the keyhole?"

Gresham had to smile at that. "I don't believe so."

"No. Which leaves us to decide if they were talking or the shooter had himself a poke."

"She wouldn't seek him out unless they had a history."

"Meaning you don't think Price has what it takes to charm a woman off the street."

"Not *that* woman."

"I happen to agree with you, Gilmer. Now tell me this: Are you a great believer in coincidence?"

"Depends."

"A shooter comes to town first time and runs into a

lady friend. Make that a married, respectable lady friend who follows him back to his room."

"It's thin."

"Transparent," Rankin said. He cogitated for a moment, frowning at his thoughts, before he said, "I need to find out more about this gunny."

"And the Mercers?"

"They're not going anywhere. Keep track of Price until I tell you otherwise."

"Alright."

Gresham stood waiting for another word, more detailed orders, but Rankin bent his head back to the map. Two sweaty minutes passed before he raised his eyes again.

"Are you still here?"

Chad Saxon slid back to the bar a step ahead of Gresham, who was leaving Rankin's office. The old man was hell on eavesdroppers and Saxon didn't want to queer his job.

"Old Gil looks fit to shit," said Perry Hart.

"That's what he gets for selling out."

"Like us, you mean?"

Saxon put down his whiskey glass and turned to eyeball Hart. "Don't tell me what I mean," he said. "We're nothing like that tub of guts. At least *I'm* not."

He saw the words sting Hart. Perry's quick temper made him want to answer back, but he knew Saxon well enough to swallow it.

"I didn't mean nothin'," he said.

"You know the difference between me and Gresham, Perry?"

"You don't got a badge."

"The badge is nothing. It's the man behind it makes a tin star count, and *Gilmer* ain't no kind of man at all. He may've been hot stuff when he was younger, but he's lost the edge."

Hart sipped his snake water and didn't answer back.

"There's somebody in town might be a challenge, though."

"Who's that?"

"A shooter by the name of Price."

Hart cut his narrow eyes around to pin Saxon. "Would that be Matthew Price?"

"What if it is?"

"He's downed many a man. I heard his piece run out of notchin' room."

"Big talk."

"Maybe."

"You want to know what else I heard?"

"Go on ahead."

"The old man thinks he's here to work some mischief with the Mercer woman."

"From the dry goods?"

Saxon nodded. "She was up to his hotel room."

Hart's scarred lip crinkled at that. "I wouldn't mind some of that mischief. She's a looker, that one."

"Rankin thinks there might be something more to it."

"Like what?"

"What do you think?"

"I'm askin' you," Hart answered.

"How's about she wants some payback for the mister?"

"Rankin tell you that?"

"I'm way ahead of him."

"Uh huh."

"Alright, then. If you got no use for bonus money, I won't trouble you."

"What bonus money?"

"Price has Rankin spooked. He's got the law dog watchin' him, for all the good that does."

"Does what he wants it to, I reckon."

"Maybe so, and maybe not. If I was Rankin and a couple fellows made my headache go away, seems like I might reward those fellows for a job well done."

Hart frowned. "I don't much like the sound of this."

"No problem. If you're yellow, I'll just do it my own self."

Hart was steaming now. He clutched his whiskey glass, white-knuckled. Squeezing the words between his teeth he answered, "No man calls me yellow."

"I'm just saying what the other boys're bound to say when they find out you wouldn't even talk to Price."

"Talk to him?"

"Two of us and only one of him. I figure we can get a word in."

"Well—"

"But if you're still afraid, I understand. First man starts any giggle talk about you losin' nerve answers to me."

Hart took another hit of gut-warmer and slapped his empty glass down on the bar.

"I'm listening."

Chad Saxon smiled. "Here's what we do," he said.

The shock of Belle's announcement left Price dumbstruck. He'd been groping for a question—something on the lines of *Are you sure he's mine?*—when she took pity on him and explained.

Belle hadn't known she was with child the night he killed the Farrell brothers and she sent him packing with their blood still warm and tacky on his feet. It might've made a difference, she supposed, but that was second-guessing fate and no one ever won that game.

She'd been almost a month gone when Price left, and by the time she knew for sure it didn't take a genius to count backward and decide the date, within a night or two.

"He's definitely yours," she'd told him, standing in the open door of his hotel room. "Just in case you're wondering."

"It crossed my mind," he'd said, shamefaced.

To which she sadly smiled and said, "I thought it might."

For a time she'd thought Price would return to her, despite her shouting at him in the lamplight that she never wanted to see hide or hair of him again, that he was poison, and she couldn't bring herself to lie down with Death. She'd hoped he would defy her and come back—not begging her, that wasn't in him; simply giving her a chance to tell her secret, let *him* choose to stay or run.

He hadn't, though.

Her words had cut too deeply. Price had taken them to heart.

When she was two months gone and starting to imagine that it showed, wondering if she should see a certain Chinaman in town and try a sample of his special medicine to finish it, the peddler had turned up in Amarillo.

He made all the difference in the world.

He saved their son, and over time Belle came to think he might've saved her soul, as well.

Price didn't know much about souls. He hadn't spent an hour in any given year since childhood pondering what preachers called The Afterlife. The few sermons he could recall in bits and pieces all agreed that good folk went to Heaven, while his kind were sent the other way. Price wasn't sure if he believed it, but he recognized that other people spent a fair amount of time preoccupied with fear of what would happen to them when they passed.

Belle hadn't seemed the type, but he supposed that carrying another life inside could change a person's point of view.

She'd made her mind up and was on her way to see the Chinaman when she'd run into Jared Mercer on the street. Distracted by her errand, Belle had literally run into him, knocking heads and tumbling backward, twisting her ankle in the process. She must've had the same effect on Mercer that she'd had on Price the night they met. The peddler had apologized a dozen times for her mistake, before he got around to asking Belle her name.

He'd seen Belle limping and insisted that she come with him to the cafe, to rest a spell and catch her breath.

Coffee turned into lunch. When Mercer asked to call on her, she'd told him he could find her any night but Tuesday at the Lucky Strike.

"He didn't judge me," Belle explained, making it sound as if Price had.

It was the other way around, he'd almost said, but kept it to himself.

The peddler hadn't judged her, but he'd kept her from her killing errand, making her think twice. He wouldn't call on her at the saloon and rent her by the hour, either. He'd insisted on a proper, public date for supper on a Tuesday evening and ignored the bluenose biddies staring in the restaurant when Belle had entered on his arm. They'd talked around her work, around her life, the peddler spinning dreams that sounded sweet to Belle, the more she heard of them.

Their second evening out, Mercer had popped the question. He'd been love-clumsy about it, offering to make an "honest woman" out of Belle. She had been nearly three months gone and Price was somewhere in the wind. She'd broken down, told Mercer everything— or most of it, at least. He hadn't minded, wanting only to care for Belle and the child. He'd settled up her debts in town and bought out her contract at the Lucky Strike. They'd married on a Saturday and rode out Monday morning, headed south.

To Redemption and the rest of it.

"He treats you well, I take it?" Price had asked her.

"Always," she assured him. "More important, he treats Jesse like his own. There's never been a moment when I didn't know he loves us both."

"You're lucky, then." There had been nothing else to say.

"He still won't go," Belle said, before she closed the door between them. "I suppose it's funny if you think about it. First I send you off, and now I can't make Jared leave. I'll cost Jesse his father twice."

She had a surgeon's skill for wounding. Price had managed not to follow her outside, but he had reconsidered leaving town that afternoon. It wasn't so much a decision as a wait-and-see evasion of deciding.

He could stay another day or two and have a look around. It wouldn't cost him much and he had nowhere else to be.

Maybe he'd catch a glimpse of Rankin and decide what sort of man he was, what it would take to back him down.

I have a son.

The thought stayed with him as he went downstairs and out into the street. There was no sign of Belle as Price turned left and moved along the sidewalk, headed east.

A voice called out behind him, from the street.

"Yo, saddle tramp!"

Price didn't slow his pace or glance around.

The voice was raised again.

"I mean you, Mr. Price!"

The more he thought about it, Perry Hart suspected bracing Matthew Price wasn't the best idea he'd heard since breakfast. He knew Price's reputation as a shooter—some of it, at least—and would no more have challenged him in normal circumstances than he would've kissed a diamondback.

Unfortunately, these weren't normal circumstances.

Chad had called him yellow once already, for suggesting they should let Price be. Hart had been close to drawing on him then, although in truth he wasn't sure he had the necessary speed to pull it off. If Chad repeated it, there'd be no way around a killing moment—and if he was bound to fight, Hart guessed the two of them would have a better chance with Price than he'd have facing Chad alone.

The good news was Chad said they likely wouldn't have to fight at all. They'd talk to Price and tell him how things were, who ran the town and all. Drop Rankin's name and let the shooter see that siding with the big man's enemies would be unhealthy for him in the end.

There was no reason anyone should die today.

Unless Price took it wrong.

That possibility gave Hart some nagging second thoughts, but there was no way out of it once they had left the Nugget and started walking down toward the hotel.

He couldn't turn tail now, without Chad knowing he was boogered. Worse yet, there'd be no way to deny it.

"There he is, I'll bet."

A tall man coming out of the hotel and passing on the far side of the street.

"You don't know that," Hart said.

"Look at him, will you? Who else could it be?"

The stranger passed them without glancing over, headed back the way they'd come. Chad turned to follow him and stepped into the street.

"Yo, saddle tramp!"

Hart watched the stranger, wondering if he would turn or even flinch, but nothing showed.

Chad tried again. "I mean you, *Mister* Price!"

That got him. Hart felt something wriggle in his stomach as the stranger stopped and slowly turned around. He saw the shooter's right hand graze gun leather.

Chad was moving, making Hart decide to keep pace or be left behind. The way he grinned through two-day stubble, Chad seemed to be having quite a time.

The stranger stood and waited for them on the wooden sidewalk, in the shade. Hart felt the dark eyes judging him and wondered what they saw.

It was a step up to the sidewalk. Chad was there, but Hart came close to stumbling and it made him look a fool. He bit his tongue and felt the angry color rising in his face.

"You know your name, at least," Chad said.

The shooter seemed to watch them both at once. He said, "I don't know you."

"Chad Saxon. I'm well-known around these parts."

"Nobody's mentioned you so far."

Hart winced at that. Chad lost his grin.

"I work for Mr. Rankin, lately." Chad was stiff with injured pride. "I guess you've heard of *him*."

"So you're a messenger, I take it."

This was bad. Hart thought about the hammer loops still fastened on his twin Schofields.

"I'm more'n that," Chad said. His right hand shivered closer to his Peacemaker. "You stick around Redemption, you might find that out."

"What's wrong with here and now?" Price asked.

It was the moment when you had to jump or walk away. Hart saw it coming, smelled his own fear-sweat and hated Price for making him afraid.

Chad moved, but he was nowhere close to fast enough. Price cleared his holster in a blur. Hart fumbled with his own and waited for the shot, but what he heard instead was an explosive grunt from Chad, as Price clubbed him across the face and put him down. Chad's pistol clattered on the boards.

Hart froze, his guns still anchored in their holsters. Staring cross-eyed down the barrel of a six-inch Colt, he heard Price thumb the hammer back.

"What'll it be?" the shooter asked.

"I got no quarrel with you."

"Then maybe you should help your friend back home."

"I'll do that very thing," Hart said.

"Your boss man wants me, I'm at the hotel. Same goes for anybody else."

"Yes, sir."

It took three tries for Hart to get Chad on his feet. By that time, Price was out of pistol range and passing Molly

Deegan's on his way to the Trail's End. Hart watched him shove in through the bat-wing doors and disappear from view.

Gil Gresham found Price at the Trail's End half an hour later. Coming through the door, he saw Price seated at a table in the corner farthest from the bar. Price kept his back against the wall and didn't seem to see the marshal coming until Gresham was within earshot.

"I thought you'd be a little quicker."

Gresham eyed the table's second chair. "You mind if I sit down?"

"Free country, Marshal."

Gresham settled in, and put his elbows on the table, both hands clearly visible and nowhere near his gun. Price held the beer mug in his left hand, while the right remained invisible.

"You knew I'd be around," he said to Price.

"It stood to reason."

"I believe we spoke about my vision of a peaceful town."

"You should've told those other boys."

"I'm telling you."

"Sedge Rankin whistles, you sit up and bark. Is that the deal?"

Gresham felt his gut twist. "Who said anything about Sedge Rankin?"

"Them he sent to try and spook me out of town."

"It's news to me."

"Somebody doesn't fill you in, I guess."

"It's risky making accusations, Mr. Price."

"Talk to the mouthy one when he wakes up. See what he has to say."

"I might do that."

"You should've done it first," Price said.

Gresham was torn between a flush of anger and a chill of fear. It wasn't every day he looked death in the face, but stubborn pride demanded a response.

"You'd tell me how to do my job?"

"In my experience," Price said, "most lawmen take their orders from the folks who own their badges."

"I could take offense at that."

"Your choice."

That hand beneath the table spooked him.

"Way it stands right now," he said, "three witnesses in shops along Main Street tell me Chad Saxon drew his pistol first."

"You'll want to lock him up, I guess."

Gresham ignored the jibe. "Most men he draws on wind up under ground."

"My lucky day," Price said.

"I'd hate to see you stretch that luck too thin."

"It's good to know you care."

He had a mind to drop Annabelle Mercer's name and see how Price reacted, but the shooter's dead eyes changed his mind.

"I care about Redemption and its people," he replied.

"Some more than others, I suppose."

Gresham ignored the bait. "I'll have a word with Saxon. In the meantime, you'd be wise to leave off making enemies."

"I take folks as I find them, Marshal. If a man comes after me, he needs to bring his best."

Gresham could feel Price watching him the whole way to the door, eyes like the muzzles of a double-barreled gun. Squinting at sunshine, Gresham took stock of his situation and decided the best thing for him to do right now was nothing.

Rankin had an axe to grind with Price, or maybe it would be the other way around. Whatever, Gresham didn't relish the idea of being caught between them when feud drew blood.

"I don't remember telling either one of you to run the stranger out."

Sedge Rankin lounged behind his massive desk, eyes boring tunnels into Chad Saxon and Perry Hart. They stood before him, hats in hand. An oblong purpling bruise marked Chad's left cheek. The eye above it had acquired a spastic twitch.

"Refresh my memory on that," he prodded them, "if I've forgotten anything."

"No, sir. You didn't tell us anything like that."

He'd known it would be Hart who broke the silence first. Saxon would set his teeth around a grudge and gnaw it to the bone.

"That's good. You had me scared my mind was failing me."

"No, sir."

"So one of you dreamed up this brilliant plan. Was this your brainstorm, Perry?"

"Well . . ."

"I guess not. Hell, you're anybody's dog who'll hunt with you."

He watched the harelip color up, but Hart was wise enough to keep his mouth shut. Rising, Rankin walked around the desk to stand in Saxon's face.

"Tell me about it, Chad."

The left eye twitched as Saxon said, "I thought we'd help you out."

"How's that?"

"I heard you talkin' to the marshal and—"

"Spying?"

"No, sir. Nothing like that. I heard a bit, is all, and thought you might appreciate it if we kept this boy from stirrin' up a ruckus."

"Way it looks to me, this *boy* put you to bed."

"He suckered me."

"Uh huh. Now let me get this straight. You thought I might *appreciate* your *help* if you went out and wound this shooter up by giving him my name. Is that about the size of it?"

"It didn't work out like I planned."

"You thought he'd be impressed. He'd take one look at you and ride out hell-for-leather."

Saxon held his peace.

"This shooter who's let daylight through more men than you've got teeth."

"I ain't afraid of him."

"Then let me ask you one more thing."

"What's that?"

"Did Price knock *any* sense into your skull at all?"

"I told you once, he suckered me."

"That's what I thought."

Rankin swung from the hip and smashed his fist into the hireling's face. Saxon went down, blood spouting from his nose.

"I guess he didn't hit you hard enough."

His knuckles ached, but he could live with it. He let Chad wobble up on hands and knees, then caught him with a kick that put him on his back.

"Consider this an education, son."

Gasping, Chad fumbled for his Colt. Rankin reared back and booted it across the office. He stooped and grabbed Chad by the vest, lifting him off the floor, and shook him like a dusty rug.

"You ride for me," he snarled, "I tell you what to do and when to do it. Are we clear?"

Chad muttered something. Rankin swung around and drove his skull into the desk.

"I can't hear you!"

"Yessir." It came out as a sob. "It's clear."

He let Chad drop and turned on Perry Hart. The freckled redhead braced himself for the assault, eyes narrowed down to slits. He made no move to raise his hands.

"And you."

"Yes, sir?"

"Next time some fool decides to take my name in vain, you come straight here and tell me. Is that understood?"

"Yes, sir!"

"Alright, then. Get him out of here and close the door

behind you." As an afterthought he said, "Don't give that pistol back until you're sure he's thinking straight. I may not be in a forgiving mood next time."

"Yes, sir."

When they were gone, Rankin straightened his rumpled jacket, gave his vest a tug. It was important for a well-respected businessman to always look his best.

7

His second morning in Redemption, after having spent another restless night alone, Price calculated he should have a look around the countryside. He hadn't paid much notice to it riding in, but now he thought examining the land Sedge Rankin coveted enough to kill for might help him decide what he should do.

I have a son.

That wasn't strictly true, of course.

Price didn't doubt the conception part—Belle wouldn't spin a lie like that to make him stay—but there was more to fatherhood than planting seeds.

His father was a decent man, a Christian in his way, but he'd been shackled to the soil and it had broken him. Instead of following his father's footsteps, all young Matthew Price could think about was how to burn the breeze, headed for God-knew-where.

He'd made it out alright, and never looked back, but where had the long run taken him? And at what cost?

Price couldn't kick about the life he'd chosen, even if it sometimes seemed to have crept up while he was sleeping and attached itself to him without a by-your-leave. Things happened day by day that made a man change course without intending to—ride south, when in his heart he wanted to be heading east or west. The desert ate his backtrail and his destination faded into a mirage.

Price knew he wasn't cut from whatever it took to make a father. Besides which, the boy—*Jesse, "his name's Jesse"*—already had a father in his life, the only one he'd ever known. Nothing worthwhile would come of tampering with that.

Belle hadn't sent for him to meet their son. She didn't want or need his help in that respect, and Price had nothing more to offer Jesse than he'd had to offer Belle ten years ago.

His life was trail dust and gun smoke, driven by the wind. The only things he left behind were fading tracks and shallow graves.

The hostler had his Appaloosa fed and watered by the time Price reached the livery. He paid for two more days and saddled up, slipping his Winchester into its scabbard. His canteen sweated in the morning heat.

Price rode out to the east, for no reason except that he'd come into town the other way and it was fresh to him. The land he'd seen so far hadn't been fenced or posted, but he'd take the risk of trespassing to have a look around. If he ran into Rankin's people they could have a little talk.

Price still hadn't decided whether he would fight for Belle—or for her man, the way it really was. It was a hard thing to decipher, with the boy in mind. Belle knew the best thing was to pack and leave, but she'd had no luck selling it.

Price thought he understood the way her peddler felt. The man had run his rainbow down and found the pot of gold, but someone else was bent on taking it away. Price would've gone for Rankin first, but Jared Mercer played the game another way.

Price couldn't call him yellow, since Mercer stuck around even after he was gelded by a bullet, but that didn't make him a hero. It was one thing for a man to stand in trouble's way and let himself get trampled, something else entirely to defend his loved ones and himself effectively.

So far, all Jared Mercer had accomplished was to prove his stubbornness—while jeopardizing Belle and Jesse in the process. Rankin hadn't been afraid to have the peddler shot; he wouldn't back down from a cripple in a wheelchair.

Rankin owned the local law and there was no one else in town with grit enough to stand up in his face and say, "Enough." Words wouldn't cut it anyway once blood was spilled. When Rankin tired of using Mercer as a lesson to his enemies, he'd move against the shopkeeper again.

If Mercer wouldn't fight or run, he'd die.

Where would that leave Belle and the boy?

Jesse.

Price wondered where the name had come from. It embarrassed him to realize that he knew nothing of Belle's family—who they were or where they came from. She had kept such secrets to herself in Amarillo, leaving Price to talk about whatever crossed his mind.

Mostly, they hadn't talked at all.

The rowdy side of town was quiet as he passed, no foot traffic around the whorehouse or the two saloons. He half expected Rankin's man to come out spoiling for a fight, but no one trod the boards. Another minute and he showed the town his back, nudging the Appaloosa to an easy trot.

Price had nowhere special to go and all day to get there. A half-mile out of town he changed course to the north and rode with the sun off his right shoulder, still three hours short of its zenith. The day was bound to be another scorcher, but he didn't mind. Price wouldn't push

the Appaloosa if he didn't have to. They could find a
pace that suited both of them and make it last.

The land he rode across was open range without a steer
in sight, the dry grass ankle-high. Belle had mentioned
that Rankin had struck oil, but there was nothing on this
side of town, as far as Price could see, to match the ugly
derricks he had seen around Fort Worth last year.

Black gold, they called it, but it looked and smelled
like muck.

An hour north of town, Price knew he had a tail.

He felt it first, the way he sometimes knew when he
was being watched, before he caught a shooter staring at
him. Price reined in atop a gentle rise and eyeballed back
along his trail, due south.

The prairie shimmered, heat haze warping vision, but
he still picked out the dark speck of a rider coming on behind him. Price sat waiting for another moment, making
certain it was only one, before he turned and started north
again.

Coincidence?

Price wished he had a spyglass, but his eyes would
have to do. Waiting to see the rider's face and learn his
business meant a confrontation, and he didn't fancy
meeting up on open ground. A fair hand with a Winchester or Sharps could pick him off before he knew the other
man had shouldered iron.

No good.

He might not get the first shot, but he wouldn't be a
sitting target either.

Half a mile ahead, three-quarters at the most, a line of
trees smudged the horizon. Price could shelter there and
shade his Appaloosa while he waited for the other rider to
catch up.

And if he recognized the man he'd gun-whipped yesterday, there would be time to watch him over rifle
sights, deciding whether he should live or die.

Price dug his heels in, widening his lead. He didn't
look around to find out if his shadow picked up speed.

Unless the Appaloosa broke a leg now, there was no way for the other rider to catch up with him before he made the tree line.

It was mostly cottonwood and hackberry, with some bur oaks scattered through the mix. Price rode well in and out of sight before he cut left and doubled back, stopping thirty yards west of the point where he'd entered the woods.

Beyond the trees, he watched the grassland baking under Texas sun. He drew the Winchester and levered up a round into the chamber, then relaxed the hammer with his thumb. There'd be no *click-clack* noise to warn his target if Price saw a need to fire.

He thought about the shooter he had buffaloed yesterday, pictured him brooding overnight and swilling courage by the glass. The tinhorn had survived one stand-up fight with Price, but maybe he was short on gratitude.

Or maybe it was someone else.

From what he'd heard of Rankin's men, backshooting wouldn't cost them any sleep. Price didn't favor it, himself, but he was satisfied to let the dealer call the game.

Come on, he thought. *Let's get it done.*

The boy was starting to believe he'd made a serious mistake. Trailing a man like Matthew Price was dangerous. He'd known that, starting out—but it was an adventure, too.

And there were questions he was bound to ask, if he could find the nerve.

He knew the shooter's name the way boys always know such things, by word of mouth. The way he knew John Wesley Hardin, Wild Bill Hickok and Doc Holliday. Hickok and Holliday were dead now, and Hardin was in prison after gunning a Comanche County lawman. Jesse'd read about them in the dime novels his parents sometimes carried at the store.

There weren't many left like Price, these days.

That wasn't it, of course.

The reputation was enough to make him gawk at Price across the street, like boys will, or to try and get a closer look at him in the saloon. It wouldn't make him bring the palomino pony out and trail Price all over creation, though.

His ma and pa had seen to that.

They'd woken him last night with one of the discussions they reserved for after he was sent to bed. Fierce talk, it was, and angry-sounding, though they tried to keep their voices down.

He'd come out once, when they were loud, and caught them at it. Both of them had turned blank faces toward him for a moment when he'd asked why they were fighting. Then his ma had walked him back to bed, explaining on the way that proper men and women didn't fight; they had *discussions* to resolve their disagreements in a manner that was *civilized*.

It still sounded like fighting, but they tried to keep it quiet now.

There had been more discussions after bedtime since his pa was crippled up. They didn't use that word at home—*crippled*—but he still heard it from the other boys. Some said it without thinking; others meant to see if it would make him bawl, but he was learning how to pay them back.

Ma didn't like him fighting, but his pa kept quiet when he brought a shiner home. They would *discuss* it later, thinking that he couldn't hear, seeming to blame each other for scuffling.

"Why can't we just *leave* this godforsaken place?" his ma would ask.

And Pa would answer back, "A man can't run away," or some such thing.

Of course, most men could *walk*, but when he thought such things the boy felt guilty and his eyes burned hot with tears.

Last night they hadn't quarreled about the town or failing business at the store. It had been Matthew Price, the boy's ears pricking up at mention of his name.

"He's got no business here," Pa said. "A man like that."

"It's what he does," Ma said.

"Well, not for me," said Pa, right back at her. "No thank you, ma'am."

"It wouldn't be for you," Ma told him, in her scolding voice.

"And thank you for reminding me of *that*," Pa said, his chair *creak-creaking* as he rolled himself away to bed.

He hadn't understood the argument, but there'd been frost around the breakfast table, neither of them saying much except to tell him he should clean his plate. Children were hungry somewhere, even if he'd had enough.

It seemed to him the other kids got hungrier each time his ma and pa had a discussion overnight.

He had a list of chores to do, it being Saturday, but he had thrown them over when he saw Price on the street, long-legging toward the livery. He'd followed on an impulse, questions brimming in his mind.

How did his parents know this shooter who had downed so many men?

Where was he going?

Was he leaving town?

Because of something Ma or Pa had said?

A sudden impulse gripped him when he saw the shooter riding out of town. There would be hell to pay with Ma for shirking, though she didn't hold with whipping, and there might be other risks as well.

What if he met Sedge Rankin's riders on the way?

They don't know you, he'd thought and took off running for the livery.

Señor Dorado always wore a sad face when the boy came in. He'd ask how Pa was doing at the store, when what he really meant was *Is there any hope?*

Señor Dorado let him borrow Dancer sometimes, take the palomino pony out to run and get his exercise. Dorado always talked a bit first, slow and easy, but the boy had prodded him today and cleared the edge of town while Price was still a speck on the horizon, headed east.

He'd made up his mind not to follow Price too closely, and to turn back in an hour if it looked like Price was leaving town. A part of him would've been happy to keep riding, all the way to Indian Territory and beyond. He could turn his back on Pa's creaky chair and the muttered *discussions,* light out for someplace he had only seen in half-remembered dreams.

He'd even pictured teaming up with Price, but that was crazy thinking. He brought nothing to the table, no skills worth the claiming, and he'd only slow the shooter down. Price didn't need a kid riding his dust and asking questions all the time.

That sort of thing could get him killed.

But maybe someday.

He'd almost given up and turned around then, when Price changed his course and headed north. An hour into it, and Ma would miss him at the store soon.

He could almost feel the tiny angel on one shoulder, telling him to double back. The devil on his other whispered, *Keep on. Otherwise you'll never know.*

He'd kept on riding.

Once, he thought he'd seen Price hesitate but couldn't tell for sure. A simple breather, maybe.

Was he looking back?

The boy was suddenly afraid, but he pressed on. He saw the trees ahead, the best part of another mile to go before he reached their shadow. Price got there well ahead of him and disappeared from sight.

Go back! the angel cautioned him.

Go on! the devil countered.

He rode on.

Waiting. He's waiting for me in the trees.

Or maybe not.

Price wouldn't stop unless he knew for sure that he was being followed.

Or he'd found a stream and was letting the Appaloosa drink.

That would be something, riding up on Price by accident, surprising him. The boy wondered how fast Price really was, and if his mind was quick enough to stay the hand before he dropped a kid.

Go back!

Go on!

The trees were closer now but kept their secrets draped in shadows. He had never ridden out this far alone, but still knew where he was. The Kelsey place was farther on, a mile or so beyond the woods. He knew Tom Kelsey from Redemption's one-room school.

The woods looked nice and cool. He'd ridden off without a hat, and now the sun was baking him. Dancer seemed to enjoy it, but the boy thought both of them could use a break.

A little farther, then.

If Price was waiting for him, watching, would he fire?

The boy hunched lower on his borrowed saddle, but it didn't help. He made a target either way, and even if the first shot missed him, Dancer might go down.

He didn't think Price was the kind to shoot a kid, but who could say? Bill Hickok once shot his own deputy, mistaken for an adversary in the heat of battle. The boy was a stranger to Price, trailing him without reason and far out from town.

He rode on, waiting for the shot. It seemed to help a little when he squinted—anyhow, the sun wasn't so bright that way.

He was still squinting when he crossed the tree line into welcome shade. Dancer picked out a path between the trees, making himself at home. The boy looked down but couldn't tell if there were any tracks to follow.

What if I get lost in the woods?

Price could ride on, ignoring him, and leave the boy to wander aimlessly all day and night. Who'd save him if he couldn't find his way back home?

The rush of fear embarrassed him. He knew from listening to others that the woods weren't all that big. He couldn't lose himself and *die,* although when Ma got hold of him he might wish he was dead.

The boy was concentrating on his mission when he heard the small click of a hammer drawing back. A graveyard voice was right behind it.

"You lose something, boy?"

Price watched the kid rein up. His mount was undersized but well behaved. Unless it was a twin, he'd seen it stabled at the livery in town.

"No, sir," the boy responded to his question. "I'm just riding."

"You should never start a conversation with a lie."

The boy blushed pink beneath a thatch of sandy hair. The color made his scattered freckles stand out plainly.

"Are you gonna shoot me, sir?"

"I'm studying the matter." Price resisted an impulse to smile. "You heeled?"

"No, sir. Don't own a gun."

"If that's a lie, whipping will be the least of your concerns."

"My folks won't let me have one."

"And the good news is they may've saved your life today."

"Yes, sir."

He was polite enough, Price gave him that.

"I know your animal from town," he said.

"She isn't mine. I borrowed her."

"To follow me."

He watched the boy consider lying, working out the risk. Young eyes kept darting to the Winchester Price carried with the butt against his right hip, muzzle pointed skyward.

"Yes, sir."

"Then you have me at a disadvantage. What's your name?"

He blinked. "Name, sir?"

"That thing your mama calls you."

"Jesse Mercer, sir."

Price felt a chill that didn't fit the hour or the place. He thumbed the rifle's hammer gently down and put the Winchester back in its saddle scabbard.

"Do your folks know where you are?"

"No, sir. I reckon I'm in trouble now."

"It could be worse," Price said. "Hard country hereabouts. Hard men, I'm told."

"Yes, sir."

"What made you follow me?"

Another stall, the boy examining a compromise with truth. "You're famous, sir," he said at last.

There's more, Price thought, but didn't press it.

"Famous, am I?"

"Yes, sir."

"Like Abe Lincoln?"

"No, sir. Like John Wesley Hardin."

"He was doing time, the last I heard."

"Yes, sir."

"You calling me a jailbird, boy?"

"No, sir! You're fast is all I meant. You've seen things. Had adventures."

"I've seen things, alright," Price said. "Now *you've* seen *me,* and you'd best ride that pony back to town."

His face looked like a rain cloud, fit to burst. Price didn't know if Jesse was about to cry, laugh, or explode.

"Sir, if you wouldn't mind—"

He stopped there, flustered, and his eyes dropped to his saddle horn.

"There's something in your craw," Price said. "Best spit it out."

Jesse screwed up his nerve and said, "I wonder if you'd mind me riding on with you a spell."

It's a mistake, Price thought.

"You want to get me strung for kidnapping?"

"No, sir! I'll keep it to myself, I swear. Somebody asks, I'll tell them I took Dancer out to run a bit."

"Suppose somebody spots us, then?"

"There's no one left out here except the Kelseys, sir. We wouldn't have to ride that far."

Nobody left.

He thought about Sedge Rankin's guns and said, "I'll tell you what. You want to ride along until we clear these woods, I wouldn't mind."

"Yes, sir!" Big smile.

"I'm not done yet."

"Sorry."

"If we should run across somebody on the way who looks like trouble, I expect you'll take that pony and skedaddle back to town."

"Trouble?"

"Is it a deal, or not?"

"Yes, sir."

Price nudged the Appaloosa closer. "Then let's shake on it."

"Yes, sir!"

The boy had a fair grip. His hand was small and warm.

I have a son.

"Gumdrop?"

"Yes, please. Ma says I have a real sweet tooth."

She used to say the same thing about me.

Price felt the burn behind his eyes and blinked it out. Taking a small bag from his pocket, he tapped a candy into Jesse's palm, then chose one for himself.

"You like that animal," he said when they were moving through the trees.

"Yes, sir. She's fine."

"Not yours, though."

"No, sir. Señor Dorado lets me ride her now and then."

"That shows some trust."

"He knows my folks, and I help out around the livery sometimes."

"A working man."

"Yes, sir." The smile lit Jesse's face.

"That's good."

"My pa says work builds character."

"I think he's onto something there."

"I'd rather travel, though, and see the world."

"Takes money," Price reminded him.

"Yes, sir. Ma says it's better to have roots."

There was a time she hadn't thought so. People change.

"Two things I've been schooled not to do," Price said. "The first is not to contradict a boy's mother."

"What's contra—contra— . . ."

"Contradict."

"Yes, sir. What's that?"

"It means to say the opposite of someone else."

"And what's the other thing?"

"Pardon?"

"You said *two* things."

"Oh, that. I never bet that I can fill an inside straight."

Jesse wasn't sure he followed that. Instead he asked, "Is this your first time in Redemption, sir?"

"It is."

"Do you know anyone in town?"

Price frowned. "I've met the marshal and a couple more. Now, I know you."

"Before you came, I mean."

Price saw the snare and edged around it. "Hard to say. I haven't asked around so far."

Was he imagining the disappointed look on Jesse's face? Price would've bet his life that Belle had kept their secret from the boy to spare him.

Jared Mercer knew the truth—or part of it, at least. Was it a quarreling point between them, now that times were hard?

"You pistol-whipped Chad Saxon yesterday."

"I don't recall you being there," Price said.

"It's hard to keep a secret in Redemption. People talk."

"What do they say?"

"Chad called you out, with Perry Hart. You backed them down."

"That's all?"

"Nobody has the why of it."

"That's how it is, sometimes. Things don't always make sense."

"You could've shot them, though."

"It wasn't called for."

Jesse frowned. "They don't forget."

"How's that?"

"They're Rankin's men. The marshal won't do anything. They'll come back on you sometime, to get even."

"Thanks for telling me."

"I reckon you already knew."

"It crossed my mind."

"They're bad men," Jesse said. "You should've done it while you had the chance."

"I never take it lightly. If they want to try again, we'll see what happens."

"If you see them coming. Pa says—"

Jesse caught himself and dammed the flow of words.

"Says what?"

"Nothing."

Backshooters.

Did Belle's husband think one of them put the bullet in his spine? Would he have said so, speaking where the boy could hear him?

They broke through the northern tree line, riding into sunshine once again. Price felt the difference, hard sun beating down.

"You ought to wear a hat out here," he said.

"Yes, sir." Jesse screwed up his courage. "Sir, I'm wondering if you—"

"Hold up."

There was a hazy smudge of smoke on the horizon, maybe two miles out from where they sat their mounts. Price studied it.

White smoke would mean a grass fire.

This was dusky gray.

"The Kelsey place!"

"You know them?"

"Tom, from school. Nobody else lives out this way for miles."

It wasn't Price's business, but he thought about what Belle had told him. Squatters being driven off the land or planted in it.

"I'll go have a look," he said. "You head on back to town and send the marshal out."

"But, sir—"

"Don't 'but' me, now. We had a deal."

He kicked the Appaloosa up to speed and left Jesse behind him, riding hard into a breeze that carried wood smoke to his nostrils.

8

Caution took over when he was a hundred yards out from the homestead, riding hard. Price cleared his Winchester and rode another twenty-five before he reined the Appaloosa to an easy trot.

If guns were waiting for him, they already had the range.

The house and barn had burned out overnight. Price knew that much at fifty yards, seeing both structures crumbled down to heaps of ash, charred timbers jutting here and there like ribs on an overcooked carcass. There was no good hiding place in sight, but Price still took it easy.

Nothing good had ever come from letting down his guard.

He reached the barn first, riding in, and circled it, sniffing the breeze. There was a fading smell of roasted meat around the place, but it was coming from the house. Off to the north, upwind, he spied two horses grazing on the flats, keeping their distance from the slaughter ground.

Some of the livestock made it, anyway.

The people, Price imagined, weren't supposed to.

Chickens pecked dirt in the yard and fled before his shadow as he rode on toward the house. It had been situated twenty yards northeast of where the barn once stood, the distance ruling out an accidental leap of flame between one building and the other.

Hoofprints in the yard were numerous and hopelessly confused. Price wasn't schooled in tracking, but he guessed the riders numbered four or five, at least. In any case, there'd been enough of them to do the job.

He circled once around the smoking ruin of the house, looking for any sign that someone may have gotten out alive. A part of the adobe fireplace had survived, its tumbled-down chimney a broken finger pointed at the sky.

The roast-meat smell was stronger here, but Price wouldn't have bet that much remained of those who'd slept within.

What was the name?

Jesse had mentioned it—a boy he knew from school— but Price couldn't remember now. He wondered if his inattention was an insult to the dead.

If so, it wasn't prominent among his sins.

The hoofbeats of a horse approaching brought the rifle to his shoulder. Pivoting on saddle leather toward the sound, Price had his target framed and focused when he recognized the boy.

My son.

Price stowed his rifle, waiting by the ashes of the funeral pyre.

"I sent you back to town," he said, as Jesse reined the palomino in.

"I had to see."

Price couldn't fault him there. Children lived in a perpetual state of curiosity. Couple that with a classmate's tragedy and his own father's shooting—

I'm his father, a small voice said.

He doesn't know that. He doesn't need *to know.*

"I smell something," said Jesse.

"Wood smoke."

"Something else."

He could've said, *You smell dead people,* but he didn't. It would be a pointless cruelty. Jesse would work it out himself.

Price was about to give some noncommittal answer when he realized that he smelled something else, aside from charcoal and incinerated flesh.

It smelled like—

"Kerosene."

Price flicked another glance at Jesse. "I believe you're right," he said.

The smell was sharper and more obvious once Price identified it. He could almost taste it, a metallic flavor far back on his tongue.

"You think it was an accident?"

Price didn't want to lie. He settled for, "It's possible."

"I don't think so," said Jesse, answering himself as if Price hadn't spoken. "More like nightriders. Prob'ly Mr. Rankin's men."

"You don't know that."

"Sedge Rankin wants this land. He wants to own the world, my pa says."

"Loose talk's dangerous sometimes."

"I know." There was a world of hurt in his young voice. Jesse sat staring at the ashes for another while before he said, "Maybe the Kelseys got away."

"Reckon they'd head for town if that's the case."

Because God knows there's nothing left for them out here.

"I should go back and see if Tommy's there."

"Sounds like a good idea."

"Would you come with me, sir?"

Price felt the tug. "I'll be along directly, for the marshal."

"Waste of time, sir. Marshal Gresham won't come out."

"We'll see."

"Pa says Marshal Gresham's as useless as teats on a bull."

Price had to smile. "You mayn't want to say that back in town."

"No, sir. I watch myself."

"That's wise."

"They missed the outhouse," Jesse said, pointing.

Price saw that he was right. The privy stood untouched, some thirty yards beyond the ruins of the house. It looked like an embarrassed sentry who'd been caught sleeping and missed the action.

There was no point in checking it. If anyone had fled the house in that direction they'd have been pursued and taken down, either left where they fell or dragged back to the pyre.

"I never talked to Tommy much," said Jesse. "He was just a kid."

"Don't let it worry you."

"He prob'ly thought I didn't like him."

"I bet he had some friends his own age," Price replied.

"Not really, living way out here."

Price heard the tears in Jesse's voice.

"Things happen sometimes, Jesse. Chewing on them doesn't help. Whatever happened here's no fault of yours."

"I know that, sir. It's still a shame."

"Yes. It is."

"I'll head on back to town now."

"You do that."

Halfway across the yard, he reined the pony in and said, "Be careful, sir."

"You, too."

Price would've ridden back with Jesse if he'd thought the boy might come to any harm. The men who'd lit this fire were night crawlers. They obviously wouldn't shrink from hurting children, but Price reckoned they'd be sleeping off a gutful of tonsil varnish about now, or maybe tending hangovers with a little hair of the dog that bit them.

And he didn't want to leave just yet, though he would've been hard-pressed to explain.

Price hadn't known the Kelseys, hadn't even thought to ask how many there had been, and now he'd missed his chance. He wasn't saddened by their passing in the sense that someone who had known and cared for them would be. He'd witnessed too much death to feel the loss of strangers.

But he could feel the wrong that had been done here.

And he thought about a means to put it right.

Belle Mercer wasn't frantic when she checked Main Street again for Jesse, but she recognized the warning signs. It wasn't like him just to wander off, and in Redemption's present climate there were risks for children as well as adults.

Some children, anyway.

Don't think that way, she told herself, but couldn't stop.

Sedge Rankin didn't care what leverage was required to get the upper hand. He'd start with bribes and graduate to threats if his intended victim wouldn't name a reasonable price. His threats weren't empty, either, as she'd seen more times than she cared to remember.

Living proof of that sat waiting for her in the dry goods store.

Jared had not seemed overly concerned when Jesse skipped his morning chores. He hadn't shrugged it off, exactly, but he didn't leap to any grim conclusions either.

That was Belle's job.

Rankin doesn't care about us anymore, she thought. *He's satisfied.*

That was a lie, of course. She saw through it like glass. Rankin pursued a scorched-earth policy with those he marked as enemies. It didn't always come to shooting, but he left them broken all the same.

And we aren't broken yet.

Jared was crippled, but he still spoke up to anyone who'd listen in the course of any given day. The audience had dwindled sharply after he was shot, though, right along with business at the store. They still had friends and customers in town, but if they lost a few more by attrition there'd be red ink in the tally books by Christmastime.

There was a time it would have shocked and angered her, losing the store, but most days lately it seemed like a blessing in disguise. If Rankin shut them down, Jared would have to leave. He couldn't sit and watch his family starve for pride's sake.

Could he?

No.

And if Rankin could squeeze them out by tightening the purse strings, then he wouldn't need to send his shooters back a second time.

Belle worried that she might've started something when she wired Matt Price. It was a desperate ploy; she hadn't really thought he'd come.

He had, though, and she wondered now if calling on him might've made things worse.

Not just with Jared—she could smooth that out, given sufficient time—but for herself and Jesse. Rankin might find out she'd sent for Price, and when he did . . .

Belle didn't want to think about that now. She wanted Jesse safe where she could see him, maybe touch him if she needed to.

He had a hellfire lecture coming to him, at the very least, for scaring her this way. If he thought—

"Ma! Wait up, Ma!"

Turning, Belle saw Jesse running toward her down the middle of Main Street, from the direction of the livery.

I should've known he'd be with Dancer.

Jesse loved the little palomino as if it were his. They'd talked about a pony for him, back before the trouble started in Redemption, but he wouldn't get one this year.

Maybe never.

Jesse caught up to her on the sidewalk, winded. He was too keyed up to register the disapproval written on her face.

"The Kelseys, Ma! They got burned out last night!"

She hesitated on the verge of scolding him. "Who told you that?"

"I saw it for myself. They missed the outhouse, though."

Belle felt a chill despite the early afternoon's oppressive heat.

"What do you mean, you saw it?"

Jesse flushed pink with embarrassment. She had to ask a second time, then it spilled out of him, the story coming almost faster than her mind could follow.

He had followed Price—a ticket to disaster, in itself—and caught up with him somehow, on the way. Belle couldn't name the feeling she experienced, imagining her son—*their* son—alone with Matt for the first time. It was a mixture of relief and dark foreboding that she'd never felt before.

She barely understood when Jesse started in about the Kelsey place. Belle made him tell it twice. The house and barn in ashes. Chickens in the yard. A smell of kerosene.

She had to ask, when Jesse didn't offer. "Was there anybody there?"

He stared down at the sidewalk. "In the house, I think."

My God.

"Did you *see* anyone?"

"No, ma'am. Just Mr. Price."

"And where's he, now?"

"Still at the Kelsey place, I guess, or riding back. He's gonna talk to Marshal Gresham."

"I see."

Belle could feel the anger rising to replace her fear. Matt should've ridden back with Jesse, to protect him. What if Rankin's men were still—

She braked the train of thought before it carried her away. The one thing Matt knew best—better than anyone alive, perhaps—was risk. Belle knew he wouldn't have done anything to put their son in danger's path.

He didn't know this country, though.

He didn't know Sedge Rankin.

Though shuddering inside, Belle kept her voice and manner firm. "You had us worried sick, young man, on top of leaving chores undone. Do you know that?"

Small shoulders slumped. "I'm sorry, Ma."

"As well you should be."

"Yes, ma'am."

"And you shouldn't think those chores have done themselves, while you were out with Dancer and your new friend, Mr. Price."

"I know."

"You owe your father an apology before you start to work."

"Yes, ma'am."

She stopped him with a gentle hand. "No need to tell him where you've been, though. Let's keep that between the two of us."

"But, Ma—"

"I mean it, too! You've worried him enough for one day, don't you think?"

"Yes'm, I guess so."

"I *know* so." Stroking Jesse's hair, she said, "I'll tell him all about the Kelseys after dinner, and we won't let on you stole away from town."

He nodded silently and followed her along the sidewalk toward the dry goods store, Belle praying silently that nobody had seen her son with Matthew Price.

Gil Gresham was adjusting WANTED posters on his wall, getting them just so, when Price came in behind him, trailing midday heat.

"Looks like you're busy there," the shooter said.

Gresham took his own time, squaring a final poster on the wall, before he said, "Come by to tell me that you're leaving town?"

"You aren't that lucky. I've got work for you."

"Somebody else you pistol-whipped?"

"A burned-out homestead north of town."

The Kelsey place? It had to be.

Gresham played dumb. "How far outside?"

"Not too far. Three, four miles."

"That's far enough," Gresham replied. "My jurisdiction stops at the town limits."

"I mistook that for a badge pinned on your vest."

"You should've read it." Gresham tapped the tin star with a square-cut fingernail. "It says, 'Town Marshal.' Who you want's the county sheriff, down in Sanderson."

"How far is that?"

"A smidgen over thirty miles, southwest. You can't miss it. Nice town."

"Who owns the law down there?"

Gresham could feel the steam heat his face but said, "I don't rile easily, Mr. Price."

"I noticed that about you."

"So, if we're all done—"

"People are dead."

"It's county business. I've got laws to follow."

"Orders too, I bet."

"If I was looking into this, first thing I'd have to ask would be what you were doing on a stranger's land."

"Having a look around the countryside," Price said.

"And you just *found* this place burned out?"

"Smoke's hard to miss out there."

"I guess you have a witness, then."

Price stared at him, deadpan. "Is that the way you do it here?"

"Do what?"

"Put someone in the frame. You tag the first one who reports something?"

"I'd have to think about the person's reputation," Gresham said. "See what comes up."

"Solve many crimes that way?"

"We don't have many crimes here in Redemption. As for what goes on outside—"

"You don't much care."

"Put any twist on it you want to," Gresham said. "The law's the law."

"Then take your badge off for a day. You're still a man, and you've got neighbors murdered."

"Now it's murder? I suppose you saw the bodies."

"Smelled them cooking."

"Well, now, that could be a tragic accident."

"Go have a look."

Gresham pretended to consider it, then shook his head.

"You want to fill out a report, I'll see the sheriff gets it. Mail goes out on Tuesdays."

"Gives the buzzards ample time to feed, I guess."

"We've got an undertaker handles that. You would've seen his place when you rode in."

"Does *he* work out of town?"

"I reckon he'll go anywhere, if someone pays him."

Moving toward the door, Price said, "Don't worry, Marshal. Someone's bound to pay."

He didn't like the sound of that, but Gresham wasn't fool enough to follow Price outside and make an issue of it. He could go warn Rankin, but the thought of one more meeting in the Nugget's back room thrilled him even less.

Rankin could take care of himself. He didn't pay Chad Saxon and the rest for minding cattle on his spread. They were supposed to do his dirty work, and the less Gresham knew about what happened outside his narrowly defined jurisdiction, the better he liked it.

Being marshal of Redemption wasn't meant to be a high-risk job. It wasn't Tombstone or El Paso, where the border trash raised hell six days a week and passed out cold on Sunday. Gresham hadn't fired a shot in anger since he took the job and only had to coldcock rowdy drunkards around major holidays.

It was an easy job and meant to be. If Gresham's neck cramped now and then from looking the other way it was a little thing and getting smaller all the time.

Try spending dignity instead of cash sometime, and see what happens.

I should still do something, though.

Like what?

He didn't have to ask which spread Price meant. The Kelsey place was north of town, and nothing else beyond it for a half-day's ride. Rankin had offered them a price. They'd turned him down. Now they were gone.

It's not my jurisdiction.

That was true enough. The limits of his dubious authority had been spelled out in black and white before he drew his first paycheck. He even had a map to prove it, with Redemption's dead line drawn around the town in bright-red ink. His badge ran out of steam a hundred yards beyond each end of Main Street. Anything that happened on the other side of that imaginary line was someone else's problem.

It was simple.

He could always wire Butch Stoddard, but the county sheriff didn't like to be disturbed. Gresham supposed that came from taking Rankin's coin, but Stoddard didn't say and Gresham hadn't asked.

Some things he didn't want to know—like what a certain gunslinger had cooking underneath his hat.

Rankin already had an eye on Price, and there was no percentage for Gresham in nagging him about it. The smart thing, Gresham thought, would be to plan ahead for what came next.

Trouble was coming. He could smell it like a dead rat in the walls.

Gresham's response would naturally depend on the shape that trouble took. If Rankin's men killed Price outside of town, he could ignore it. If they killed the shooter in Redemption, he could fudge the evidence and squeeze the witnesses until it came out self-defense.

Suppose they couldn't take him, though.

What then?

He didn't want to think about that, yet. It would be ugly, and he'd have to side with Rankin or leave town—assuming there was time and opportunity for him to get away.

A headache started throbbing at the base of Gresham's skull. He walked around his desk, sat down, and took his secret bottle from the bottom right-hand drawer.

It wasn't seemly for a lawman to be drinking in the middle of the afternoon, but Gresham didn't care. His life had been unseemly for as long as he could recollect.

And now he was afraid it might be drawing to a close.

Redemption's undertaker was a gangly stork named Aloysius Grymdike. He was probably the tallest man in town, at six-foot-five, but he gave up a good three inches to a slouch that made it seem as if he bore upon his shoulders all the grief he had absorbed in twenty years of planting dearly departed. He wore black six days a week but switched to charcoal gray for church on Sunday, as a small concession to the Risen Lord.

Grymdike was a fourth-generation undertaker, schooled from solitary childhood in the tricks of the trade. He would've left the business to his sons, but he'd chosen poorly in a wife. Louise was barren, and she'd passed away the year after they moved from Dallas to Redemption, Grymdike looking for a town with growth potential and a minimum of competition.

Finding a replacement for Louise had been more difficult than he'd imagined. His appearance didn't captivate the gentler sex; Grymdike had been compared to Lincoln once, but the smart-ass was quick to add *two days after Ford's theater* when he made the remark. Grymdike's correspondence with spinsters and widows through a Houston matrimonial agency had likewise been more costly than productive, dialogue breaking down in each instance when he named his profession.

Never mind.

He was a young man yet, at only forty-three. And there was always Molly Deegan's, down the street, if he required particular relief.

Grymdike was polishing his most expensive casket— cherry wood with silver fittings—when a stranger walked in off the street. He made a point of recognizing everyone in town, all future customers, but this face stopped him cold.

"Good afternoon, sir. May I help you?"

"Depends," the stranger said. His clothes were dusty from the trail, his holster tied down low. "The marshal recommended you."

"That's very kind of him, I'm sure."

"You do the planting hereabouts."

"I care for the departed, sir."

"You've got some waiting for you on a homestead two or three miles north of town."

"Why, that would be—"

"The Kelsey spread, I'm told."

Grymdike nodded, frowning. "You're not a member of the family, I take it?"

"Never met them in my life."

"And you are Mr. . . . ?"

"Price."

"I see."

In fact, he saw too much. Grymdike was not a wholly friendless man. He heard most rumors as they made their way around Redemption, and he'd known a gunman was in town. The incident with Chad Saxon and Perry Hart had been reported to him over beer last night at the Trail's End.

He forced a smile. Shooters were often good for business.

"About the Kelseys, sir—"

"You'll need shovels," Price said. "Maybe an extra pair of hands. I'd leave the fancy duds at home."

"Forgive me, but I'm not quite sure I understand."

"Somebody torched their place last night. They didn't make it out."

"Good Lord!"

"He wasn't watching either, from the looks of things."

"You say that Marshal Gresham sent you?"

"He's fresh out of energy," Price said. "Killings weren't close enough to home for him to saddle up. He seemed to think you'd want the customers, though."

"Of course. But if the law's involved—"

"Your marshal knows his limitations."

Grymdike let that pass. "I take it there were no survivors?"

"None I saw."

All four, and Rachel Kelsey in a family way. *Dear Lord.*

"I normally do business with the next of kin," he said.

"Makes sense. I doubt they'll be around, though."

"No, I see your point. Unfortunately—"

"You're a businessman," Price said. "How much?"

"Excuse me, sir?"

"To get them off the ground and into it. How much?"

"Ah, well. We have the caskets to consider."

"You're not wrapping Christmas presents," Price reminded him. "The house burned down with them inside it. Keep it simple."

"Certainly. Unfinished pine, perhaps. I have two part-time helpers for the heavy work. They're Mexicans, but decent fellows all the same."

"Do tell."

"Oh, yes indeed. Shall we say fifteen dollars each?"

"Say ten and I can pay you now."

Grymdike did the arithmetic. Plain boxes—and if Price was right about the fire, he might get by with only one or two. Call it a family plot, and no one had to be the wiser. He could get the Mexicans for next to nothing, pesos on the dollar for their time and sweat.

"Your generosity to strangers is deserving of reward," he said. "We'll call it ten apiece."

Price palmed a roll of greenbacks, counting forty dollars into Grymdike's outstretched hand. The undertaker made it disappear before he spoke again.

"If I may say so, Mr. Price, it's most unusual to find a stranger passing through, no roots in town, who takes such interest in the grief of those he's never met."

"Unusual, you say?"

"From personal experience, I'd say unprecedented."

Price surprised him with a smile. "I've been called lots of things, but that's a new one."

"I assure you, sir, I meant no disrespect!"

"None taken. I might even throw you some more business in a day or two."

Startled, Grymdike had trouble coming up with a reply. Price was already in the doorway when he said, "I'll be at your disposal, sir."

"That last bit needs some work," Price said, and let the door swing shut behind him.

Aloysius Grymdike found that he was trembling. It embarrassed him. He'd spent a lifetime courting Death, but it had never walked into his shop before.

That last bit needs some work.

Perhaps. And Grymdike needed something for his nerves.

He locked the shop and moved along the sidewalk double-quick, toward the Trail's End.

9

It was approaching sundown when the undertaker and his Mexicans returned from their ex-
cursion to the Kelsey place. They had the bodies
wrapped in canvas and laid out in a wagon as if they
were sacks of grain. The undertaker, riding between his
helpers on the wagon's tall box seat, wore a stovepipe
hat that made him nearly two feet taller than his slouch-
ing bookends.

Price watched from the open window of his hotel room
as Grymdike's wagon passed beneath him. He counted
four bundles, one of them child-size, none of them large.
Fire eats what it wants to and spits out the rest.

A small crowd gathered on the street outside the undertaker's place to hear about his latest customers and
maybe sneak a peek. The Mexicans climbed down and
went to work unloading, while Grymdike stood and addressed his audience from the wagon seat, behaving like
a politician on the stump.

Price couldn't make out much of what the undertaker

said. He concentrated on the upturned faces of the audience instead. The barber was among them, frowning at the news; also the pinch-faced woman who clerked days at the hotel. The marshal stood well back, outside the circle, listening impassively.

Price didn't recognize the others, but he marked them down as ordinary town folk. None among them dressed above a common merchant's means, and one or two were on the shabby side. None of them rated any deference from the rest, which told him that Sedge Rankin hadn't come to see the Kelseys off.

Why would he, if he'd been responsible for their demise?

It was a leap with nothing to support it, but it made sense to his mind and felt right in his gut. Price was a man who trusted instinct when it spoke to him.

Rankin was driving squatters off the land around Redemption. Four of them were dead now, in a fire someone had set with kerosene. It didn't take a team of Pinkerton detectives to decide that Rankin was a likely suspect.

Call it four times murder, plus the string of other incidents Belle had described to Price. Rankin would rate a stiff rope and a short drop if there'd been a lawman in the county who was straight and diligent enough to build a case against him. He stood unchallenged, though, and plainly meant to have his way at any cost.

Price thought it might be time for him to have a look at Rankin, maybe see what Belle was up against. Big men acted the same wherever Price had been, but some of them were gutless wonders when they couldn't hide behind a wall of mercenary guns. Their money made them big, but they were small inside.

The other kind of big man grew up tough and mean, fighting for every inch of ground he gained, winning more battles than he lost. He nurtured memories of hunger from his youth, and he'd stand firm whether he had an army at his back or not.

Both kinds of big men had one thing in common, though: they bled and died like everybody else.

Price wouldn't know what kind of man Sedge Rankin was until he had a look. One thing was reasonably certain—namely, that the would-be master of Redemption didn't soil his hands with dirty work if he could help it.

That's what gunslingers were for, as Price himself could testify.

He'd fought his share of range wars as a gun for hire, and while he hadn't always been particular about which side came out on top, Price balked at shooting unarmed men from ambush. He had never dropped the hammer on a woman or a child, and he'd turned on more than one employer who expected Price to earn his pay by killing innocents.

Price wasn't a crusader, but he walked a line and made no secret of it. He would fight for money, but he wasn't an assassin. Some could never see the difference, but their stubborn blindness didn't spoil his aim.

He waited for the crowd outside Grymdike's to scatter homeward, watched the undertaker drive his empty wagon out of sight, then buckled on his Colt and went downstairs. Price had forgotten all about the midday meal during his ride with Jesse and their grim discovery, but he was hungry now.

The clerk who'd checked him into the hotel on Thursday night gave Price a nod as he passed through the lobby, showing him a poker face. Price nodded back and felt the gray man watching him until the door swung shut between them, jangling its fairy-bell. It had begun to cool a bit outside, but not enough to keep the sweat from trickling under Price's arms as he crossed the street to O'Malley's.

The restaurant was doing fair business, but he found a table near the window that enabled him to watch the entrance, kitchen door, and street without straining his neck. Price didn't have a wall to guard his back, but he checked out the graying couple seated there and reckoned neither of them was a shooter in disguise.

The waitress took his order for a steak well-done, with beans, biscuits and fried potatoes on the side, coffee to wash it down. Price looked around the other tables while he waited for his food. It was a solemn group tonight. The scraps of conversation he retrieved told Price the Kelseys were on everybody's mind.

"It was a fire, I understand."

"All four, they say."

"She was expecting, don't you know?"

"A shame, that's what it is."

He saw no tears, no evidence that appetites were suffering. Four deaths had put a damper on the crowd, but nobody was calling for investigation of the incident, much less a hanging rope.

Because they knew who was responsible and feared him? Or because they'd seen too much to care, beyond a rote expression of uneasiness?

His meal was on the table but he hadn't tasted it when Price glanced up and saw a lean man coming through the door. Hatless and dressed in banker's tweed, the new arrival looked around the room briefly, then fixed on Price and made a beeline for his table.

Price looked him over and decided he was probably unarmed. The stranger's jacket was a snug fit that betrayed no pistol bulge. He still might have a pocket derringer, but drawing it before Price reached his Colt would be a dead man's play.

The stranger stopped six feet away from Price, heads turning at the other tables to examine him while he stood fidgeting. Price made a show of setting down his knife and fork.

"You want something?"

"I do," the stranger said, "if your name's Matthew Price."

"I'm Price."

The stranger seemed relieved. "My name is Arlis Duffy. May I sit?"

"You're fine right there."

"Of course, sir. As you wish."

"Food's getting cold," Price said. "I'll eat; you talk."

Keeping his voice pitched low, the stranger said, "I have an invitation for you. My employer—"

"Who'd that be?"

"Sedge Rankin," Duffy said. "Perhaps you've heard of him?"

"Same fellow sent two boys around to warn me out of town? I've heard of him. They didn't fare so well."

The tweed man frowned. "I'm authorized to say that was a grave misunderstanding."

"Could've been."

"Excuse me?"

"Could've been a grave misunderstanding," Price elaborated. "They were breathing when I left 'em, though."

Duffy paled. "Oh, yes. I see. The men responsible were disciplined by Mr. Rankin for exceeding their authority."

"What's that, exactly?"

"Sir?"

"You mention their authority. I didn't see them wearing badges yesterday."

"No, sir. I simply meant—"

"What's Rankin want with me?"

The man was getting flustered, trying not to show it.

"He requests the pleasure of your company for drinks this evening at the Nugget—if you're free, of course."

"I'm never free," Price said. "Sometimes I'm reasonable, though."

It went over Duffy's head, leaving a slightly pained expression on his face.

"May I tell Mr. Rankin you accept his invitation, sir?"

"Free drinks? You might as well."

"If I may ask you, sir—"

"Tell him I'll be along after I finish here and give the spuds a chance to settle."

"Yes, sir. The Nugget is—"

"I know the way."

"Of course. Good evening, sir."

Price filled his mouth with steak in lieu of answering and left Duffy to decide if he should stay or go.

He went, glancing around him as he left and nodding to a couple of the diners on his way.

The pleasure of my company, Price thought, smiling.

He'd never heard it phrased that way before.

Rankin was up to something, plain enough. Price could've snubbed him, but the meeting suited his desire to find out more about Redemption's leading citizen. This way, he'd get it from the horse's mouth—one version of it, anyhow, cleaned up for presentation to a stranger—and he'd measure Rankin for himself.

Price knew the meeting could turn out to be a trap, even with a formal invitation from a go-between, but he saw no percentage for the town's Big Man in setting up an ambush at the Nugget. Even with the marshal on his payroll, Rankin couldn't be that sure of taking Price.

Sometimes a reputation helped, as much as hurt.

Price took his time with the meal, stretching it out, and got two refills on his coffee afterward. He would've liked the apple pie but let it go, afraid that one more bite would make him sluggish when he needed speed to stay alive.

Full night had fallen by the time he left O'Malley's, pausing on the sidewalk for a look each way along the street. He saw no shooters lurking in the shadows, but that didn't mean he was alone. Rankin could have one of his gunmen try to snipe Price on the way if he was spooked enough, but then the invitation would've been superfluous.

No, Price decided, Rankin meant to have a word with him, whatever that might be. The big man could be curious about what Price was doing in his town, or he might try to warn Price off. Whatever Rankin had in mind, though, Price was fairly certain that it didn't hinge upon the pleasure of his company.

Not even close.

Price released the Colt's hammer loop and loosened the pistol in its holster before he turned eastward, moving toward the rough end of town. Ambush or no, he was on hostile ground, going to meet a man of certain power who wished him ill—or likely would before the night was over.

He was on the same side of the street as Rankin's Nugget, picking up the sounds of music and hilarity when he was still a block away. A group of men who looked like aging farmhands stood outside the whorehouse, opposite, talking and spitting carelessly into the street. Most of the group wore guns but none of them were watching Price as he passed by.

He stood outside the Nugget's bat-wing doors and swept the smoky room with cautious eyes before he pushed his way inside. The crowd was average for a small-town Saturday night, male customers exclusively, while half a dozen working girls showed off their wares in low-cut beaded gowns. No less than half the men inside were armed, but none of them were visibly alert and all were strange to Price.

Get on with it, he thought, and stepped across the threshold.

Several faces turned to eyeball him, displaying shades of normal curiosity. He watched for darting eyes or twitching hands but came up empty.

Maybe it was just supposed to be a meeting, after all.

He started for the bar, then saw Arlis Duffy coming from his left, winding among the tables with his hand raised like a child in school who needs to use the privy.

Price held up and waited for him near the middle of the room.

"Good evening, sir! I see you found your way."

"Must have."

"If you'll just follow me?"

"Depends on where we're going."

"Mr. Rankin has a private room in back, away from all this noise."

"You lead," Price said.

He followed Duffy past the bar to an open doorway blocked by a length of plush rope. Duffy unhooked it on the right and stood aside to let Price pass. Price shouldered by him, gun hand hovering, then waited for his guide to replace the rope and lead him onward.

Rankin's private office was directly opposite a storage room. Both doors were closed. While Duffy knocked on one, Price tried the other, opened it, and checked the storeroom out.

No lurking shooters there.

"Um . . . Mr. Price?"

He turned to find Duffy holding the other door open. Price crossed the hall and stepped past Duffy, who immediately took himself away.

Sedge Rankin was a large man, filled to bursting with a grand opinion of himself. His hair was thinning but he didn't try to hide it, letting Mother Nature have her way. He wore a stylish broadcloth suit, dark gray, accented with a shiny gambler's vest and gold watch chain. Two heavy rings on either hand bespoke success and gave him an advantage if a conversation came to blows.

"Good evening, Mr. Price. Thank you for coming on short notice."

Rankin's grip was powerful, but he refrained from making it a test. Up close, he smelled of sweet cologne and twenty-cent cigars.

"Your boy mentioned a drink," Price said.

"Of course, of course!" Big smile. "Please have a seat. Bourbon?"

"Suits me."

He waved Price to a chair that put the desk between them, poured whiskey at a small bar near the door, and brought two glasses back, three fingers each. Price took a sip and let it warm him.

"That's expensive."

"I enjoy fine things."

Price looked around the office. There were trophies on the walls: a puma skin, some kind of fish nailed to a plaque, an eight-point buck's head.

"You're a hunter."

"Now and then. Cigar?"

"No, thanks."

Rankin clipped one and lit it for himself.

"You're wondering why I asked you here."

"It crossed my mind," Price said.

"Before we get to that . . ."

Instead of finishing the sentence, Rankin snapped his fingers. Price saw movement in the doorway, turning with his hand firm on the Colt.

Chad Saxon entered, hat in hand. Behind him, Arlis Duffy lingered in the open doorway. Price picked out his pistol brand on Saxon's cheek and wondered who had given him the other purpling bruises.

"Chad has something on his mind," Rankin explained.

The battered gunman cleared his throat and spoke through swollen lips, his eyes downcast.

"I'm sorry for what happened yesterday," he said. "I had a few too many drinks. It wasn't Mr. Rankin's doing."

"Fair enough?" asked Rankin, through a cloud of fragrant smoke.

"Suits me," Price said. "Your boy seems prone to accidents."

"He's working on it. That's all, Chad."

"Yessir."

There was a gleam of something in the shooter's eye

as he turned toward the door. Something besides repentance, that would be.

"Come back and see me anytime," Price said.

Saxon stopped short but didn't turn around. A frown from Duffy got him moving. Duffy closed the door behind him, leaving Price alone with Rankin.

"I hope that dispels any suggestion that I may've sent the boys around to pester you," said Rankin.

"Everybody makes mistakes."

"More bourbon?"

"I'm still working on it."

"Well, to business, then."

"Do we have business?"

"That should be my question."

"Are you asking it?"

Rankin smiled around his cigar. "You have a reputation, Mr. Price, if you don't mind me saying so."

Price shrugged and sipped his drink.

"I do believe this is your first time in Redemption."

"That's a fact."

"We've had some trouble in the recent past."

"You mean last night?"

"The Kelseys, yes. A tragedy. I understand you found them?"

"More or less."

"Well, that's a blessing, I suppose."

"How so?"

"A man of your experience, I meant to say. A simple farmer might've panicked. God forbid a woman or a child had come upon the scene."

Price kept the thought of Jesse tucked behind his deadpan face. "Your marshal wasn't too concerned when I reported it."

"A lawman's bound by rules and regulations, Mr. Price. I'm sure you understand. The county sheriff's been informed, of course."

"That's a relief."

"The trouble I was speaking of goes back awhile. We have some bad blood hereabouts. It's fairly common in a growing territory. Someone's always envious of a successful man."

"Makes sense."

"You've seen your share of that, I guess."

"I've worked for some successful men," Price said. "And worked against some, too."

"I'd hate to think you're working against me."

"Nobody's offered me the job."

Rankin eyeballed him through cigar smoke. "Do I have your word on that?"

"You do."

Belle hadn't offered money, but he would've lied to Rankin anyway. To hell with him.

"I take it you're not working at the moment, then?"

"Not so you'd notice."

"In that case," Rankin said, smiling again, "I may have something for you."

"Meaning what?"

"A job, if you're inclined to take it."

Price pretended to consider it. "Depends on what it is."

"The trouble I referred to could resume at any time. The next few months, I plan on making some important moves. We've got the railroad coming in next year. I run some cattle, I'm in oil—"

"Sounds messy."

Rankin blinked at him, decided he was joking, and gave out a barking laugh. "That's good. I like it. Some folks say I've got no sense of humor, but you know how that is."

"Folks say lots of things."

"Exactly. I expect they've wagged a tongue or two behind your back."

"It happens."

"Blaming you for things you never did or even thought of doing."

"Talk's cheap," Price agreed.

"You see my problem, then."

"Not quite."

"A man makes enemies on the way up. Sometimes he needs help."

"You have somebody after you?"

"No one specific, at the moment."

"Well, then—"

"You've seen the quality of men available to me. Chad means well, but he doesn't have your style."

"You want to hire me, then?"

"What else have I been saying?"

"Just to watch your back."

"And deal with any problems that arise."

"Such as?"

"You name it."

"No, *you* name it."

Rankin's eyebrows came together as he took a pull on his cigar.

"We have disputed land titles from time to time," he said. "Some rustling on my range. Trouble with squatters."

"Like the Kelseys?"

"You've been misinformed, my friend. But now that you mention it, I may put down an offer on their land. No reason it should go to waste."

"I guess I'll pass," Price said.

"You haven't heard my offer yet."

Price took another sip. "Let's hear it, then."

"Two hundred a week for the summer, assuming it's quiet. Any special work you have to do, we'll renegotiate."

"That's it?"

"That's it."

"I'll pass," Price said again.

"May I ask why?"

"I hadn't planned to stick around that long. Haven't seen much to recommend the place."

The big man cocked an eyebrow at him, blowing smoke.

"Is that a fact?"

"On top of which, I've got some business waiting up by Colorado Springs."

That much was true enough. Bill Hardwick's feud with the McAllisters was in its second year and showed no signs of slowing down.

"If it's a question of the money—"

"No."

"I see. You never said what brought you to Redemption, Mr. Price."

"You didn't ask."

"I'm asking now."

"Would you believe just passing through?"

"No, sir. With all respect, I don't suppose I would."

"And you'd be right."

"The question stands."

Price wondered how far he could push it. "I've got friends in town. Thought I might catch up on old times, see how they're making out."

"These friends of yours have names?"

Price nodded, smiling back at Rankin.

"I'm just wondering, since I know everyone in town."

"And some outside," Price said.

"That, too."

"You knew the Kelseys, I suppose."

"Knew of them, anyway. They had hard luck from day one, right on through."

"Hard luck for them, good luck for you."

"It happens."

"So I'm told."

"You sound to me like the suspicious type."

"Careful's more like it."

"Careful is the way to be these days."

Price drained his glass and set it down on Rankin's desk. "Thanks for the drink."

"We're finished, then?"

"I'd say."

"Are you a cautious man?"

"I've learned to be."

"It's not the best idea to get mixed up in business you don't understand."

"That's true."

"Or take a tale to heart before you hear both sides."

"Which tale is that?"

"Annabelle Mercer blames me for her husband being crippled," Rankin said.

Price didn't have to ask how Rankin knew about Belle's visit to his room. It could've been the hotel clerk or anybody else who saw them talking on the street.

"You're innocent, of course," he said.

"It wouldn't be my choice of words," Rankin replied. "I've got my share of sins to answer for, like anybody else. Like you, I guess. That doesn't mean I'm guilty of attempted murder, just because some female with her knickers in a twist decides to point a finger."

"Why blame you, if it was someone else?"

"I had some business conflicts with her husband. I came out on top."

"The shooting's just coincidence?"

"A man like Jared Mercer rubs some people the wrong way. I heard he had some trouble with a couple of the squatters over unpaid bills."

"Your marshal checked that out, I guess."

"Still working on it, I believe."

"He doesn't like to hurry, that one."

"Being thorough's what we call it."

"My mistake."

Price rose to leave and Rankin came around the desk.

"I'll walk you out."

They had the hallway to themselves. Rankin unhooked the velvet rope, leaning in so Price could hear him speaking softly.

"I don't blame you, really."

"Glad to hear it."

"Hell, no. Money isn't everything. A man has other needs—and women, too."

Price saw where he was going, but he let the big man finish it.

"I guess that Annabelle can pay your tab in ways I'd never manage. No, sir, I can't blame—"

Price hit him with an elbow, careful not to risk the knuckles of his shooting hand. The blow caught Rankin full across one cheek and sent him sprawling.

All at once, the room went deathly still. Jangly piano music, female laughter, conversation, and the slap of cards were all cut off as suddenly as if Price had been stricken deaf.

He saw Chad Saxon turning from the bar and swung around to face him. Price could feel the younger man itching to draw his six-gun, fairly choking on the need to prove himself. He wouldn't make it, but the smoky room was full of others who might try it, too.

Price couldn't take them all.

"Alright, now," Rankin said, behind him. "Everybody just stand easy. No harm done."

Price kept his eyes on Saxon while the big man rose and came around to face him.

"You're my guest this evening, Mr. Price. You get that one for free."

"You won't mind walking with me to the sidewalk, then."

"Don't mind at all."

They crossed the silent room together, Rankin nodding affably to several men along the way. They nodded back at him but couldn't find the wherewithal to smile.

The room came back to life after they stepped outside. Price didn't have to guess what Rankin's customers were jawboning about.

"You made a bad mistake tonight," the big man said.

"It wouldn't be the first time."

"Try the last."

Price left him standing in the spill of yellow light, westbound toward the hotel. He'd covered half a block when Rankin called to him.

"Enjoy it while you can, shooter! You're running out of time!"

10

A small town's like an echo chamber. Even whispers travel, and a shout reverberates like gunfire. Secrets are illusory, impossible to hold.

Price didn't know how long it would take the news of his encounter with Rankin to make the rounds in Redemption, but he guessed most residents would know some version of the story by the time they finished breakfast. Most of them would get it wrong or add embroidery before they passed the story on.

That was the way of twice-told tales.

Price knew a man like Rankin couldn't let it rest. He'd been humiliated in the presence of his hirelings and his customers, the kind of insult that requires an answer if a big man wants his reputation to survive and grow.

He didn't think the next move would be personal. Rankin had courage of a sort, melded with arrogance, but if he'd meant to call Price out his best chance had already slipped away. The more Rankin considered it, the more reasons he'd think of for somebody else to pull the trigger when the time came.

In truth, Price worried less about retaliation than about Rankin connecting him to Belle. He'd known it wasn't any deep, dark secret after she turned up at the hotel, but hearing it from Rankin's lips reminded Price that Belle and Jesse were in danger's way.

Before the incident with Rankin he still could have ridden out and left things as they were. Belle could have worked on Jared in a woman's way and possibly convinced him that his family was more important than his pride. It would've been a risky coin toss, but at least they'd had a chance.

Now, thanks to him, that chance was gone.

Rankin knew he was linked to Belle, and while Price would've bet his life the big man didn't know about their son, that was beside the point. Rankin would hate Belle for involving Price. He'd want revenge for his embarrassment and he might blame them equally.

Whatever Price did next, Belle's family was at mortal risk.

Which meant he couldn't leave.

Damn it!

Price hadn't known what to expect when he rode in on Thursday night. Belle's plea for help had lulled his common sense. Redemption wasn't where he'd choose to die, if he was given choices, but he'd learned to play the cards as they were dealt.

Nobody's dead so far, he thought.

At least, by Price's hand.

He had to smile at that. Two showdowns in as many days, and he had yet to fire a shot. That kind of record couldn't hold, but he almost enjoyed the change of pace.

Almost.

He had been making enemies and leaving them alive.

It was an invitation to disaster.

Spilt milk, he thought. All Price could do about it now was watch himself, each step along the way.

A small sound pricked his ears. Was that the floorboard halfway down, between the stairwell and his room?

Price stood up from the bed, strapped on his pistol belt in case he had to run, and drew the Colt. Footsteps came toward his door, along the hall. He stood off to the side and waited, where a gunshot through the door would miss him by at least three feet.

He listened for the knock, and when it came he replied, "Who is it?"

"Belle."

"Are you alone?"

"I am."

He'd only heard one set of footsteps, but it still took faith to cross the last six feet and turn the doorknob. By the time he got that far, he'd put the Colt away.

Belle's hair was down. She wore a shawl around her shoulders, a concession to the night. Her dress was blue, with flecks of white that could've been snowflakes or tiny flowers. She was beautiful.

Price edged past her, smelling her perfume as he checked out the hall.

"I told you I'm alone."

"What are you doing here?"

"I heard."

He didn't need to ask her *what* she'd heard.

"Word travels fast."

"The bad news, anyway." She flicked a pointed glance beyond the open door. "Where are your manners, Matt?"

"This is a bad idea."

"Too late for secrets, don't you think?"

She had him there. "Alright," he said. "You may as well come in."

Price closed the door behind her, locking it. He couldn't trust a squeaky board to help him twice.

Belle took the chair she'd occupied last time. Price left his gun belt on and sat down on the bed.

"I guess you saw the clerk downstairs."

She shook her head. "I came in through the back this time."

"Your husband know you're here?"

"He does."

"Won't like it much, I guess."

"He's not my keeper."

"I should meet him someday."

"Not tonight. What happened at the Nugget, Matt?"

"I thought you heard."

"Broad strokes," she said. "I'm looking for some details."

Price considered how much he should tell her. Everything she loved was balanced on a razor's edge. Her presence in his room would only make it worse, if anyone found out.

"Rankin made me an offer. I declined. He didn't take it well."

"You knocked him down in front of fifty witnesses."

"I'd be surprised if there were forty."

"You think this is funny? He's obliged to kill you now. You shamed him in the public eye."

"He'll *try* to kill me."

"He has men."

"I met a couple of them."

"Yes." She frowned. "I heard that, too. He owes you twice."

"Owing's one thing. Paying's another."

"Matt, you're just one man!"

"Same man you wired for help three weeks ago."

She broke eye contact, concentrating on the hands clenched in her lap.

"I've been regretting that," she said.

"The wire, or that I came?"

"Both, I suppose. It wasn't fair of me to ask."

"What's fair? If you can't ask your friends for help, what good are they?"

"I wasn't sure if you still were. My friend, I mean."

"Well, now you know."

"But people want to kill you."

"Wouldn't be the first time," he replied.

"The others weren't my fault."

"Nor this. We all make choices, Belle. Sedge Rankin made a choice tonight. He crossed a line."

"It's not your fight."

"Is now."

"You met Jesse, I understand."

Price felt a sudden tightness in his throat. "He loves that palomino pony."

"Dancer. Yes, he does."

"How is he?"

"Fine. He's fine."

"I tried to send him back. First sign of smoke, I told him he should go back home."

"He gets the headstrong part from me."

"Maybe from both of us. I'm sorry, Belle."

She met his eyes again and said, "He's fine. Really."

"Well, if you're sure."

"I'm sure. Jared's another matter, though."

"Can't help, you being here," Price said.

"I'll handle it. You know . . ."

"What?"

"Never mind."

"Tell me."

"I don't know where to start."

"Pick anyplace."

She thought about it for a moment, then began.

"Sometimes I feel like everything I do's a waste of time."

"Not Jesse."

"No, not him. But still . . . Redemption was supposed to be a whole new start. I thought we'd have a family—"

"You do."

"—and build a life."

"You have."

"It's slipping through my hands," she said. Tears glistened on her cheeks. "We've lost so much."

"That's Rankin's fault, not yours."

"Sometimes it feels like punishment."

"For what?"

She made a handkerchief appear from somewhere, dabbing at her eyes.

"I never should've run you off," she said.

"Oh, that." His smile was soft, not mocking her.

"Yes, *that*. You must've thought I hated you."

"You did the right thing, Belle. Both for yourself and for the boy."

"I'm not so sure."

"What kind of husband would I be? What kind of father?"

"One who could protect his son, maybe."

Price shook his head. "It's hard to dodge a back-shooter. I've seen more than my share."

"You look alright to me."

"I might not be, if I was playing storekeeper."

"You make it sound like I blame Jared."

"Do you?"

She gave up mopping tears and said, "He's not the man you are."

"Most folks'll tell you that's a good thing."

"Most folks do their best to stay away from me, these days. You'd think it's catching."

"They're afraid."

"Cowards. They didn't mind when Jared took the lead and tried to make things better in Redemption. Now he's stuck in that damned chair and our fair-weather friends all wish we'd disappear."

"That's people for you."

"Right." Her tone was bitter now. "You're better off alone."

"You don't mean that."

"Don't I? You've no idea how many times I've thought about what would've happened if I'd never met Jared that day. "

"You would've seen that Chinaman and kept your job

at the Lucky Strike," Price said. "And Jesse wouldn't love that palomino."

"I just thought . . . I thought . . ."

"I know."

"You *don't*!" Her sudden anger startled Price. "How could you?"

"Tell me, then."

"I thought he was my second chance, and maybe my only one. You spend your whole life waiting for a break, until you start believing it'll never come. Then, when it does—"

"You grab it, if you're wise."

"And let it drag you down."

"A dream can't drag you down. People do that."

"Exactly. Jared should've seen this coming, Matt. *I* saw it coming. Christ, he could've gotten us away from here in time."

"Running's a habit some men never cultivate. Others can't seem to shake it."

"Which are you?"

"Been running all my life, from one scrape to another."

"But you always win."

"Who says I'm winning?"

"You're alive."

"So is your husband, Belle."

"It's not the same."

She left her chair and came to sit beside him on the narrow bed. There was at least a foot of empty space between them, but Price could've sworn he felt her touch.

"When I met Jared, it was like a new door opening," she said. "I saw a world outside of Amarillo and the Lucky Strike, where no one would look down on me for who I was or what I'd done. I wanted that. I *needed* it."

"Makes sense to me."

"We had such hopes. It felt like magic."

"That's the way it should be."

"Jared loved me then. I think he loves me now, in spite of everything."

"Why wouldn't he?"

Why wouldn't anyone?

"He's never blamed me for what happened, Matt."

"Because it's not your fault."

"You don't think so? He picked Redemption as a new start for the three of us. Without Jesse and me, he could've made his peace with Rankin or moved on to someplace else. He wouldn't leave because he was afraid of what I'd think. He stays on now because he won't let Jesse see him run away."

"You make him out a strong man."

"Yes, he is."

"Then you can't blame yourself for every choice he makes."

"You don't know what it's like. I watch him roll around the house, around the store, pushing that goddamned chair. He used to have a proud walk, Matt. He used to be—"

Price waited for the tears to pass.

"I did that to him, don't you see? And now I'm doing it to you."

"You've done nothing to me," Price said. "I rode in on my own."

"Because I asked you to."

"I was ready to leave. The day I got your telegram, I killed a boy. He may've been twice Jesse's age. I'll never know. He thought his gun made him a man."

"He called you out?"

"If that's a consolation."

"I remember what you told me once."

"What's that?"

"You said the other fellows lose to you because they care who lives or dies. It was the saddest thing I'd ever heard. Still is."

"Don't let it worry you."

"I've missed you every day since Amarillo."

"Some days more than others, I expect."

"Sometimes, I used to make believe I'd married you, instead of Jared."

"Don't tell him."

"He's crippled, Matt, not blind or stupid."

"That's a lot to carry."

"Other days, I thought it might work out."

"Still might."

"What if we've lost too much?"

"You can't tell that by running out."

"I'm frightened, Matt."

"You should be. Rankin's all stirred up right now. I'll try and find a way to calm him down."

"You're staying?"

"For a bit, at least."

"You can't take on the world."

"Sedge Rankin's not the world, Belle. He just *thinks* he is."

"'Round here, he's close enough."

"Things change."

"That's what I'm telling you."

Price blinked and saw she'd closed the space between them when he wasn't looking. When she touched his hand it almost made him jump. His pulse went from a canter to a gallop.

"Belle—"

"It's been a long time, Matt. So very long."

It felt like desperation talking, but he didn't care. When Belle leaned toward him, Price met her halfway, wishing he'd had time to shave again. Her lips were soft, her breath sweet from what could've been a mint or glass of wine.

The first kiss took a second and forever, wrapped up into one. It snatched Price back through time, until he half-imagined he could hear the clamor of the Lucky Strike saloon downstairs. Nearly ten years since he'd set foot inside the place, and he was back.

His eyes snapped open of their own accord to find

Belle watching him, so close her warm breath brushed his lips. He knew that look but hadn't seen it in a decade.

He couldn't think of anything to say, mind racing, filled with images that blurred and undulated, calling up sensations from a time long past. She stole the moment from him with another kiss, her fingers tangled in his hair as she lay back and drew him down on top of her.

The second kiss was liquid fire. Belle opened to him and her tongue found his. She made a little mewling sound as Price responded, letting her take his weight, hands roving. She arched her back, firm breasts filling his hands—until a thought of Jesse stopped Price cold.

He drew back, hard and aching for her, feeling her confusion and surprise. She tried to hold him, but he gently, firmly pried her hands away. Price missed the closeness instantly, as if a hand had reached inside his chest and grappled something loose.

"I can't do this," he told her.

"Wha— Why not?"

"Wrong place, wrong time."

"Wrong woman?"

"Someone else's woman."

She pushed off from the mattress, sitting up.

"So, you've got scruples now?"

"Not many, but the ones I've got are troublesome."

She laughed at that, a sad, ironic sound. "We make a strange pair, you and I."

"It's not so strange," he said, brushing the hair back from her face. "It's just too late."

"We have a son."

"He has a father who's been with him all his life. We can't steal that away from him."

"He reads about you," Belle said. "We get those dime novels at the store."

Price shook his head. "I swear to God I never met Geronimo or Wyatt Earp."

"I used to think it was a sign."

"Of what?"

"That you were meant to find him in your own good time."

"Time's not so good, right now."

"It could be."

"I don't think so."

She trembled on the brink of saying something both of them would probably regret, then reeled it back and said, "Alright. Your choice."

"The only choice."

She smiled through tears, bewitching him.

"You'll kick yourself tomorrow."

Price returned the smile. "Tomorrow, hell. I'll kick myself tonight."

"You don't need to."

He shook his head. "No, Belle."

"This isn't how I pictured it."

"It never is."

"What must you think of me? I'm sorry, Matt."

"You know exactly what I think of you," he said. "And you've done nothing to be sorry for."

"I would've, though. I wanted to." She let him see the need in her. "I *still* want to."

"People depend on you for strength," he said.

"I guess they're out of luck, then."

"I'd say they've got luck to spare."

"You mustn't think I called you here for . . . this," she said, smoothing the rumpled comforter with one soft hand.

"I know better."

"We can't change what we are, Matt. Once a whore—"

"Stop it!" His sudden anger startled both of them. Price had no memory of reaching out to grab her arm, but now it took an effort to release her. "Don't say that."

"You have another name for it?"

"We all get lonesome."

"Even you?"

"From time to time."

"How do you handle it?" she asked.

"I mostly think of you."

Her eyes brimmed over. "I'm right here, Matt."

"But you're needed elsewhere."

"Yes, I am." She rose and Price stood with her. Reaching out to lightly touch his chest, she said, "Promise you'll leave. Get out tonight, while there's still time."

"The livery's closed."

"Wake someone up. Break in, if you have to."

"I'm tired," he said. "It's been a long day."

"Please don't let it be your last."

"You used to have more confidence in me."

"I couldn't bear to see you hurt, or—"

"Let's see how things look tomorrow."

"Matt . . ."

"Your family's waiting for you, Belle."

She left without another word. Price closed the door behind her, but a long, slow moment passed before he heard her footsteps moving toward the stairs.

"I've called you here because I owe Chad an apology."

The faces ranged around Sedge Rankin's desk were solemn. Three of them mirrored surprise in various degrees; the fourth was sullen, waiting.

"I flew off the handle yesterday when Chad and Perry tried to help me out with something on their own initiative. You might say I misjudged the situation and it's turned around to bite me on the ass."

Rankin reached up to stroke his bruised cheek with a fingertip. He had a dull ache on the left side of his head, but whiskey helped. Chad still looked worse, and Rankin knew he wasn't buying it.

Not yet.

"It takes a big man to admit he's wrong, sir."

"I appreciate that, Perry."

Hart wasn't averse to brownnosing if it would help him out. Saxon shot him a glare that stopped him short of puckering.

"Turns out this shooter's not just passing through Redemption like I thought," Rankin continued. "He's got friends in town. The Mercers, maybe more."

"The gimp," Lee Fowler asked.

"His wife, at least. The more I think about it, I believe he's here to settle up accounts."

Rankin saw Saxon fidget in his chair. Beneath the sullen anger there was something else, not quite a nervous tic.

"You think he wants whoever plugged the storekeeper?" Joe Orland asked.

"What else?"

"Maybe he's looking for some poon."

Hart's yelp of laughter at his own joke turned into an awkward coughing fit when no one joined him.

Rankin let it pass and said, "I think we need to count Price with the other side. Maybe the Mercer woman's all he cares about right now, but that could change. I guess you've heard he found the Kelsey place this morning."

That brought nervous glances all around, but Saxon couldn't let his anger go that easily.

"So what?" the battered gunman asked. "Somebody had to find them. He's no lawman. What's he gonna do about it?"

Rankin let the question hang there for a minute, watching as his hired hands thought it over. "Maybe nothing," he replied at last. "He may just let it go and concentrate on what was done to Jared Mercer."

"That's old news."

"I hear you, Chad. But then I have to ask myself if Price thinks so."

"The hell with what he thinks!"

"You've got some sand, I give you that."

"I'm wondering," Hart said, "what Price thinks he can do about it, anyway?"

"You'd have to ask *him* that."

"I mean, nobody knows who did the shooting, right? The marshal closed it out."

Rankin leaned back in his expensive chair and watched the others busily avoiding eye contact. All but Chad Saxon, who was glaring holes in Hart.

"I'm sure that's what a reasonable man would say," Rankin replied. "But I'm afraid Price may be the suspicious type. He might jump to conclusions."

All heads turned to Saxon. Fuming, he said, "What the hell's that got to do with me?"

"Why, nothing, Chad—except you did go over there and try to spook him. You and Perry."

Hart cringed at the mention of his name. He seemed about to say something, but he thought better of it, worrying a thumbnail with his teeth.

"Man could put that together," Orland said. "Maybe convince himself he's found the boys he rode in lookin' for."

"What's that supposed to mean?" Chad challenged him.

"Just what I said."

"You need to watch it."

Orland shifted in his chair, hand sliding closer to his Remington. "You need to get a grip."

"Now, boys." Rankin leaned forward, big hands on the desk, and waited for the two of them to face him. "I know you're upset about this thing, the same as I am. There's no call for bickering among ourselves, though. We've got grief enough, right there in the hotel."

"Somebody needs to run Price outa town," Lee Fowler said.

"You wanna do it?" Orland asked him, smiling.

"I'm afraid that may not do the trick," said Rankin. "Take a man like Price, who kills for money. He's more dangerous when you *don't* see him, if you catch my drift."

"You think he'd try to dry-gulch Chad?"

"Goddamn it, Lee!"

Fowler recoiled from Saxon's anger. "I'm just askin'."

"Honestly," said Rankin, "I'd not care to guess what he might do—or where he'd stop."

That set them thinking, got their minds off Saxon for a bit. Orland spoke up. "He's got nothin' on me."

"Nor me," Fowler echoed.

"That's what I'm saying," Rankin told them. "He's got nothing that would stand in court. How could he? But as Chad already pointed out, Price doesn't wear a badge. He's not a great respecter of the law."

"Like us, you mean," Lee Fowler said, grinning.

"I mean he may be less concerned with proof than pay-back."

"We oughta do something," Hart said.

"Maybe go south a spell," Fowler suggested.

"I'd think about that, Lee. Running could make him think you're guilty," Rankin said. "And thinking that, a man like Price would follow you."

"Running ain't what I had in mind," said Hart.

"Enlighten us, by all means."

"Huh?"

Rankin smiled through his headache. "Kindly share your thoughts."

"Oh, yeah. I'm thinkin' we should throw the saddle tramp a party, let him know 'zactly how glad we are to have him in Redemption."

"Are you sure that's wise, Perry? He knows your face."

"He wouldn't see us comin' if we went in there tonight."

"When you say 'us'—"

"I mean the four of us, right here."

"Hey, now!" Lee Fowler raised a hand.

"The *four* of us," Hart said again, turning a glare on Fowler. "Just to do it right. He'll be asleep most likely, anyhow."

"Why just the four of us?" Rankin found Saxon staring at him, frowning with his swollen lips. "If Price blames one of us for plugging Mercer, who's to say he won't blame all? He knows who pays our wages."

Rankin's smile had steel behind it, frost around the edges. Chad surprised him. He'd finally developed some guts. Rankin knew he'd better keep an eye on him. No one could be allowed to question his authority. Ever.

"You men understand I can't involve myself in anything so public. I'm a businessman. I have a reputation to protect."

"Who built that reputation for you?" Saxon asked, angrily.

"I don't forget my friends, Chad."

"Friends and hired hands. There's a difference."

Now Chad was getting *too* brave, Rankin thought as he put a few degrees of warmth into his smile. "Point taken. I believe we'll all be better off without this obstacle to progress in Redemption, but we won't split hairs. Let's say five hundred dollars to the man who takes him out."

"And for the rest?" Joe Orland asked.

"A hundred each to those who pull their weight."

"Who does the judging?"

"You can work that out amongst yourselves."

Chad kept his eyes on Rankin. "Just be sure you have the money waiting when I get back here."

"You'll get what's coming to you," Rankin said. "Now go on, boys, and make me proud."

II

"I still don't like it," Lee Fowler said. His hands were busy with his Colt dragoon, checking the load. "It don't feel right."

"The man's *asleep*," Perry Hart answered. "It don't get any easier than that."

"If it's so easy," Fowler said, "then why's it take all four of us?"

Chad Saxon had heard enough. He turned on Fowler, stepping close in to the older man and locking eyes. "It don't take four," he said between clenched teeth. "I thought you'd wanna share the prize is all. If you'd rather sit it out, go back inside and tell the man. Same goes for anybody else who's short on guts."

Fowler stiffened. "You want to call me yellow, say it to my face."

"I'm in your face," Saxon replied. "You've got a pistol in your hand. We gonna do this now, or what?"

Fowler stood trembling in his anger. Chad reckoned he had a bit of wiggle room. "You want me to, I'll turn around," he offered. "Make it more like Lawrence, where the mighty Quantrill let you shoot them unarmed men and boys."

"I didn't see you in the goddamned war."

"You see me here, Lee. Are we gonna have a war right now, or can it wait until we done our job?"

Giving the older man an out was only common sense. As keyed up as he was, Chad wasn't sure how well he'd do outdrawing Fowler with the gun already in his adversary's hand. In fact—

"You shoot each other now," Hart said, "it's bound to wake up Price."

"Don't wanna do that," Joe Orland stated, then ducked his head and turned away, embarrassed.

Easing back a notch, Saxon addressed himself to Fowler. "So, what'll it be?"

The old guerrilla fighter spat tobacco juice and put his Colt away. "Hell's bells. Let's go'n get it over with."

"Alright."

They moved along the sidewalk two abreast, with Perry Hart at Saxon's side, Fowler and Orland bringing up the rear. It was the time when a backshooter might make his move, but Saxon didn't think Fowler could cock the Colt dragoon without him hearing it. Besides, the old man's nerve had failed him once tonight already.

They were coming up on the hotel, Chad slowing down to peer in through the lobby windows. He saw empty chairs, nobody visible behind the registration desk or on the stairs. Cautiously, he backed away and looked up at the windows facing on the street.

All dark.

"Bedtime," he said, rejoining his companions on the sidewalk. Muffled sounds of celebration from the Nugget and the Trail's End reached his ears, but there were no stray witnesses abroad as far as he could see.

"All set?" he asked the rest.

They checked their hardware, spinning cylinders and clicking hammers.

"Ready," said Orland, smiling.

"I'm good," Hart replied.

Fowler nodded but kept his mouth shut.

"Right," Chad said. "Let's go."

And he forgot about the goddamned bell above the hotel's door. It startled him and nearly made him jerk his Peacemaker before he realized they weren't under attack.

The night clerk came from somewhere in the back, nervous and frowning. "Can I help you gentlemen?" he asked.

Chad frowned right back at him. "Which room's the shooter in?"

Instead of playing dumb, which would've meant a thumping at the very least, the clerk just said, "Four D."

"Which floor's that on?" Joe Orland asked.

Chad grimaced at the pain of being forced to work with idjits. "Just c'mon," he said, before the clerk could speak. "We'll work it out."

His gun hand was already twitching as he started up the stairs.

Redemption's one hotel was modern when it came to coping with a call of nature in the middle of the night. Instead of sending guests out to a privy full of spiders in the dark, the hotel had flush toilets—gents and ladies, separate of course—on the third floor. For Price, it still meant putting on his pants and hiking down a few flights of stairs, but it was better than a midnight cactus patch. He wore his gun from force of habit, hanging it upon a hook inside the lavatory door while he was occupied.

He didn't miss the sleep, fitful at best since Belle's last visit, and his interrupted dreams were troublesome. Price didn't bother picking over half-remembered fragments. He was more concerned with what tomorrow would bring, now that he'd worn out his welcome with Sedge Rankin.

He didn't know the big man well, but rather knew the

type. Rankin couldn't afford to let a public insult go un-
punished, if he meant to keep the common folk in line.
Already damaged by the fact that he'd let Price escape
the Nugget after slugging him, Rankin needed to make an
example of Price, and the sooner the better.

Price wondered who—or how many—he'd send to do
the dirty work. Rankin must have more guns than those
Price had already met. If those turned out to be his best,
though, there was still a chance he might come through
the rest of it alright.

Or, maybe not.

He'd been surprised that Belle remembered what he'd
told her once in bed, about not caring if he lived or died.
It wasn't that Price courted death—if anything, he
would've said it was the other way around—but he'd
seen and caused so much of it, it held no mystery or ter-
ror for him anymore. A faster gun was waiting for him
somewhere, bound to be, and that would be the end.

Good riddance, some would say, and Price would be
hard-pressed to argue they were wrong. He thought Belle
might have tears laid by for him, but Jesse wouldn't
know the difference and Price figured that was for the
best.

The boy was his by blood, but not in any other way
that mattered. They were strangers who had crossed paths
once, ridden together for a little while, shared gumdrops
and the smell of death. Boys mostly put that kind of thing
behind them as they grew. As Price recalled, it was the
best part about being young.

These days, he found it harder to forget.

Price was emerging from the lavatory when he heard
the shooters on the stairs. They'd passed the third-floor
landing and were halfway up to four, not talking, but
their boots scuffled as if their feet were weighted down
with lead. He guessed there must be three or four of
them—and he knew exactly why they'd come.

Rankin was quicker than he'd thought, or else the
shooters simply didn't want to wait for daylight. Price

had never shot a sleeping man, himself, but he found no fault with their reasoning. Why risk a bullet when you didn't have to, if the payoff was the same?

He fed his Colt a sixth round while he waited for the other men to clear the stairs and move down toward his room. A friendly floorboard creaked above him, and he started up behind them with the pistol naked in his hand.

Jesse was riding Dancer at a gallop through a field of tall grass, laughing with the warm wind in his face, when gunfire sent him tumbling headfirst from the saddle. Jerking bolt upright in bed, it took a moment for him to remember where he was—his bedroom, at the northeast corner of the second floor above his parents' dry goods store—and to be sure the palomino really hadn't stumbled, spilling him.

There was no pony in his room, of course; no grass or sunshine, either. What had wakened him?

A second ragged volley echoed in the street.

No, that was wrong. He knew the sound of pistols fired outdoors, when somebody got drunk at one of the saloons and took a notion to hurrah the town. Sometimes—*most* times—the drunkard's friends came out and dragged him back before the marshal woke, got dressed, and tracked him down.

This sound was different, though, and Jesse knew the guns were being fired indoors. He threw the covers back and tiptoed to his window facing on the alley, opened it with care and listened to the night.

The gunfire sputtered out like distant fireworks at the tag end of a celebration. Definitely fired indoors, he thought, and from a building somewhere to the west of where he stood.

But the saloons and Molly Deegan's clustered to the east, behind him. That meant—

The hotel!

His pants were neatly folded on a chair beside his bed.

He struggled into them, hopping to keep his balance, listening for any sound of movement in his parents' room. He pulled on his small boots and made a special effort not to clip-clop on his way back to the window.

Jesse was forbidden to go out alone at night, but he'd been favored with a rope ladder to use in case of fire, should he be cut off from the stairs. He used it now, to keep from passing by the master bedroom's doorway, and descended quickly to the dark alley below. He skinned his knuckles on the shop's siding and bit his lip to keep from crying out in pain. A moment later he was running west.

He'd missed the best of it already, that was clear. A gunfight in the middle of the night, at the hotel, and that could only mean Matt Price was killing men or being killed himself.

The latter thought made Jesse slow his pace a bit, but it was not enough to stop him. History was being made a few yards down the street, and he wasn't about to miss it. He needed to be careful, though. Bystanders were at risk in any shooting scrape, the more so after midnight, running toward a battle in the dark.

Price heard the shooters kick his door in, picking up his pace now that stealth didn't matter. He made the fourth-floor landing in time to see the last man disappear inside his room, before they started firing in the dark. He reckoned that most of their shots would be aimed at the bed, but he also heard a crash of glass—mirror? window?— that told him someone had fired wild.

Price didn't count the shots. They fired enough to do the job and damn near deafen anyone inside the room—at least a dozen, maybe twice that with the blasts all run together. They were using pistols and at least one shotgun.

Damn it all, Price thought. He turned off the wall-mounted gas light at his end of the hallway and settled in to wait.

There came a lull after the gunfire, while a match flared and a couple of the shooters started arguing. Price couldn't make out what they said, but from the tone of it he knew they were unhappy. Down below, on three, he heard a couple of the hotel's other tenants calling worried-sounding questions back and forth between their rooms.

The shooters took another moment to reload. Price couldn't see them, but he knew they wouldn't want to leave his room with empty guns. They would be jumpy now, nervous and angry in approximately equal parts. And they'd be wondering where in hell he was.

Right here.

Price didn't recognize the first man through the door—tall, rangy, bearded—but he shot the stranger anyway. His bullet spun the man around and dropped him on the carpet as a second shooter cleared the open door.

They fired together. Price's target couldn't see what he was shooting at, maybe the muzzle flash from Price's Colt. The man got off two shots before he doodle-bugged back through the doorway into Price's room. One of the rounds peeled back wallpaper on Price's left; the other hummed past on his right.

Four shots remained in the Colt as it became a waiting game. Price thought it might be interesting to see what happened if the marshal came around, whether he'd even make a pretense of arresting Rankin's men or maybe feel obliged to join the fight himself. If he was smart, Gresham would take his sweet time putting on his pants and let the shooters settle it amongst themselves.

Somebody stuck a pistol out the door and fired two shots, but nothing came of it. The slugs went high and wide, neither passing within six feet of where Price crouched against the wall. He didn't bother firing back before the tiny target was withdrawn.

They had to rush him soon, though, if they didn't plan to spend the night. The window had no ledge, and Price didn't imagine the remaining shooters would enjoy a drop exceeding twenty feet. The thought of hobbling home on broken ankles should dissuade them from the jump, if pride and anger couldn't flush them out to face his gun.

The last thing Price expected was to see the first shooter he'd dropped get up and try again, but there he was, struggling to hands and knees, then getting one foot under him. He nearly lost it reaching for his pistol, had to brace himself with his free hand, but then he had it, leaning on the wall and pushing off as he stood.

Price let him turn around before he fired again. This time the bullet struck his man dead-center in the chest and sent him stumbling backward toward a window at the far end of the hall. The glass couldn't hold him when he hit it and buckled with his weight, before the man tipped over backward and was gone.

"Alright," Price called down to his room. "Who's next?"

A half-block short of the hotel, Jesse slowed down to a jogging pace, then to a walk. The sound of his own footsteps worried him, made Jesse wish he'd left his boots behind, but then he would've bruised and gashed his feet. He hesitated in the narrow alleyway between the hotel and the barber shop, looking for places he could hide if someone challenged him.

He was still looking when there came another gunshot, followed rapidly by several more. Jesse looked up in time to see a window on the fourth floor shatter, raining glass. He stumbled back, raising an arm to shield his face, and heard a heavy *thud* in front of him.

When Jesse dropped his arm, a man lay where he'd fallen, limp and twisted as if all his bones had turned to jelly in midair.

The taunting voice chilled Perry Hart. The break-top Schofield .45's were dead weight in his hands. Dizzy

from breathing gun smoke, he imagined he would suffo-
cate unless he found a way out of the hotel room.

"Bastard's got us penned in here," Joe Orland said.

"There's only one of him," Saxon remarked.

"And three of us that started out with four," Hart said.
"Lee's gone for sure."

"You don't know that."

"Man blew him out the goddamned window, Chad.
You think he's comin' back?"

"We don't need him."

"We sure as hell need *somethin'*," Orland said.

"You need some guts, Joe," Saxon hissed at him.

"I don't see you out chasin' him."

"You think I won't?"

"Go on ahead. I'll follow you."

A little more of this, Hart thought, and they were
bound to kill each other. Chad and Joe were glaring fit to
bust with guns in hand. Hart knew it wouldn't take much
of a spark to set them off.

"We got one fight already," he reminded them. "Man's
likely sittin' out there listening to you two carry on."

"He can't hear shit," Chad said.

"You wanna bet your life on that?"

"Be nice to get someone behind him," Orland said.

"You may've noticed we're a little short on help right
now," Hart said.

"I know that, damn it! But if Mr. Rankin sends somebody else—"

"He won't," Hart said. "He'll figure four of us should
be enough to get it done."

"We *are* enough," Chad said.

It didn't feel that way, from where Hart stood. His
mind replayed the image of a dark hall—what had happened to the lamp down by the stairs?—and gunfire
winking at him from the shadows. It was suicide to go
out there, but what choice did they have?

As if reading his mind, Joe Orland said, "Somebody

could go out the window, right? Then sneak around and take him from behind."

"You got a ladder in your pocket?" Chad asked. "Or you just wanna jump and break your neck?"

"Legs, anyway," Hart said. "It's twenty feet if it's an inch."

"Ain't one way outa here but through that door," Chad said. "We go out shooting, all together, there's no way he can take three of us."

Hart didn't share Chad's confidence on that score, and he didn't want to be the one Price killed before the others gunned him down, but Chad was right. They either had to make a move or sit and wait for Price to come for them.

"Hey, what about the marshal?" Orland asked.

"That yellow bastard?" Chad retorted. "What about him? You think Gresham's gonna try his hand against Matt Price?"

"If Mr. Rankin tells him to—"

"Forget Rankin! We're all there is."

And it ain't much, Hart thought. But what he said was, "Well, let's do it, then."

"Damn right! You with us, Joe, or not?"

"You know I am," said Orland, thumbing back both hammers on his shotgun.

"That's more like it." Saxon cocked his Peacemaker and nudged Hart toward the open door. "You first," he said, grinning.

Belle cleared the back door running, headed west along the alley toward the hotel and sounds of gunfire. Jared called out once again to her but she ignored him, focused on the need to find her son.

It was a mother's automatic reflex, checking Jesse's room after the shooting jolted her awake from sweaty dreams that left her frightened and excited, all at once. She'd meant to reassure the boy but found his bed empty, that damned rope ladder dangling from his windowsill, the alley yawning like a gullet. Belle had grabbed a shawl for modesty, remembered slippers in the nick of time and left Jared in bed, demanding that she help him to his chair.

No time. There was no time to humor him.

She knew the way her son's mind worked. Jesse admired Matt Price from reading his so-called adventures, more so from their morning ride together and their grim discovery at the Kelsey place. He'd know the shooting meant some kind of trouble, probably with Price dead-center in the midst of it, and Jesse'd want to see the game played out.

Belle cursed herself again for reaching out from one life to another that was over, bringing Matthew here to risk himself—and all for what? A woman who'd rejected him ten years ago? Her crippled husband, whom he'd never met? The son he didn't know existed until yesterday?

She felt humiliated by her selfishness, ashamed of what she'd nearly done with Price at his hotel that very night. She'd wanted him with a ferocity that took her back to Amarillo in her mind—the days when she was wild, if not exactly free. She'd been his for the taking, but Price had surprised her with a strength of will or simple decency that made her blush with shame.

Belle loved her husband still and didn't want to see him die, but at the moment she was more afraid for Price—and terrified for Jesse. He had a child's faith in tomorrow, rushing into harm's way as if he were bullet-proof, untouchable.

Belle prayed he wouldn't pay for that mistake tonight.

The lull in gunfire broke before she got halfway to the hotel. A startling crash of broken glass followed the latest shots, and then another cease-fire. Belle heard voices on Main Street, Redemption waking up to sounds of violence one more time.

There'd only been one shot the night Jared was wounded, fifteen minutes ticking past before the first neighbor arrived to offer help. Tonight was more like Independence Day, a fireworks show the townspeople could watch from a safe distance without feeling any guilty urge to intervene.

She found Jesse between the hotel and the barbershop, a narrow alley there. He stood over the body of a man she didn't recognize and jumped, squealing, at Belle's touch on his shoulder.

"Jesse, it's alright."

His hair stood out all over, from his pillow. Tears left bright tracks on his cheeks. "He's dead, Ma," Jesse said.

"We're going home now."

"Mr. Price—"

Whatever Jesse meant to say, Belle lost it to the sudden roar of guns.

The first one out the door was Perry Hart. Price recognized him by his harelip and the twin Schofields, blazing before he cleared the threshold. Saxon followed with a Peacemaker, and bringing up the rear a slender man Price hadn't seen before. He recognized the sawed-off shotgun, though, about the time the stranger let both barrels go.

A storm of lead broke over Price, gouging the walls and ceiling, raining dust and splinters. They'd have nailed him if he hadn't stretched out prone, in preparation for the rush he knew was coming, and the concentrated fire was still too close for comfort. Even with the dark to cover him, Price couldn't hold his ground for long against four guns.

Time to reduce their number, then. Two of the three kept firing, while the stranger with the empty shotgun fumbled for a cross-draw Remington. Price shot him from the floor, then swung his Colt toward Hart without waiting to see how well he'd scored.

Hart's two guns made him theoretically more dangerous than Saxon, even though he'd wasted half his cartridges without finding the mark. Price took no chances, aiming for a point an inch or two above Hart's belt buckle and squeezing off the shot. Hart staggered, slumped against the wall, and managed two more aimless shots before he settled to the floor.

Hart wasn't dead, but he was down, and that left Saxon on his feet. He had a fix on Price now, from the muzzle flashes of his Colt, and Saxon's next shot burned past Price's ear with no more than an inch or two to spare.

Price rolled out to his right, firing along the hallway, missing clean. His Colt was empty now, Saxon still on his feet, and damn all if the third man hadn't rallied with his Remington, kneeling against the wall and using both hands to support his pistol as he fired.

Price wormed his way backward in darkness, digging in with knees and elbows. He would need a moment and some cover to reload, if Saxon or the wounded stranger didn't kill him first. He felt as much as saw a door beside him, wondering if rooms were left unlocked when they weren't occupied. Price reached up for the knob, tried it, and felt it turn. He pushed the door open, rolled through, and kicked it shut behind him as the Remington unloaded two more rounds.

Reloading in the dark, by feel, Price worked his way around the pistol's cylinder, ejecting empty cartridges, replacing each in turn with fresh ones from his belt. Outside, he heard his adversaries shuffling forward—one wounded, the other simply cautious.

"Which room was it?" one asked.

"Shut up!" said the other.

Price stood motionless, holding his breath and listening. He heard the footsteps stop outside his door and dropped into a crouch, well back and to the left.

"Go on!" somebody whispered, and a shotgun blast ripped through the door, blowing a foot-wide hole. A second blast came right behind it, taking out the doorknob, flinging what was left of the door wide open and back against the wall.

Chad Saxon filled the smoky doorway, fanning his

Peacemaker from the hip. Price shot him through the right side of his chest and once again before he fell, two killing wounds.

"Jesus!"

He caught the wounded shooter with his shotgun broken open, trying to reload, blood soaking through the left leg of his pants and beading on his dusty boot. He dropped the gun and paper cartridges, raising his hands.

"Hey, now! I just—"

Price shot him in the face before he had a chance to finish whatever he'd meant to say. It was too late for words.

"Help me!"

Price stood over the one named Perry Hart and watched him bleed. One of the Schofields lay between his outstretched legs, the other just beyond arm's reach. Hart didn't try for either one of them as Price approached him, more concerned with clasping hands over his belly wound.

"I'm done," he said.

"Looks like it."

"Where's Chad?"

"He's gone on ahead of you."

"Oh God, it hurts!"

"It's meant to. Was this Chad's idea or Rankin's?"

"Rankin? Is he here?" Hart's voice was weakening. His fingers writhed in blood.

Price put his Colt away and said, "Don't worry, boy. He'll join you soon."

12

Gil Gresham took his time responding to the gunshots. The first rounds had barely woken him, sedated as he was with four shots of tequila and a cold beer chaser. Tangled in his sweaty sheets, he'd lain and waited for a second burst of fire to let him know he hadn't dreamed the first. It came and kept on coming, for a good five minutes anyway. He'd known exactly what was happening, of course. The only question in his mind was why it took so long to kill one man.

He'd been in no great hurry dressing after that. There was a lamp to tend, yesterday's clothes to shake the wrinkles out of, thinning hair to comb. Gresham considered making coffee, but he didn't want to push it. Even in Redemption, there were still appearances to be maintained.

When he was dressed and more or less alert, he left the house Sedge Rankin paid for and walked down to the hotel. He didn't run because it was unseemly for a lawman and the dead have all the time they'll ever need. Gresham saw Aloysius Grymdike there ahead of him and wondered what had drawn the undertaker with a flock of others to the alley east of the hotel.

Price made it to the street somehow, he thought. That would explain the time and all the shots it took to finish him.

The onlookers had dressed in haste, if you could call some of them dressed at all. Gresham wished there was still a newspaper in town, to send somebody over with a camera. He would've paid a quarter for that photograph and hung it on his office wall, as a reminder to the good folk who looked down their noses at him that they weren't so high and mighty after all.

Belatedly, he thought to look around for Annabelle Mercer, but she was nowhere in sight. Afraid, most likely, now that her long-riding hero was gone. If she was smart, she'd toss her boy and crippled husband in a wagon, make the trip down south to Sanderson, and buy three tickets on the next train going anywhere at all. They should get out while there was still time.

Or maybe it was already too late.

Gresham shoved past the vultures, being none too gentle with them, and found Grymdike crouched beside a corpse. The undertaker's Mexicans were standing by to haul the meat away when he was done. He wondered—not for the first time—where Grymdike kept those two and how they nearly always made it to a killing scene in town before the corpse had time to cool.

"What have we got?" he asked Grymdike.

Still poking at the dead one, Grymdike glanced around and said, "We have Lee Fowler, Marshal."

"What?"

"He's shot—at least a couple times, I think. One of them put him through the window."

"I'll be damned."

That put a whole new light on things. The small crowd parted to release him this time, so he didn't have to make contact. Before he entered the hotel, Gresham checked out the street again and saw nothing of Rankin. There

was no surprise in that, of course. The big man wouldn't
put himself out if there was a hireling for the dirty work.

One less tonight, he thought and stepped into the
lobby, grimacing as always at the jangling bell above the
door. Heck Fleagle was behind the counter, either waiting
for the marshal or some late-arriving customers who
hadn't shown up yet. There were a few stray gawkers in
the lobby, keeping well back from the stairs, but they got
out when Gresham glared at them and cocked a thumb
back toward the street.

"Looks like you had some trouble, Heck."

"Yes, sir."

"Got more upstairs?"

"I haven't been to see."

"How many's up there, do you know?"

Heck didn't want to say, but Gresham was prepared to
wait him out. The clerk saw that and said, "Four men
went up a while ago. They haven't come back down."

"One of them did," Gresham corrected him. He didn't
ask for names, having a fair idea of who the others were.
The only question now was whether any of them were
alive. "And Price?" he asked.

The night clerk shook his head. Gresham drew the gun
he hadn't fired at anything but tin cans in the past two
years and started up the stairs. He tried to keep it quiet,
but he knew a shooter waiting on alert would hear him
coming. Watching the staircase above for bushwhackers,
he tripped three times before he reached the second floor
and wound up creeping like an old man the remainder of
the way, disgusted with himself.

A reek of gun smoke met him on the third-floor landing, but he didn't smell the stiffs until he reached the top-
most floor. Blood spilled in quantity has a metallic smell,
and men killed violently are prone to spilling other fluids
too. The fourth floor had a slaughterhouse aroma Gresham hadn't smelled in years—not since a certain shooting match in Abilene, when he was on the sunny side of

forty and he'd never given any thought to putting on a badge.

Three men were laid out in the hallway, dead or dying by the look of them. Gresham had never gone beyond third grade in school, but he could count to four and that meant somebody was missing. He would have to check the bodies to determine who it was, and if he couldn't find Matt Price—

The hammer on his six-gun was ungodly loud as Gresham thumbed it back. He should've done it on the way up from the lobby, but he'd been afraid of stumbling on the stairs and firing wild. Too late to fret about it now, though. If the shooter was alive and waiting for him, he'd already know that Gresham had arrived.

The nearest corpse was slumped directly opposite an open doorway, nothing but a wedge of carpet visible by gaslight from outside the room. Gresham ignored the body as he crept up on the doorway, conscious of a sudden tremor in his shooting hand. The taste of last night's liquor nearly gagged him, but he swallowed it and focused on the shadows that could kill him if he dropped his guard.

Up close, he saw the door was barely there, torn through with close-range shotgun blasts. No body on the floor told Gresham both had missed, but he'd still have to check the room before he turned his back on it. He paused and listened, squinting as if that would help him hear better, then rushed the door before his nerve could fail him.

It was empty. Gresham checked the tiny closet to be sure, then had a look under the bed and got up feeling foolish. Better that than feeling dead, he thought, but now he had to leave the room again, knowing a shooter could have waited for him in *another* room, maybe stepped out while he was distracted and be waiting for him in the hallway now.

To hell with it.

He went back to the first dead man and recognized Joe

Orland, even with his face all bloody and the hole plugged through his forehead. Price had caught him with the Greener empty, trying to reload, and that was it for Joe.

Chad Saxon had a dazed look on his face, beneath the bruises that would never have a chance to heal. His Peacemaker lay where he'd dropped it after bullets opened up his chest. The trademark sneer was gone, replaced by an expression that said Chad had died bewildered, wondering how such a thing could happen.

That left Perry Hart, lying in blood down near the far end of the hallway. He was gut shot and had needed time to die, while Gresham put his clothes on and debated making coffee down the street. A doctor might've saved him, Gresham thought, but it was no great loss.

He heard the door open behind him, froze and waited while a grim voice asked him, "Did you come to talk or shoot?"

"Looks like there's been enough shooting," the marshal said.

"Then you can put your gun away," Price told him.

Gresham eased the pistol's hammer down and holstered it. "Mind if I turn around?"

"Feel free."

The marshal turned to face him, frowning when he noticed Price's Colt still in its holster. He was having second thoughts, deciding whether it was worth the risk.

"It's your decision, Marshal."

Gresham blinked at that and broke the spell. "We've got a problem here," he said.

"Do we?"

"Four dead men, I'd say so."

"I'll simplify it for you," Price replied. "These boys dropped by in hopes of catching me asleep. As luck would have it, I was otherwise engaged. They shot my bed up for awhile, then tried to leave without saying good-bye. I've never liked rude people much."

"That's your side, anyway."

"Talk to the clerk downstairs."

Price caught a flicker in the marshal's eye. "Maybe I will," he said.

"Maybe you have already," Price replied. "How else do you explain your four friends being here?"

"Not *my* friends."

"Rankin's men. It's the same thing."

"You think I'm Rankin's man, why are you still alive?"

Price had to smile at that. "Because you're old and slow and smart enough to know it. If you want to try your hand, though, like I said before, it's your decision."

Gresham might've been a shooter once, but he was out of practice, years beyond his prime. Soft living made a gunman rusty. He had more to lose and so began to fear its loss. That understood between them, Gresham still took half a minute to decide.

"I didn't come up here to fight with you," he said at last. "I've got a job to do."

"You'll need to see what Rankin says, I guess. See if he wants to claim his boys were moonlighting."

"Loose talk like that could lead to trouble," Gresham said.

"Trouble's already here, Marshal."

"I can see Chad coming for you, after yesterday," the lawman said. "Perry, same thing. You made 'em look small to the town. It wouldn't take much tonsil varnish for the others to pitch in. You have a way of making enemies."

"You don't put Rankin on the list?" Price asked.

"Some reason why I should?"

"You're out of touch, Marshal. Go ask around the Nugget when you've got some time."

"You want to tell me something?"

"Get it from the horse's mouth. You'll like his version better, I expect."

Gresham surveyed the bodies, broken window, and the bullet-splintered walls. "This damage and the funerals," he said, "somebody has to pay."

"I covered four of Rankin's kills this afternoon. Let him pick up the tab on these."

"That's slander, now."

"Rankin can sue me, I suppose."

Gresham wasn't amused. "This has to go before a justice of the peace in Sanderson. If he decides it's wrongful death, I'll have to take you in."

"You'll have to try."

"Don't think I won't."

"Why don't you check with Rankin first? He may have other plans."

"Whichever way it goes, you may not find the climate in Redemption very healthy from now on."

"Sunshine, blue skies," Price said. "What's not to like?"

"I'm saying you'd be wise to get out while the getting's good."

"So you can tell your justice of the peace I killed four men and ran away? No thanks, Marshal."

"That's *your* decision," Gresham echoed.

"And I'll live with it. Think you can do the same?"

"I'll do my job."

"You'd best get to it, then. Try not to let Sedge Rankin get you killed."

The marshal seemed like he had more to say but kept it to himself. Price watched him go, moving slump-shouldered toward the stairs, then went back to his room. He had the window open, letting gun smoke out and scraps of conversation from the sidewalk in.

There was no lynch talk yet. He doubted whether anybody in Redemption had the nerve to try it without Rankin pushing them, and he was betting that the big man would try something else next time. Unless he ran, all Price could do was wait and find out what that something was.

"Looks like we wait," he told the bullet-fractured mirror. His reflection stared back at him, a lopsided face shot through with jagged scars.

At Sunday breakfast there was only one topic of conversation in Redemption—which is not to say the townspeople were of a single mind, or even that they were agreed on what had happened overnight. Four men were dead, shot down at the hotel, but once that basic information was conveyed the story had a way of taking wing, transforming to accommodate the teller and his audience.

One version had it that the stranger, Matthew Price, had pistol-whipped Sedge Rankin at the Nugget, whereupon a group of Rankin's men had set out to avenge him without much success. Another, whispered cautiously by Rankin's enemies in town, related how Chad Saxon and his no-good friends had lain in wait for Price at the hotel and wound up getting more than what they'd bargained for. A neutral version of the shooting claimed that Saxon and his friends were drunk as always on a Saturday and picked a fight with the wrong man this time.

Word also got around, as word will do in small towns everywhere, that Annabelle Mercer had some acquaintance with the shooter who had done in Saxon and his friends. In fact, the gossips whispered, she had called on Price *in his hotel room* one day prior to Saturday's quadruple killing. One could only speculate—and speculate the local gossips surely did—about her motives and intentions, but it was unseemly for a wife and mother to keep company with an assassin while she left her son and crippled husband to their own devices. No great leap of intuition was required to draw a link between the shooter and the proper lady at the dry goods store—but was she really all that proper, if she knew a man like Price? And what about her crippled husband, anyway? It was a tragedy of course, but if a man can't tend his garden, who's to say what may come out of it?

Small towns are easily divided by the simplest things. A quarrel between two neighbors can become a civil war as friends take sides and parcel out the blame. If reputations are at stake, so much the worse—and money is the worst of all. Before the church bell rang on Sunday morning in Redemption, lines had already been drawn between the folk who viewed Sedge Rankin as the town's salvation and an element that saw his presence as a curse. Ongoing violence made the latter group cautious of speaking out, but old wounds were reopened and picked over, all the same.

Something was in the wind, most of the town's folk would agree, for good or ill.

Some said it smelled like death.

Belle Mercer fixed a normal Sunday breakfast for her family—smoked ham and scrambled eggs, with biscuits on the side—but Jared wasn't hungry, grumping over loss of sleep and inventory waiting for him in the store downstairs. They closed on Sundays, but he couldn't let it wait and wouldn't let Belle help him with the pulley on the service elevator they'd installed to hoist him up and down after the shooting.

He was brooding over Price, she knew, and worried about what would happen now that blood was spilled between Matthew and Rankin. Jared judged himself relentlessly, examined and exaggerated his prospective failings until guilt and anger merged to put him in a funk that might go on for days. Real danger only made it worse, their lives more tenuous.

Jesse, by contrast, had recovered from his brush with death at the hotel and brought a badger's appetite to breakfast. He was full of questions, forcing Belle to think when she'd have rather let her mind go blank.

"Ma, do you reckon Mr. Price came out alright?"

"He has a way of landing on his feet."

"You're worried for him though, aren't you?"

The question startled her. "What makes you say that, Jesse?"

"Oh . . . nothing."

Belle left the sink and sat beside him at the dining table. "Did your father say something?" she asked.

"No, ma'am." He made a show of concentrating on his breakfast. "I just hear things."

"Things?" She tried to keep the worry from her voice. "What sort of things?"

"Sometimes, when you and Pa have your discussions." Jesse glanced up from his plate. "I wasn't ear dropping, I swear."

"Eavesdropping," she corrected him.

"Yes, ma'am. I wasn't doing that."

"Alright."

"But I hear things, sometimes, when I'm not trying to."

"I'm sorry if we've troubled you," Belle said.

"It isn't that, so much."

"What is it, then?"

He hesitated, poking at his food. "You never told me you knew Mr. Price."

"It was a long time back."

"Before me?" Jesse asked.

"Before I knew your father."

"Were you friends?"

"I'd say we still are, Jesse."

"But you haven't had him over since he came to town."

"That's true."

"Why not?"

"You'll find friends grow apart sometimes. It isn't always easy to explain."

"Pa doesn't like him much," said Jesse, cutting through it.

"No."

"How come?"

How best to answer that? A lie, of course. "They've never met," Belle said. "It's nothing Mr. Price has done, so much as what he is."

"A gunfighter?"

"That's right. Your pa worries that having Mr. Price in town may cause more trouble, like last night."

"You don't think that was his fault, do you?"

"Not directly, but a gunman has a way of finding trouble everywhere he goes."

"We already had trouble here," Jesse reminded her.

"You're right again."

"Did you ask Mr. Price to help us, Ma?"

"It crossed my mind," she said, hating the lie, "but now I'm not sure it's a good idea."

"Maybe he'll help us anyway."

"It's possible," she said. And wondered whether she was lying to the boy or to herself.

Sedge Rankin drained his whiskey glass and pushed it back. He could've used another drink to ease the nervous tension in his gut, but discipline required that he abstain. It wouldn't do for him to show weakness in front of a subordinate. The look on Arlis Duffy's face told Rankin that his aide was already on shaky ground, in need of strength to prop him up.

"I spoke to Grymdike," Duffy said. "He's asking fifty dollars."

"Too damned much," said Rankin.

Duffy blanched. "For all four, sir?"

"Ah. That's more like it."

"I'll tell him to go ahead, then?"

"Might as well."

Chad and the rest weren't getting any fresher at the undertaker's parlor, Rankin thought. The sooner he was rid of them, the better. One small job he'd trusted to them, and they couldn't get it done. They'd been so clumsy at it, in the bargain, that Gil Gresham couldn't even run the shooter out of town, much less throw hemp around his neck.

He needed someone who could deal with Price and

clean this mess up fast, before it spun out of control. Rankin had lost enough prestige and men already. Any more would undermine his hard-earned power base and leave him painfully exposed. Someone . . . but who?

"I need to send a telegram," he said at last.

"Yes, sir?"

"To Farley Pilcher, up in Austin."

Pilcher was a captain with the Texas Rangers. He knew shooters in the same way other men knew dogs and horses. If a gunman had a name worth knowing, chances were that Pilcher knew his pedigree by heart, chapter and verse.

"If I may ask, sir . . . ?"

"Price is good at what he does, but no one's perfect, Arlis. He's made enemies along the way, and some of them are still alive. Not many, I suppose, but all I need is one or two."

"Sir, I'm not sure I follow—"

"Shooters," Rankin interrupted him. "In case you haven't worked it out, we're suddenly in short supply. Dumb bastards didn't take Price with them when they had the chance. What I need now is one or two good men to pick up where the others let me down."

"And you think Captain Pilcher knows someone who fits the bill?"

"Farley knows every working gun from Little Rock to Tucson, count on it."

"Yes, sir." Duffy was taking mental notes. "You want someone as good as Price—"

"Or better."

"Yes, of course. Someone who knows him?"

"*Knowing* him won't cut it, Arlis. That could be a friend of his, for all we know."

"Sorry, I didn't think—"

"I want someone who knows and *hates* Price bad enough to ride halfway across the country for a shot at him. Get me a shooter who'd pay *us* to tell him where

Price is. That way, the bounty on his head will make it twice as sweet."

"Good thinking, sir."

"Just send the telegram," Rankin replied. "I'm too damned tired to let you kiss my ass right now."

Duffy turned red and muttered an apology as he was making for the door. Rankin ignored him, unconcerned with ruffled feathers at the moment. Duffy wouldn't quit his job over an insult, since he earned a damn sight more from Rankin that he would've somewhere else. And if he did quit, what the hell?

The only thing that mattered now was Farley Pilcher and the list of shooters that he carried in his head. Rankin had paid the Ranger captain well for favors in the past, and he would pay again to rid himself of Matthew Price. One gun was all he needed, maybe two.

Damn Saxon and the others for their foolishness! The way Gil Gresham told it, they'd waltzed into Price's room and shot his bed to pieces without checking first to see if anyone was in it, then got killed themselves as they were leaving. Stupid bastards. All four dead because collectively they didn't have the brains to strike a match.

Rankin despised embarrassment. He'd built a name around Redemption as a man of influence and power, ruthless when he had to be—the kind of man, in short, who wasn't lightly crossed. Now Price had made a fool of him in public, twice within a single night. The shooter should be dead, but it was Rankin's men stacked up and waiting at the undertaker's place.

Not good.

A reputation was a fragile thing, sometimes. One lapse could scuttle years of calculated effort and destroy the whole façade. If Rankin let the drifter slap him down and kill four of his riders with impunity, he'd soon find opposition sprouting all over the county and his hard work would've been in vain. He could lose everything. It was unthinkable.

Surrender went against the grain for Rankin, always

had. He'd failed to buy Price off, and now the first attempt to kill him was a bloody bust. If Rankin hadn't bought the law when he was starting out in town, he would've been locked up by now, looking at prison time or worse. That end of things was covered, though. If he could only rid himself of Price before the insurrection had a chance to spread, he would regain control.

And he would pay the Mercers back for all their meddling, when the time was right. It would be folly to go after them right now, when he was short of guns and Price was on the prod. Rankin knew he must deal with first things first.

Price had to die, and soon. Somewhere within the reach of Rankin's bankroll there must be a shooter who could do the job. All Rankin had to do was find him, strike a bargain, then sit back and watch the show.

13

The wire caught up with Cole Hardwick in Trinidad, Colorado. He was taking it easy, enjoying himself in his way, when the Western Union runner found him sitting at a corner table in the Royal Flush Saloon. Hardwick sat alone, with his back to the wall, taking his time with a bottle of cheap whiskey. He saw the runner coming and switched the shot glass to his left hand, letting his right disappear beneath the table.

"Mr. Coleton Hardwick, sir?" The runner's nervous eyes flicked toward one side of Hardwick's face, checking the mark.

"I'm Hardwick."

"Sir, you have a telegram." He laid the flimsy bit of paper down in front of Hardwick as if it were something precious, worth its weight in gold.

"How much?"

"Excuse me?"

"What's the damage?"

"There's no charge to you, sir."

"You're excused, then."

"Yes, sir." Still the runner hovered. "If you'd care to answer—"

"Then I'll come down to the office when I'm ready."

"Yes, sir. Very good, sir."

Hardwick didn't touch the envelope at first. He watched the runner leave, then brought his right hand out of hiding and tipped another shot of whiskey into his glass. It burned going down, making him grimace at the taste.

Hardwick could've afforded better, after last week's job in Durango, but he'd been raised by thrifty parents who taught him not to throw money away on frills. They'd also taught him to pray over meals and fear Jesus, but it was the penny-pinching bit that stuck.

When he was ready, Hardwick set his shot glass down and tore into the Western Union envelope. It was his second telegram, the first—twelve years ago—being the notice of his father's death from typhoid fever. Hardwick hoped for more good news, but he was unprepared for what he read.

REQUEST THE PLEASURE OF YOUR COMPANY FOR MEETING WITH MUTUAL ACQUAINTANCE. MATTHEW PRICE AVAILABLE FOR CONSULTATION. EXPENSES AND NEGOTIABLE SETTLEMENT. RESPOND ARLIS DUFFY, REDEMPTION, TEXAS.

Hardwick was smiling by the time he'd read the telegram a second time, feeling the long scar crinkle on the right side of his face. A stranger watching Hardwick might've reckoned he was scowling over some unwelcome news, but it was just the opposite.

He didn't know who Arlis Duffy was or how the stranger had located him, but three words in the middle of the telegram hooked him immediately. MATTHEW PRICE AVAILABLE. The "consultation" part was smoke, the kind of double-talk that kept his clients from revealing what they really had in mind. A lawman looking at the telegram might guess what it was all about, but proving it was something else.

"Mutual acquaintance, my ass."

Hardwick had bought the bottle and he took it with him, heading back to his hotel. It was the cheapest one in town that still had single rooms with locking doors. He was a skinflint when it came to money, always had been, but a man in his profession needed privacy.

The hotel clerk had learned to skip his normal greeting when Hardwick appeared, bending to his register in rapt concentration. Hardwick returned the favor by ignoring him and climbed creaking stairs to his second-floor room. Inside, he locked the door, took another long pull on his bottle, then quickly stripped to the waist. He left his gun belt on. The familiar weight of his twin ivory-handled Peacemakers centered Hardwick, anchored him against a feeling that he might start floating if he wasn't tethered down.

That feather-light sensation came to him more often lately, alternately spooking and amusing him. There'd been a time when Hardwick only felt that way in the heartbeat before he killed a man, but now he sometimes wondered whether it was taking over, tiny bits and pieces of himself evaporating day by day, until he ceased to be. The notion didn't bother Hardwick all that much, as long as he had time to settle one last score before he dwindled down to nothing.

Matthew Price.

Why not?

He'd been postponing it, taking other jobs and making up excuses, letting his hatred simmer, but now it felt right. A man he'd never heard of was delivering Price like a gift, with money thrown into the bargain.

It was perfect.

Hardwick stood before the vanity mirror, examining his face. He could've used a haircut, but there wasn't time. Why waste the money, anyway? The beard he'd grown to hide a portion of his facial scar was going, though. His mind was set on that. Hardwick wanted Matt Price to see the scar and remember everything before he died.

It was only fitting that Price take the image with him on his way to hell.

Hardwick shaved with tepid water and a razor that was half-past dull. He used a tiny bar of hotel soap in place of lather, gritting his teeth at the pain as his long face was slowly revealed. There was a moment when he barely recognized himself, imagining another face instead.

"Leland?"

There was no answer from the glass, and Hardwick saw through his mistake. His brother had been five years in a grave in Farmington, New Mexico. If there was anything remaining of him now, it would be dust and bones.

Matt Price had done that, killing one Hardwick and leaving the other for dead. It was a grave mistake, not finishing the job.

"You should've killed me too," he told the glass, and flashed another of his grimace-smiles.

When he was finished with the razor, Hardwick put his shirt and hat back on, surveyed the room, and locked the door behind him when he left. It was a short walk to the railway depot but he took his time, enjoying it when men he didn't know sidestepped to clear the way. He felt them staring at him, taking in the scar that stretched from his right nostril almost to his ear, and their revulsion gave him strength.

A nervous-looking clerk told Hardwick that Redemption, Texas, wasn't on a railroad line as yet. The nearest stop in Terrell County would be Sanderson, a long day's ride to the southwest. A closer stop was Sheffield, to the north in Crockett County, which would cut the last leg of his trip in half.

Hardwick laid out the money for his ticket, thankful that a man he'd never heard of would be picking up the tab. After he sold his horse in Trinidad he ought to come out well ahead. The cash was secondary, though, for once.

Matt Price was waiting for him, and the bastard didn't even know it yet.

There was a moment when Price thought the hotel management might try to put him out, but no one broached the subject as he went about his business—what there was of it—on Sunday morning. It was mostly killing time, with all the stores shut down while merchants either went to church or took their day of rest at home. O'Malley's still served breakfast and the undertaker's parlor showed a certain bustle of activity, but otherwise Redemption had its mind made up to spend the Sabbath in a sleepy daze.

Price didn't buck the trend. He'd thought of going for a ride but changed his mind and settled for a visit to the livery instead. The Appaloosa snorted greetings, asking for a run, then settled for a bag of oats. Price watched him eat awhile, then walked back to his room.

If Rankin wanted a repeat performance of last night, he'd have to send more shooters down to the hotel. Price wouldn't make it easy for a bushwhacker by traipsing off across the unfamiliar countryside.

He kept an eye open for any sign of Belle or Jesse on his way back from the stable, but there was no trace of either one. The townspeople he met along the way avoided eye contact and gave him ample room to pass, as if he carried some disease they feared to catch by brushing elbows. Price had seen it all before and told himself he didn't mind.

He passed the day anticipating Rankin's next attempt to kill him. There was no doubt in his mind Rankin would try again; the only question now was when and where. A man in Rankin's place couldn't allow some drifter to insult him, kill his shooters, and generally defy

the status quo. It was bad for business and might give
some others ideas.

An early supper at O'Malley's was Price's last outing
on Sunday. Alone in a new room on the hotel's fourth
floor, he locked himself in and pulled the blinds, wedg-
ing a chair under the doorknob before he lay down to
sleep with his Colt close at hand. He woke before dawn,
stifling in the closed room, and sat up to watch the sun
rise from his window, wondering what the new day
would bring.

It brought workmen after breakfast, surveying the
damage from Saturday's fracas. The shot-blasted door to
4-D was replaced in an hour, but the scarred walls and
bloodstained carpet required more discussion, conducted
in whispers. The workmen would relax when he was
gone, so he got out and left them to it.

Where to go?

It came to him as inspiration sometimes did, for good
or ill. Price needed ammunition to replace his dwindling
supply, and where else in Redemption would he find it
but the dry goods store? The simple logic of it overrode
his recognition of a bad idea.

Price needed cartridges and Belle's shop sold them.
He'd heard nothing from Belle since her unexpected visit
on Saturday night, before all hell broke loose, and it occurred to him that Rankin might retaliate against her family while he bided his time, building up his nerve for
another run at Price. She might appreciate a warning
now, before it was too late.

Or so he told himself—and knew it was a sham before
he'd traveled halfway down the street in the direction of
the dry goods store. He wanted to see Belle again, but
warning her of danger she already recognized was merely
an excuse—a flimsy one, at that.

So be it. Price would call it what it was, a lure that had
drawn him across three states to face death on behalf of a
woman who'd never be his, a son who would never carry
his name.

Price hesitated for a moment on the street outside the dry goods store, then pushed his way inside. Another fairy-bell jangled above his head, making him wonder if there'd been a special sale on them in town. He'd barely closed the door when he heard squeaking noises behind him and a male voice asked, "May I help you?"

Price was unprepared for Jared Mercer in the flesh. He was a handsome, square-jawed man with dark hair lightly oiled and neatly combed, showing no signs of the erosion others suffered at his age. He wore a white shirt buttoned at the collar, filled with shoulders that had started strong and grown more so from exercise provided by his wheel-chair. While trying not to stare, Price noted the discrepancy between the merchant's torso and his narrow legs, awash in charcoal-colored pants, with brightly polished shoes on useless feet.

They'd never met, but Price saw recognition click in Mercer's eyes, translated to a tightening along his jaw. The merchant forced a smile that showed off healthy teeth but never reached his eyes.

"I'm looking for some cartridges," Price said.

"I shouldn't be surprised," said Mercer, through the rigid smile. "You're new in town."

"A few days," Price replied.

"Just passing through?"

"It started out that way."

"But now you've found something to make you stay?"

"Maybe a little while."

"Redemption's like that, for some people."

"Off the beaten track, though," Price suggested. "I suppose a man could lose his way."

"It happens." Wheeling closer in his chair, the store-keeper stuck out a hand. "I'm Jared Mercer, Mr. . . . ?"

"Price. Matt Price."

Mercer's grip was firm without being aggressive. Whatever might be going on behind his eyes, he wasn't looking for a test of strength. "What caliber?" he asked.

"Sorry?"

"Your cartridges."

"Colt forty-fives. Two boxes, if you have them."

"Sure thing. If you'll just follow me, we'll have you on your way."

He wheeled around and led Price toward the back wall of the store, where a few long guns were racked and cartridges were shelved by caliber. Price scanned the arsenal and wondered whether Jared Mercer ever thought of loading up a rifle, rolling down to Rankin's place and evening the score.

"Two dollars, if you please."

Price paid and took the cartridges. He knew there should be more to say, something between himself and this man who had taken Belle away from him, but all he felt was sadness at the way her life had turned. The memory of kissing her was almost blotted out by thoughts of all she'd suffered for this man and for their son.

Almost.

"Be careful here in Terrell County, Mr. Price," said Mercer. "Things aren't always what they seem. A man gets turned around sometimes and thinks he's making progress, when he's really not at all."

"I've felt that way before," Price said.

"We have something in common, then."

"Maybe."

The merchant's smile was losing ground. "Good luck to you."

I need it, Price thought, but he left the store without another word and started back along the street toward his hotel.

Jesse stood trembling in the backroom shadows and watched Matthew Price leave the store. He'd come downstairs moments earlier, in time to catch most of his father's conversation with Price, and while his stomach churned with guilt for eavesdropping, his curiosity over-rode the sick feeling.

It was strange, seeing Pa and the shooter together like that. From the way his parents argued over Price at night, Jesse'd expected angry words if the two men ever met. Instead, they'd been stiffly polite to each other, the way his folks sometimes were after church, shaking hands with townspeople he knew they really didn't like.

Jesse didn't understand grown-ups. Maybe he never would. They talked about honesty and "character" but put on masks that wouldn't fool an eight-year-old when dealing with each other. Only in the dark of night did they allow their true feelings to surface, and even then they held something back, as if afraid they might be over-heard, somehow exposed. Jesse didn't know where honesty came into it, but he was growing more adept each year at seeing through the smoke, looking behind the smiles. He didn't always like what he found there, but it was closer to the truth.

Though vague on details, Jesse now believed that his parents had drawn Matt Price to Redemption. Make that his mother, since Pa and Price had plainly never met before today, and from their conversation Jesse guessed they'd never pass for friends. His mother was a friend of Price from somewhere, sometime in the past. He wasn't sure what that meant, but it was enough to bring the shooter in and make him stand alone against Sedge Rankin. Four men dead so far, and Jesse knew it wasn't over yet.

He hated Rankin. His parents told him it was wrong to hate, but Jesse couldn't help it. Pa hated Rankin too, but in a quiet way that wouldn't let him show it off. Ma was a worrier, more than a hater, but he still saw fury in her eyes when Rankin's name was mentioned. Both his folks blamed Rankin for the shooting that had left his father crippled, but they only talked about it indirectly, Ma wishing they'd leave Redemption, Pa insisting they should stay.

Jesse sometimes wished he was a grown-up, armed and dangerous like Price. He'd kill Rankin or run him out of town and let his parents—all the decent people, really—live in peace. He'd be a hero then, with everybody lining up to shake his hand.

Okay, not *everyone*. He knew some of the folks in town sided with Rankin, although Jesse wasn't sure exactly why. Pa said it had to do with money—"filthy lucre," whatever that meant—and called it the root of all evil. At the same time, though, his parents worked for money in the dry goods store. Jesse had figured it out on his own that money wasn't evil in itself. The evil part was what some people did for money, how they craved it more than anything.

Whether from fear or greed, he could've guessed no one would stand with Price against Sedge Rankin. How could one man defeat a small army? Maybe by killing them four at a time, the way Price had last night.

Jesse still felt queasy when he thought about the dead man in the alleyway. It wasn't how he'd expected to feel, after all his reading on shooters and gunfights. Things were different, though, since he'd seen his father lying in blood with a dazed look of shock on his too-pale face. Jesse'd still been drawn to the action, as any boy would be, but now he thought there'd been another reason too. He wanted to see Rankin's gunmen die, hoping that one of those Price killed might be the man who'd put his father in the wheelchair.

It was justice, in a way, but Rankin wasn't finished yet. He would come back at Price with more men, more guns—if not today, then sometime soon. Jesse wished he could help Price somehow, but what could a boy his age do?

Maybe nothing. Then again . . .

He would have to work fast, without letting his parents find out. Price himself would require some convincing, but Jesse was persuasive when it counted. Ma once told him he could wheedle with the best of them, smiling as she said it, taking pride in him.

Excited now, he ducked out the back door and into the alley, retracing his path from the dark run on Saturday night.

Sedge Rankin studied his reflection in the mirror and decided that he looked like hell. It wasn't anything a man could put his finger on, exactly. He was shaved and neatly dressed the same as always, with his hair slicked back. There was no bruise to speak of from the elbow shot he'd taken Saturday, although his cheek was slightly swollen, still sore to the touch.

What was it, then?

The eyes, for one thing. They were bleary and blood-shot from lack of decent sleep. He hadn't slept at all on Saturday after the massacre and only for a few short hours Sunday night. On top of that, his visage had a sallow, almost jaundiced hue. It didn't help that he'd been drinking more than usual and smoking twice his normal number of cigars.

To hell with that. A man had to do something for his nerves.

Rankin had picked one of his black suits for the funerals that afternoon. Grymdike had his hands full, between the Kelseys and Rankin's four shooters, with a capacity turnout expected for Redemption's first-ever eight-holer. Rankin had considered skipping it, putting some distance between himself and Saxon's bungling crew, but on second thought he'd decided that missing the Kelsey service might be construed in some quarters as a tacit admission of guilt. More gossip was the last thing he needed right now, with tongues wagging all over town as it was, so he'd be standing graveside in his Sunday best, singing the hymns like everybody else.

But he damn sure didn't have to like it.

Reviewing the ledgers that morning had helped put

Rankin in his present sour state of mind. Business was
down across the street, at the Trail's End, but it had
picked up at the Nugget after his embarrassing encounter
with Matt Price. More money should've made him smile,
but Rankin bristled at the thought of people stopping in
to stare at him, watching the bat-wing doors and hoping
Price would come back for a second show.

Worse yet was when he caught himself watching the
door, praying the shooter *wouldn't* come. Rankin had
worked hard for his reputation as a man immune to
fear, secure behind his money and hired guns, but now
he felt it slipping through his hands. Four of his shooters
were already dead and two more had been missing from
the breakfast table at his ranch that morning. Others
might desert unless he offered them more money, but the
nine or ten remaining weren't worth what he paid them
now.

A cautious knocking on his office door distracted
Rankin from the looking glass. "Come on ahead."

The smile on Arlis Duffy's face told Rankin it was
good news for a change. "We have an answer, sir," he
said, and put the telegram in Rankin's hand. Rankin was
smiling by the time he read it through.

NEED TRANSPORTATION FROM THE SHEFFIELD DEPOT
TUESDAY, 4:15 FROM LUBBOCK. FIVE HUNDRED +
EXPENSE. KEEP PRICE IN TOWN.
C.C.

"He's not exactly eloquent," Duffy observed.

"I don't care if the sumbitch is a certified illiterate, as
long as he can finish this, once and for all."

"Yes, sir."

"Go up and meet him with a couple of the boys tomorrow, Arlis. Take two hundred dollars with you. He can
have the rest if he's alive on Wednesday and the job's
been done."

Duffy was frowning now. "Will you be speaking to the gentleman yourself, sir?"

"What you mean to ask is whether your ass will be dangling in the breeze if anything goes wrong."

"Well, um . . ."

"You can relax, Arlis. Bring him to me first thing, when you get back to town. Come in the back way, though. I don't want any of these yokels seeing me with Hardwick in advance. We don't know which of them might tip Price off."

"Yes, sir." Relief was written on the young man's face.

"I think I'll have a drink to celebrate. Join me?"

Duffy seemed on the verge of making some excuse, but he thought better of it. "Yes, sir. Thank you, sir."

Rankin poured double shots of bourbon into crystal, passing one to Duffy. He'd been drinking too damned much the past few days, but recognizing that was half the battle. Even so, he stopped before the whiskey took control of him and made him pull some foolish stunt that placed his life and property at greater risk.

"We've got this bastard where we want him now," he said, as he slugged down the bourbon.

"Yes, sir." Duffy finished his drink, looking worried when Rankin poured him another.

"Can't dance on one leg," Rankin said.

"No, sir."

"You're coming to the funeral this afternoon." He phrased it as an order, not a question.

Duffy hastened to nod, nearly spilling his drink. "Yes, sir. Of course."

"The dead deserve respect," said Rankin. "Most of them, at least."

"Yes, sir." Duffy was looking slightly green around the gills.

"Take Price, now. That's one planting we can celebrate."

"If Hardwick's good enough." The words were barely

out when Duffy recognized his error. "What I mean to say is—"

Rankin fanned the air to silence him. "You heard what Farley Pitcher said. Hardwick's put down a dozen men, at least—maybe a couple dozen, if you believe all the stories. He's done some time, but Pilcher says it didn't slow him down. Main thing, Price killed his brother back in eighty-four and gave Hardwick a big ugly scar to remember him by. He's our boy. Wait and see."

14

Cole Hardwick woke when they were crossing into Texas at a pissant town called Texline, one of those border whistle-stops named on a whim by somebody with no imagination. They littered the map like rat droppings, tediously predictable from their look to a vague sense of money-grubbing desperation that hung in the air like trail dust.

The train stopped at Texline for water and Hardwick got out to stretch his legs. He'd never seen the town before, and yet it looked familiar to him: clapboard buildings faded by relentless sun and wind, a dusty main street wider than it ought to be, yokels who watched the trains roll in and out because their lives were just that empty and it was the only show in town.

They probably had liquor in Texline, but Hardwick didn't have the time to search it out and border towns were known for jacking up their prices anyhow. The country he'd seen coming into town was barren aside from the usual mesquite and cactus, nothing to suggest that anyone had ever plowed or fertilized the land. If they were growing anything but misery in Texline, Hardwick hadn't seen it yet.

He hung around the seedy depot, keeping his distance from locals and his fellow passengers alike. Some of the former stared at him, then cut their eyes away like spooky children when he caught them at it. Hardwick took it as a compliment and let it go. Hard to believe these hicks were so hard-up for entertainment that a glimpse of him would keep them jawing for the next few days.

You shoulda seen 'im thar. Them iv'ry-handled six-guns tied down low.

An' don't forget that scar.

They wouldn't know his name of course, but that was for the best. Hardwick had done three bitter years at Huntsville for a drunken Dallas shooting scrape where no one even died, and he had no desire to mix with Texas lawmen if he could avoid it. Not before he had a chance to deal with Price, at any rate.

Hardwick didn't see it coming, but a moment later he was back in Farmington, high country near the Colorado line. It happened that way sometimes, years melting away in a heartbeat and dropping him back in a place he'd have rather forgotten. Smell the pine trees, coming into town at midday after a hard ride from Durango, shaking the damned posse off at the border. They'd been paid for their killing and Leland was itching to drop his share at the first whorehouse they found. They'd never gotten that far, though.

They hadn't seen him, going in. Price wasn't one you'd notice in a crowd, but he was sitting at a table big enough for three and Leland reckoned that he wouldn't mind vacating for the Hardwick brothers. With a stiff drink warming up his guts, Cole had agreed it was a fine idea—but Price refused to move. He had a certain attitude, a nerve about him, when he told Leland he wasn't finished with his whiskey yet. Leland was all smiles, being helpful, still not knowing who the stranger was when he picked up the bottle and began to pour it out across the floor.

Price sat and watched him, let him tip the last drop out before he spoke. Hardwick recalled his words as plain as day. He said, "I'll need a dollar or a bottle from you boys, before you leave."

Leland had laughed at that. How could he not? Some saddle tramp with gall enough to brace the Hardwick brothers over spilt red-eye. "Why don't you just get down and lick it up?" he asked.

"A dollar or a bottle, either way," Price said again, all icy-calm.

Cole had begun to think by then that something might be wrong, but Leland would've turned on him for interrupting. "I don't think you heard me," Leland said to Price. "I told you to—"

"A dollar or a bottle," Price repeated, interrupting him.

And Leland wasn't laughing, then. Cole felt the heat that radiated from him like a well-banked fire. "You wanna stand," he said, "or take it sitting down?"

"You're not worth standing up for," Price replied, and then it happened all at once. Leland went for the gun on his right hip and Cole was sure he'd make it, but Price must've had a pistol drawn and cocked beneath the table. Nobody could draw and fire that fast when he was sitting down. The first shot hammered into Leland's chest and rocked him backward, then another took him underneath the chin and put him down.

Hardwick remembered how the scream felt, rushing out of him as he was reaching for his gun. Still no idea on earth who he was dealing with, but with his brother dead in front of him he had no choice. He'd seen the smoking pistol swing around his way, Price frowning as he thumbed the hammer back, and then a ripping impact on the right side of his face before it all went black.

The doctor told him later that it was a miracle he'd lived. Another inch or so, the .45 slug would've cored his

brain instead of plowing up his cheek and putting him to
sleep for two days straight. A preacher came around and
said he ought to learn from the experience and give his
heart to Jesus. Later on, the sheriff brought him Leland's
guns and told him to get out of town as soon as he was fit
to ride.

The lawman also gave him Price's name, enjoying it.
"I sent him packing too," the sheriff said. "You trash can
kill each other somewhere else."

The train whistle cut through his memories and Hardwick went aboard to claim his seat. It wouldn't be much
longer now. A few more hours and he could settle things
for Leland, finally.

It should've made him happy, but the shooter felt a
sudden chill.

Price heard the small voice hissing at him as he passed
the alley east of his hotel. He stopped and turned, surprised to see Jesse standing well back and shaded from
the street. The boy beckoned. Price checked the sidewalk left and right, then stepped into the alley, moving
closer to his son.

"I was afraid I'd miss you," Jesse said. His face was
flushed from running.

"Here I am."

"You met Pa at the store."

"That's right."

"I wasn't eavesdropping."

"No harm," Price said. "What can I do for you?"

"You bought more cartridges," said Jesse, nodding at
the boxes in his hand.

"I did."

"That's good. You have some extra, then."

Price didn't know where he was going with it. "Running out's a bad idea," he said.

"You had to use some up, the other night." There was
the bare hint of a smile on Jesse's face.

"It's nothing to be pleased about," Price said.

"I'm *glad* you killed those men. One of 'em prob'ly shot my pa and put him in that chair he rolls around."

Price nearly told the boy two wrongs don't make a right, but that poor logic hadn't done a thing for him when he was Jesse's age. Whatever parents said, sometimes it *did* help, striking back. It didn't make things right, but sometimes there was no "right" to it. Sometimes getting even was enough.

Instead, Price said, "I don't believe your father feels that way."

"He's scared of Mr. Rankin."

"Think about that for a minute, Jesse. If he's scared, why hasn't he packed up and taken you away?"

"The store," Jesse replied. "Nobody wants to buy it, and it's all he thinks about."

"I don't believe that."

"It's the truth! Besides, he can't fight from a wheelchair." There was something like contempt in Jesse's voice, or maybe it was just a child's embarrassment.

"There's more to life than fighting, Jesse."

"I know that. There's getting beaten up and crippled if you don't. There's getting killed like Tommy Kelsey and his folks."

"I guess you've told your parents how you feel?"

"Pa doesn't listen to me. He just tells me what to do or sends me to my room."

"Your mother, then."

"They have *discussions* when they reckon I can't hear them," Jesse said. "She wants to leave, but Pa says no."

"Does that sound like a frightened man, to you?"

"He took a stand with Mr. Rankin once before and wound up crippled. Now he talks about his pride while people laugh at him behind his back."

"You've heard them laughing, have you?"

"Kids at school." The bitterness was plain in Jesse's voice.

"They're cruel sometimes. It doesn't mean they're right."

"I know that," Jesse said. "But if a man won't fight *or* run, what's left?"

Price knew there ought to be more civilized alternatives, but his experience in talking problems out was limited. "There's something on your mind," he said.

"Yes, sir."

"Out with it, then."

The boy swallowed, then said, "I saw what happened here on Saturday."

Price felt himself go numb. "You did?"

"Part of it, anyway. There was a man came out the window and he fell back there." Jesse's head tilted toward the alleyway behind him.

"How'd you happen to be out here in the middle of the night?"

"I heard the shooting and came down to see."

"That's not the smartest thing you could've done," Price said.

"Ma said that, too. It worried her, I think."

"I shouldn't be surprised."

"I had to see, though. And I thought . . ."

"Thought what?"

Jesse was blushing now. "That maybe I could help."

"Help me?"

"Yes, sir."

Price felt a tightness in his throat. "What did you have in mind?"

"I didn't think about it."

"That could be a problem, Jesse."

"Yes, sir."

"I appreciate the thought, but there are times when boys your age should mind their parents and stay safe at home."

"My home's not safe."

Price felt like reaching out to Jesse, but he held himself in check and said, "It will be, someday."

Jesse shook his head. "No, sir. It won't, unless I learn to fight."

"How's that?"

"Whoever shot my pa, whether he's dead or not, Sedge Rankin told him what to do. He's killed the Kelseys and some others, too. He won't be satisfied until we're gone."

"You plan to face him, boy?"

"Somebody should."

"Don't take this wrong," Price said, "but you're a bit young for the job."

"Billy the Kid shot his first man when he was twelve!"

"That leaves you two years shy, if I recall."

"I wouldn't mind some help."

Price had to smile at that. "We're getting to it now, I guess."

"Yes, sir."

"So, what's the plan?"

"You teach me how to shoot."

Price didn't laugh. It wasn't funny anymore. "There's more to it than shooting."

"You can teach me all of it."

"It's not that simple, Jesse."

"I can learn. I'm not afraid."

"Nobody said you were."

"What's wrong, then?"

"You don't want to go this way."

"You don't know *what* I want!"

"I know you'll never get it with a gun," Price said. "Go down that road, and there's no coming back."

"I'll go with you, then. You need help sometimes, the same as me."

Price felt as if a fist were clenched around his heart. He didn't recognize the feeling and he wanted it to go away. "We're not the same," he said, more harshly than he meant to.

Jesse blinked at him. "Why not?"

"Because you have a family that loves you and you'd be a fool to give it up."

"I'm not a fool!"

"I didn't mean—"

"If you won't teach me, then I'll do it on my own!" Red-faced and fighting tears, he turned his back on Price and moved away.

"Wait, son."

"I'm not your son!" cried Jesse, as he broke into a run and disappeared around the corner, racing back toward home.

Jesse ran along the alley, past his parents' store and upstairs living quarters, all the way down to the livery stable. He stopped there, not because he was exhausted, but because a few more minutes on the run would take him past Sedge Rankin's Nugget and beyond the very limits of the town.

The worst part of a small-town life, he thought, was never really having any privacy. In the old days, before the trouble started, Jesse remembered lying awake in his bed some nights, listening to his parents in their room. They weren't having *discussions* then. It wasn't really talk at all, maybe some whispering mixed in with moaning, grunting noises like someone was sick with a bellyache. Sometimes his ma would squeal, and then his pa would say, "You'll wake the neighbors, Annabelle," before they fell to giggling.

Jesse didn't hear those noises from the master bedroom anymore, and what he heard seemed always tinged with anger or with sadness. He preferred the old ways, but he'd gathered from the way things had been going since his pa was shot that they were gone for good.

He was surprised to feel tears spilling down his face. Unaware that he'd been crying as he ran, Jesse swiped at his eyes with a sleeve, angry and embarrassed. Big boys weren't supposed to cry, at least not in public, and the worst part was that Jesse didn't even know what he was crying for. He wasn't sad, the way a weeper was supposed to feel. Price had rejected him, but that sparked anger. He knew Rankin would send more shooters against his family someday, but that made him afraid. Somehow, he guessed, the two emotions must've run together and spilled over through his eyes.

There'd been a moment when he'd hated Price, but it was fading now. Anger remained, like sunburn on his cheeks, but Jesse knew that was embarrassment as much as rage. He must've looked a fool to Price, asking a grown-up shooter whether he could help kill Rankin and the rest. Price must think he was simpleminded now, to even bring it up that way.

His breath hitched in another sob, but Jesse caught it in his teeth and swallowed it. Enough bawling. Price wouldn't take him on as an apprentice, but it didn't matter. None of those shooters he'd read about were schooled by anyone, unless he counted Jesse James— and that was growing up during the War Between the States. Jesse had war enough right in his own backyard; he didn't need Missouri or the likes of Quantrill's Raiders to teach him that life was hard—and sometimes cheap, as well.

His pa had guns for sale back at the store, but they'd be missed if Jesse borrowed one to teach himself the basics. Same thing for the ammunition that he'd have to steal. Coming or going, one way or the other, he'd be caught as sure as anything if he tried borrowing a weapon from the store. There was another way, though, now that he thought about it, and it might just work.

Since he'd been shot, Pa kept a pistol in the nightstand by his bed. Jesse had seen it and he knew it was a Smith & Wesson .44-40. He'd never been allowed to handle it, of course, but that could change. He'd looked into the nightstand drawer a couple times, while his parents were busy in the shop, so he knew Pa didn't carry it downstairs. It probably wouldn't be missed before bedtime, if then. Taking a box of ammunition would be harder, best left for night, while his parents were sleeping. He could take the candle from his room downstairs and pick out the right caliber. If he wasn't caught in the act, Pa might not miss the cartridges for days.

Time enough for him to practice, once he found a place. He could take Dancer out for a run, maybe back to the woods where he'd ridden with Mr. Price on Saturday. He had no gun belt, but the fast draw didn't matter. Jesse wasn't fool enough to think that he could stand against Sedge Rankin's shooters in the middle of the street. They'd laugh at him, then kill him if he tried to draw.

But there were times when being young and insignificant was helpful to a boy. No man would take him seriously or consider him a threat. The men who came to hurt his parents next time might dismiss him out of hand, let down their guard. He wouldn't mind backshooting if it did the job. Rankin's killers deserved no better, after what they'd done to his pa.

He thought about the woods north of town, imagining his first pistol practice. He'd be alone there, no one around for miles now that the Kelseys were gone. And if someone came along to interrupt him—

The Kelseys!

He had to get home for the funeral service, to pay his respects. Ma was taking him, a gesture of respect she called it, while Pa stayed behind at the store. Jesse saddened at the thought of Tommy Kelsey in a box, burned up, but he was also curious to see what happened when Sedge Rankin's shooters were laid out in line with the innocents. Whisper-talk around town blamed Rankin for the Kelsey massacre. His ma had used the term *poetic justice* over Sunday breakfast, but Jesse didn't take her meaning and his pa just grunted, mopping up his gravy with a biscuit. Later, taking down the dictionary, Jesse'd read that it meant "an ideal distribution of rewards and punishments such as is common in some poetry and fiction"—and he still didn't know what in heck they were saying.

No matter.

He knew what *justice* was, with or without poetry, and he reckoned Matt Price had dispensed some on Saturday night to Chad Saxon and the rest. Marshal Gresham must have agreed for once, or he would've locked Price up in jail. As for Saxon's replacements, whoever they were, justice might be waiting for them where they least expected it, wielded by a hand so young they never even saw it coming.

Smiling finally, he turned and started walking back along the alleyway toward home.

The black suit captured Rankin's mood as he surveyed the cemetery crowd. From where he stood—dead-center at the six- or eight-foot gap between the Kelsey caskets and his four dead hands, with Arlis Duffy at his side—it looked like damn near everybody in Redemption had turned out to hear the Reverend Dooley Bursaw send eight souls to Jesus in a batch.

There was some whispered doubt amongst the crowd, of course, as to the ultimate direction some of the departed might be taking when they left this mortal coil. It didn't take a mind reader to figure out that some townsfolk hoped Saxon and his boys were roasting in the blackest depths of Hell. Chad hadn't been well-liked and wasn't greatly missed in town, even by men who'd drunk their share of whiskey with him while he was alive, trying to find his good side and stay on it. There were some who'd say he didn't have a good side, but allowed *good riddance* might've been a fitting epitaph.

In fact, Rankin couldn't have cared less what the town's people thought of Chad, Perry Hart, or the rest. He wouldn't give two cents for their opinion of the Kelseys, either, if it came to that. What Rankin cared about, as he stood ramrod-straight before the eight pine boxes filled with death, was the town's attitude toward him.

He knew some people blamed him for the Kelseys. That was only natural; after all, he was guilty as sin. They'd blame him for the hotel shootings too, and that would be alright except for how the whole thing had turned out. He didn't mind folk fearing him—in fact, he actively encouraged it. Today, though, with his four men boxed and ready for the worms, it wasn't so much fear he felt as something else.

Contempt, perhaps? A subtle shift from healthy dread to understanding that the big man had his weak points, just like everybody else. That kind of attitude was bad for business. It would hurt him in the long run, if he didn't stamp it out.

Rankin was doing what he could in that direction, though. Cole Hardwick was arriving tomorrow to deal with the problem, bringing his guns and his hatred for Price to Redemption. He was several cuts above Chad Saxon and the others, by all accounts—a first-class killer, if there was such a thing in the world. His grudge against Price for the brother he'd lost gave Hardwick a motivation beyond mere money, suggesting to Rankin that he wouldn't back down when the going got tough.

And if he couldn't cut it—then what?

Rankin shook his head, then caught himself, wondering if anyone had noticed. A surreptitious glance around the crowd showed no one watching him specifically. He made a mental note to strive for better self-control and focused on the caskets ranged in front of him.

As for Hardwick losing out to Price, he would jump off that cliff when he came to it. There were always more guns and gunslingers. Someone out there was faster than Price. It was a law of nature: no one lived forever. All he had to do was stay alive until he found that faster gun and sealed a bargain for the job.

Preacher Bursaw took his place behind the caskets,

looking positively mournful with his long face and thinning gray hair that blew every which way as soon as he
took off his hat. There was a problem with the Bible,
thumbing through it with his hat in hand, and Bursaw
frowned a bit before he put the hat back on and found his
text.

"Dearly beloved," he began, "we're gathered here
today—"

For Christ's sake, Rankin thought, *we're here to bury
them not* marry *them.*

"—souls of these dead, departed brothers . . . and, er,
sisters . . . from our midst. They're leaving us untimely,
Lord. We pray for Thee to greet them all with open arms
and make them welcome in your land of many mansions,
where there's neither doubt nor care."

Rankin bit his tongue to keep from snorting at a mental
image of the Lord embracing Saxon and his friends.
More likely, they'd be met outside the Pearly Gates and
booted down to Hell without a by-your-leave. As for
Rankin himself, he was still working angles, avoiding
that last trip as long as he could.

Preacher Bursaw was reading scripture now. Rankin
had missed the text, but he recognized the psalm. "The
Lord is my shepherd; I shall not want."

But I do, Rankin thought. *I* do *want.*

"—beside the still waters. He restoreth my soul."

Too late for that, with Chad and the rest.

"Yea, though I walk through the valley of the shadow
of death, I will fear no evil, for thou art with me. Thy rod
and thy staff, they comfort me."

Give me a team of first-class shooters any day.

"Thou preparest a table for me in the presence of mine
enemies."

Tried that, thought Rankin, *and it didn't help. It's no
good breaking bread with them that hate you.*

"Surely goodness and mercy shall follow me all the
days of my life,"

I'll take the goodness. Never mind the mercy.

It occurred to Rankin that he'd been too merciful already. When Price was safely dead and in the ground, he'd need to do some touch-up work on certain locals who had crossed him in the meantime, starting off with Jared Mercer's brood. They'd definitely have to go.

"Amen," said Preacher Bursaw.

Rankin had to smile at that. "Amen," he said.

15

The buggy ride from Sheffield to Redemption got on Hardwick's nerves and made his backside ache, but with two hundred dollars in his pocket for the trouble he could tough it out. While driving, Arlis Duffy babbled like some kind of tour guide for a mile or so, pointing to buttes and such along the way, then Hardwick ordered him to shut his pie hole and they finished off the trip in blessed silence.

Hardwick hadn't been surprised to learn that Duffy was a spineless go-between. The men who hired assassins tended to be cautious types. Range wars were one thing, but for straight-up murder most preferred to leave no paper trail between themselves and a hired gun. The deal with Price fell somewhere in between, but Hardwick didn't mind a man who watched out for himself. The ones he had a problem with were those who didn't pay their debts on time.

He was supposed to meet some character named Rankin whom he'd never heard of and would happily forget as soon as he received the rest of the agreed five-hundred dollars and expenses. Hardwick didn't care who Rankin was or why he had decided Price should die. It was enough for him to have the opportunity and make a little something for it on the side. He didn't tell the go-between that he'd have done the job for free. Hardwick made it a point to never pass on easy money when it came his way.

Redemption wasn't much to look at in the evening shadows. Hardwick had seen a thousand other small towns like it in his time. They sprang up everywhere, it seemed, growing on gold or silver, grass and water, sometimes nothing but a dash of hope. Most of them faded in the stretch and blew away, but this one had a stubborn look about it, like a burg that might hang on. That wasn't saying it would prosper, but survival in itself would mean these folks had beat the odds.

Some of them, anyway.

Instead of driving right through town, Duffy steered the team along an alleyway that ran behind the buildings facing Main Street on the south. There was enough room for the buggy, but it still made Hardwick nervous, curtains sliding back on windows here and there along the way. He kept a sharp eye out and both hands near his guns, ready to fight if anyone did more than watch while they passed.

Duffy pulled up in back of a saloon that seemed to do good business, from the sound of things within. Hardwick climbed down and waited while Duffy secured his team. When it was time to go inside, Hardwick ignored the show of courtesy that would've let him walk in front and said, "You go ahead."

The sound of women's laughter and piano music gave Hardwick ideas. Trail dust had made him thirsty, and a shot of whiskey sometimes tasted better with a woman sitting close beside him. Only sometimes, though, when Hardwick felt the itch. It would be fair to say that he was itching now, but there was business waiting for him at the moment. He would rather have a taste of Matthew Price's blood than French champagne.

Duffy led Hardwick to a door marked PRIVATE, knocked and waited. When a voice inside said, "Come," he led the way inside. An older, well-dressed man was on his feet and circling around a desk to greet them, showing off a big smile on his face. He had an inch and forty pounds on Hardwick, but the hand he offered had a certain softness to it, like he wasn't used to doing his own dirty work. He smelled like money and cigars.

"Good evening, Mr. Hardwick. I'm Sedge Rankin. Would you like something to cut the dust?"

"Whiskey."

"Of course. Arlis, why don't you make it two, then run along. I'll take care of our guest from here on out."

Duffy poured two stiff shots and brought them to the desk. He left without good-byes, which suited Hardwick fine. Rankin was back behind his desk and waving toward a chair covered in maroon leather. "Please, have a seat," he said.

Hardwick sat down and sipped his whiskey. It was several cuts above the rotgut he'd been drinking when the telegram found him in Colorado.

"I trust you had a pleasant journey," Rankin said.

"I'm here," Hardwick replied. "That's all that counts."

Rankin was trying not to frown, the effort etching little lines between his thick eyebrows. He was a man who liked to set the mood, but Hardwick wasn't having it. "We may as well get down to business, then."

"What else is there?"

"I thought you might want to relax a spell, after your trip."

"I'll rest up afterward. Where's Price?"

"He's here." Rankin saw Hardwick stiffen and it made him smile. "I don't mean *here,* of course. But he's in town. Across the street, in fact, at the Trail's End."

"That's a saloon?"

"Indeed. My people tell me he's been there an hour or so. He also has a room uptown, at the hotel."

"You said five hundred and expenses."

"That's correct. Arlis gave you two hundred at the Sheffield depot, I believe?"

"He did."

"I'll have the rest for you as soon as you complete the job."

"Sounds fair."

Rankin was studying his face, the scar that pulled Cole's nostril back a bit and made him seem to sneer whether he tried or not. Caught staring, Rankin covered with a smile and said, "I hope you're up to this."

It sounded more like simple curiosity than any kind of challenge, maybe with a smidgen of concern. Hardwick said, "You called me, remember?"

"No offense," said Rankin. "You come highly recommended, but I ought to warn you. Price killed four of my best men on Saturday."

"Your best weren't good enough."

"That's obvious."

"I owe the bastard, from before you ever heard of him."

"And it's my pleasure to accommodate you. If you'd like some help . . . ?"

Hardwick tossed back his drink and stood. "Across the street, you said?"

"That's right. You can't miss it."

"This won't take long."

"I'll be right here," said Rankin, smiling.

Hardwick went out through the front, feeling the drinkers and their women eyeing him as if he'd just performed a magic trick, appearing from thin air. Warm night had settled on the town when he pushed through the bat-wing doors and crossed the street.

Price was sitting in a smoky corner of the Trail's End with his back to the wall when Cole Hardwick came in.

Price made a habit of door-watching in saloons—and most particularly now, when he was on Sedge Rankin's patch, daring the man to make another move.

Now it was made.

It took a moment for Hardwick to spot him, scanning the big room and finally turning toward Price, the bullet-scarred side of his face on display. In the time he had, Price ran a mental calculation on the odds of Hardwick passing through Redemption, stopping into the saloon where Price was drinking, and he reckoned they were on the shady side of slim to none. That meant Rankin had done his homework and reached out to Hardwick, finding him in something close to record time.

It should've worried Price, but didn't. Strangely, it felt right. Unfinished business winding up. Come one, come all. He sat and sipped his whiskey, watching Hardwick cross the room, drinking left-handed while his right hand found the Colt.

Just like old times.

Hardwick stopped ten feet back from Price's table. The expression on his scarred face could've been a smile or sneer. Whichever one it was, Price knew the thought behind it was the same.

"Matt Price."

He kept his left hand on the table, wrapped around his empty glass. "Hardwick."

"So, you remember me?"

"I've got an eye for faces," Price replied.

"You like it?" Hardwick turned his head a bit to let Price have the full effect.

"It suits you."

Hardwick showed him yellow teeth. "I've been looking for a chance to thank you."

Price had played this game before—both sides of it, in fact. Most towns, the law frowned heavily on shooters breezing in and blasting someone on the street without a call. It had to look like self-defense, or at the very least an equal contest. Provocation could take many forms.

The trick was to be ready when the other shooter made his move and put him down before he had a chance to use his gun.

The law would be no problem in Redemption. Price assumed that Marshal Gresham would be pleased to look the other way if Hardwick killed him, but thoughts of Belle and Jesse made him hesitate. He wasn't much against an army, but he was the only thing that stood between the Mercers and the weight of Rankin's wrath, right now. A lucky shot from Hardwick could leave Belle and Jesse at the big man's mercy. For the moment, then, he'd have to bide his time and find a way to keep Hardwick at bay.

"Looking for me?" he said. "It's been awhile."

"Five years," Hardwick replied. "I got a bit distracted."

"Huntsville's what I heard."

"You keepin' track of me?"

"Word gets around."

"Same way I found you here."

"I doubt it."

Hardwick's dark eyes narrowed down to slits. "What's that supposed to mean?"

"I'm thinking someone paid your way down here for reasons you don't know about, hoping that you and I would mix it up."

"Why should I care?" asked Hardwick. "I've got reasons of my own."

"And you've been five years getting to it, less the time at Huntsville."

Logic wasn't Hardwick's strong point. He was frowning now, whether from anger or confusion Price couldn't have said. "You have a point to make?"

"I do. He's using you."

"I'm gettin' misty here, you so concerned and all."

Price shrugged. He held the Colt and eased its hammer gently back. There was a sense of having played this scene before. "No skin off me," he said. "Man has a right to see the whole picture, that's all I'm saying."

"I see fine from where I stand," Hardwick replied. "I'm lookin' at the man who gave me this—" his index finger rose to trace the scar—"and left my brother dead."

"You recollect how those things came about?" Price asked.

"My memory's as clear as day."

Price risked a smile. "This all must look familiar, then," he said.

Cole Hardwick paled a bit beneath his tan, the long scar gone fish-belly white. He glanced down at the table set between them, as if seeing Price's hand beneath it and the gun he held. "I always said you were a sneaky bastard."

"Sticks and stones," Price said.

Hardwick drew courage from the fact that he was still alive, keeping his hands well clear of both guns as he spoke. "I don't believe you'll do it here, like this."

"Depends how much you piss me off. If you've got anything but hair under your hat, you may see we don't need to fight at all."

"I knew it," Hardwick said. There was no doubt about the sneer this time. "You're yellow."

"I've got business more important than a five-year grudge. Maybe you're smart enough to understand that, maybe not."

Some of the drinkers at surrounding tables had begun to eavesdrop, watching them. Hardwick played to the audience, raising his voice. "I look at you and see a shooter with a reputation too damn big for him, afraid to face me like a man."

"Ask Rankin how he liked the funeral yesterday," Price said.

"Which funeral's that?"

"The four he sent ahead of you. He's running short of able hands."

"I heard about those four," said Hardwick. He was

stoking fury now. "I ain't afraid of you, and I ain't leavin' town until we settle this."

"Then make your move," Price said, "or step aside and wait your turn."

He heard chairs scooting back, giving the scar-faced shooter room to work if he was so inclined. Hardwick considered it, then let his shoulders slump and splayed his empty hands. "I ain't no fool. I want a stand-up fight."

"Another time, then," Price replied. "You need to run along before my thumb gets tired."

"You watch for me," said Hardwick, as he backed away. "I won't go far."

Price tracked him to the door and out, then carefully relaxed the hammer on his Colt. It took a few more seconds for the conversation at surrounding tables to resume.

Go straight to hell for all I care, he thought, and poured himself another drink.

Rankin had waited in his office for a ruckus to erupt across the street. He might not hear the shots, but he had spotters in the Trail's End who would let him know the minute Price went down. Gil Gresham would be summoned in accordance with the law, and he would rubberstamp the claim of self-defense.

Rankin had confidence in his assassin. From the moment he'd walked in, Cole Hardwick radiated menace—not the sense of petty arrogance Chad Saxon used to wear like cheap cologne, but something altogether more impressive. Chad had killed some people in his day, but Hardwick had the feel of one born to it. More important, he'd faced Price and lived to tell the tale, anxious to have a rematch.

After fifteen minutes passed without some word, Rankin began to wonder. At the twenty mark, nervous, he rose and poured himself a drink. Come thirty, if he felt like it, Rankin decided he would stroll across and have a look-see for himself. It wasn't like he needed an excuse or anyone's permission to go calling on his own saloon.

At twenty-four minutes he heard approaching footsteps and the sound of Arlis Duffy's voice, muted enough that he had trouble making out the words. Rankin was back behind his desk, standing with arms crossed, when Cole Hardwick entered, Duffy trailing red-faced at his heels.

"Excuse us, Mr. Rankin," Duffy said. "I realize—"

"Forget it, Arlis."

"Yes, sir. But—"

"Go on, now. There's a good boy."

Duffy left them with the door ajar. If Rankin knew his stooge, Duffy was standing just outside to eavesdrop. "Arlis!" he called out, raising his voice.

"Yes, sir?"

"You have some business elsewhere, I believe."

"Yes, sir," he said, before shutting the door.

He turned to Hardwick, smiling. "That was quick."

"It ain't done yet," the shooter said.

Rankin put on a vague look of surprise. Hardwick's expression had already told him something was amiss. Rankin sat down and rolled his chair forward until his gut was snug against the desk. His right knee brushed the pistol he kept hidden underneath there, for emergencies.

"Tell me what happened, please," he said.

"I went in prodding him, the way it's done," Hardwick replied. "Thought sure he'd take the bait, but somethin' held him back."

"Perhaps you frightened him."

"That's part of it, I'd say, but he's got somethin' else in mind right now."

Rankin already knew the answer, but he had to ask. "Such as?"

"My thought would be he's set on killin' you."

"He told you that?"

"Not in so many words. I worked it out."

"Well, now, that's problematical."

"Say what?"

Rankin allowed a thoughtful frown. "I'm thinking, Cole—you don't mind if I call you Cole?"

"Suits me."

"Perfect. I'm thinking, Cole, that if he kills me, there'll be no one left to pay you the remainder of your fee."

"He worries you," the shooter said.

Rankin couldn't deny it. "It's the reason why you're here, Cole. But if you're not up to it—"

"I'll kill him for you, don't you worry." Hardwick's smile was crafty. "But I'll need a couple things from you."

"What might those be?"

"First thing, the price is goin' up. Big man like you, I guess your life is worth a thousand dollars, anyway."

"We had a deal."

Hardwick dug in his pocket for a roll of currency. "You want to play it cheap," he said, "I'll take my round-trip fare and leave you to it."

"There's no reason to be hasty," Rankin said. "You said two things."

"The money first."

"Agreed."

"And now, I need some kinda hook to make him fight. He don't swell up and bust for words, like some."

Rankin pretended to consider it, although he knew the answer instantly. He used the time to ponder means of making Hardwick pay for gouging him on terms. If he survived the fight with Price, Hardwick would have to come back for his money. When he did . . .

Rankin put extra warmth behind his smile. "I may have something for you, Cole."

"I'm listenin'."

"Price has a woman here in town. She's married to a cripple and it leaves her wanting, I suppose."

"I know the sort," Hardwick replied. A leer crinkled the long scar on his cheek.

"They've tried to keep it quiet, mind you, but we're just a small town here and people talk. They see things."

"You suppose he'll fight for someone else's woman?"

"I'd bet money on it."

"Mister, you already did. Now, if you'll tell me where to find this woman, I'll be on my way."

Rankin gave him directions to the dry goods store and promised the remainder of his thousand dollars would be waiting when the job was done. He walked the shooter out and beckoned Arlis Duffy from his table near the close end of the bar.

"Yes, sir?"

Rankin lowered his voice and leaned in close. "Our friend's gone off to try his luck a second time. I'd guess we have at least an hour, likely more. It should be long enough."

"For what, sir?"

"Why, for you to round up every man we've got and fetch them over here before Hardwick comes back."

"Sir, I'm not sure—"

"Just *bring* them, damn it! I'll explain when everybody's here. I only want to say it once."

Jesse Mercer wasn't sure exactly where his dreams cut off and waking life began. He guessed it was a dream that sent him running madly through a house he didn't recognize, through musty rooms and corridors that seemed to stretch for miles on end. Someone—some*thing*—was chasing him, but Jesse didn't want to turn and look behind for fear of seeing what it was. The sight of it, he knew, might freeze him in his tracks or stop his heart.

And so he ran for what seemed hours, terrified, without a goal or hope of getting out. Most of the doors he tried along the way were locked; the others stuck until he threw his frantic weight against them and they spilled him into more dark, empty rooms. He called for help and heard the echoes of his voice come back, mocking. He ran because a part of him knew it was death to stop.

And he knew he was looking for something—but what? A weapon of some kind? How could he possibly defend himself against the monster that pursued him through those shadowed halls?

It was almost on top of him when Jesse tried another door and barged into a room that had no exit. Panic flared inside him and he turned to flee. A hulking shadow fell across the open doorway. Trapped! He slammed the door and gave the latch a twist, for all the good it did. Backing away, deeper inside the room, he heard the beast begin to hammer on the flimsy door that separated them. It wouldn't take much more until—

Jesse woke to the sound of a door crashing open, sheet falling away to his waist as he sat up in bed. Relief came fast behind the rush of fear, Jesse starting to realize he'd wakened from a nightmare, when he heard more banging, crashing noises from the shop downstairs.

His first thought was of thieves, then he knew better. Scrambling from his small bed, Jesse took care to step lightly, keeping down the noise. Worried-sounding voices issued from his parents' bedroom, Ma and Pa trying to whisper without much success. Pa said something about his chair, Ma shushing him as best she could.

Jesse heard heavy footsteps on the stairs. The flash-back to his dream was instantaneous. It nearly paralyzed him where he stood, feet rooted to the floor. He thought of crawling underneath his bed to hide, but dream logic told him a monster in the house could sniff him out.

It's not a monster. It's a man, he thought.

That made it worse, because he'd seen what men could do. The monsters in his dreams were faceless shadows, chasing him but never catching up. It was a man who'd put his father in the wheelchair, men who'd burned the Kelseys out and left them dead. One man behind it all, with others paid to do his bidding.

Jesse looked around his bedroom for a weapon, but the

only thing he had was a jackknife, last year's birthday present from his father. Tiptoeing across the room, he fetched it from his dresser, opening the longest blade, clutching it tightly as he moved back toward the bedroom door.

What could he do against a grown-up gunman, much less several? Jesse had a hunch he'd only make things worse—but, then again, how much worse could it be when shooters broke into the house at night? If they were doomed regardless, he might as well go down fighting.

Huddled just inside the doorway, Jesse wondered if he'd meet Tommy Kelsey in Heaven. It troubled him to think he might not recognize his classmate, but he guessed that burns and such were healed when dead folks passed the Pearly Gates. Otherwise, Jesse reasoned, Heaven would be more like some infernal freak show than a land of milk and honey where the saints played harps and sang hymns all day long.

What if I go the other way? he thought, and felt tears prickling at his eyelids. Hell was hot and smelly, so the Reverend Bursaw said, with people screaming all the time. At least, if Jesse went down there, he reckoned he could bide his time and wait to pay Sedge Rankin back for all he'd done to Jesse's family.

Approaching footsteps snapped his mind back to the bedroom where he stood, small knife held in a trembling two-handed grip. He started breathing faster, working up his nerve to charge the minute his door swung open, embarrassed by the sudden tingling in his bladder.

Not now! he thought, biting his lower lip.

The doorknob turned, no hesitation, and the door opened enough for him to see a tall dark shape outside. He thrust the knife in front of him, startled to see a dim smile break across the shadowed face. Was that a scar across one cheek?

"You wanna play?" a strange voice asked. "Alright, then."

Jesse saw the six-gun leveled at his face and knew his

life was over. When the prowler thumbed its hammer back, he closed his eyes, too scared to move. Instead of gunfire, though, he heard his mother screaming, "No!"— a tone of voice he'd never heard before but recognized, regardless. *Then* the shot came, but it wasn't aimed at Jesse and it wasn't from the stranger's gun.

The tall man ducked and swung around to meet the woman rushing at him. If she'd fired again after the miss, she might've had a chance; up close and grappling with the stranger it was hopeless. He disarmed her, tossed her gun aside, and pistol-whipped her into semiconsciousness.

Jesse lunged forward, furious and frightened all at once. He slashed out at the shooter with his knife and snagged the left leg of his pants, maybe some flesh beneath. The stranger cursed, scarred face contorted with rage, and retaliated with a kick that slammed Jesse against the wall.

When Jesse got his wits back, he was sitting in the hallway by himself. He heard Pa shouting from the bedroom, calling out Ma's name and struggling to get out of bed. There was a loud thump when he hit the floor, then language Jesse hadn't realized his father even knew.

Jesse stood up and took a second to regain his balance. He was turning toward the master bedroom when he saw Pa's pistol lying on the carpet. In a flash, he knew what he must do.

Scooping up the gun, he turned his back on sounds of cursing from his father's room and bolted for the stairs. Barefoot, oblivious to pain, he ran downstairs and through the wreckage of the dry goods store, into the night.

16

Price came awake to frenzied pounding on his door. He had the Colt in hand and cocked before he recognized the boy's voice calling out to him.

"Please! Mr. Price! Help me!"

He took the pistol with him, crossing to the door. The voice was Jesse's, but that didn't mean he was alone. Price tugged the chair out from beneath the doorknob, kicking it away when it fell over on its side. He held the Colt behind him, finger on the trigger, as he pulled the door open.

Jesse lunged past him, sobbing, while Price checked the hall and found it empty. Turning back, he saw Jesse holding a small revolver pointed at the floor.

"Is that for me, boy?"

"Sir?" Jesse blinked hard against the flow of tears and glanced down at the pistol, seeming to see it for the first time. "No, sir. It's Ma!"

"Let me have that and try to catch your breath," Price said. He took the gun from Jesse, heeled the door shut as he passed, and put both weapons on the vanity. The smell of gunpowder told him the boy's piece had been fired.

"It's Ma," Jesse repeated, trembling where he stood.

"Tell me."

Jesse was winded, out of breath from running, but he did his best. "A man broke in. He came to my room. Tried to shoot me. Ma came out and shot at him. I guess she missed. He slugged her. Dragged her off somewhere. I don't . . . I don't . . ."

"Slow down," Price said. His voice was calm, despite the cold dread churning in his stomach. "Where's your father, Jesse?"

"Pa? He's home. I came for you."

"Is he alright?"

"Fell out of bed, I think."

"He wasn't shot?"

"No, sir. We have to help her!"

"Son, you're helping her right now. Calm down and tell me if you know this man."

The boy snuffled and shook his head. "No, sir."

"Can you describe him to me?"

"Tall, like you. There wasn't much light in the hall and he was wearing mostly black, I think. He had a scar, right here." Jesse reached up to stroke the left side of his face. "I never saw white guns before."

"White guns?"

"The handles, anyway. Like bone, maybe."

Price felt the muscles clenching in his shoulders. "You rest easy now," he said. "I know him. I'll go see about your mother."

"I can help you," Jesse told him, turning toward the vanity to claim his pistol.

Price got there ahead of him and took both guns. "You've done enough, Jesse. Your father needs you now."

"He can't do anything! It's his fault all this happened in the first place!"

"You don't mean that, son. Put blame where it belongs."

"I *need* to help you!"

Price was getting dressed as he replied, buckling his gun belt, tucking Jesse's pistol down in back. "I need to think about your mother and the man who took her, now. If you come with me, half my mind'll be on you. That's bad for everybody but the man I have to see."

"I don't know where he took her."

"That's alright," Price said. "He won't be hard to find. He's doing this to draw me out."

"You really know him, then?"

"I do."

"How fast is he?"

"Not fast enough," Price said, and prayed he wasn't wrong.

"I hope you kill him."

"Be a good boy now and go on home. Your father needs you."

"I don't care!"

"Go home! We're wasting precious time."

Red-faced from sorrow mixed with fury, Jesse fled the room. Price gave him a head start before he followed down the stairs. There was no sign of Jesse or a night clerk in the hotel lobby as he went through to the street. The fairy-bell rang for him as he stepped into the night, Price doubling back and reaching up to tear it from the wall.

Belle Mercer was aware of being dragged downstairs, feet thumping painfully along the way, and then out through the back door of the dry goods shop. Her head throbbed viciously, pain centered in the space behind her eyes. She kept them closed accordingly, not only to relieve a measure of the pain but out of fear of what she might see.

Dazed as she was, Belle thought she had accomplished

her objective of protecting Jesse. She'd been too quick
with the gun, not aiming properly, but she'd distracted
the assassin when he obviously meant to kill her son.
Jared was also safe, she thought, as long as he remained
at home and out of sight. Belle wondered briefly why the
gunman hadn't simply killed them all, but in a mother's
way she was relieved to sacrifice herself if it would only
save her child.

She felt dirt underfoot but was unsure of the direction
they were taking, only realizing when she smelled manure that they'd reached the livery stable. Belle had half
expected the kidnapper to head straight for Rankin's office at the Nugget, but she guessed that would've been
too obvious. It wouldn't do to have the Great Man soil
his hands, especially if there were witnesses around.

A lamp was burning in the stable, with the wick turned
down to dim the light. It still sparked new, insistent pain
behind Belle's eyes, but she kept them open now, deter-
mined not to let the pain defeat her. They were near the
stable entrance, with the hostler's quarters on her right.
Belle cast a glance inside, seeking Señor Dorado, and recoiled from what she saw.

Behind her, her abductor said, "Don't fret about the
beaner. He was too big for his britches anyway, givin' a
white man lip."

She turned to face him with a snarl. "You bastard!"

"I admire your spirit, lady, but you need to watch that
mouth. Man goes to all this trouble for a date, he likes a
bit of courtesy."

The man was dressed in black, two Colts tied down,
his gun belt bright with cartridges. Lamplight picked out
the long scar on his face and made it glisten. His eyes
roved up and down her body, following the contours of
her flannel nightgown.

"What do you want with me?" she asked, almost afraid
to hear the answer.

"I can think of half a dozen things, right off the top,"
he told her, smiling. "Got some business to take care of

first, but maybe when it's finished you and me can celebrate."

"What business do you have with me?"

"It ain't with you," he said. "I hear you got a friend in town who's interested in lookin' out for you. It's him I wanna see."

Belle knew the name before she asked, but she still had to hear it from the scar-faced stranger's lips. "What friend?"

"You playin' innocent? I like that in a woman sometimes, if we both agree she's only playin'. Matthew Price is who I'm after."

"Do you know him?"

"Not like you do, maybe, but I know him well enough." The shooter thumbed his scar. "He gave me this reminder of the day he killed my brother. Thought he'd killed me too, I guess, but he was wrong."

"You want him to correct the oversight?"

"I gave him one chance already, tonight. He wouldn't face me. Now, maybe we'll see if he can find his guts."

"How much is Rankin paying you for this?" she asked.

"Enough," the shooter said. "You wanna know the truth, though, I'd've probably paid *him* to set me up with Price."

"I hope you got your money in advance," Belle said. "Rankin's been known to cheat his so-called friends the same way he does common folk."

"No man cheats Cole Hardwick and lives to brag about it."

Belle supposed she should've recognized the name, but she had never shared Jesse's fascination with shooters. Only the one had ever captured her imagination or her heart.

Matthew.

A wave of guilt washed over her, making the headache pale beside it. This was her fault, once again. She'd brought Price to Redemption, risked his life, and now a madman from his past had joined Sedge Rankin's private army simply for the chance to kill him. If there was a way to stop him . . .

"Maybe we should have that celebration first," she said, "in case you're not around later." She could bear anything, Belle thought, if it bought time for Matthew to destroy this man.

How will he even known what happened?

In a flash, she knew the answer: Jesse.

No!

"I'll be here after, don't you worry," Hardwick said. "We'll have ourselves a party you can tell that crippled husband all about."

"I'll see you dead," she promised him.

"You'll see your boyfriend dead."

Another question had occurred to her. "You've thought this out so well," she said, "how do you reckon he's supposed to find us?"

Hardwick smiled at that. "I plan on sending him an invitation, any minute now."

"I want to thank you men for turning out on such short notice," Rankin said, as if he'd given them a choice. "We've had a problem come up that needs taking care of now, tonight."

"What kinda problem?" It was Ollie Murphy asking, not the fastest gun Rankin had ever seen, but steady when he had to be. The other seven Duffy had collected stood around and waited for his answer.

Rankin had decided that it wouldn't hurt to tell the truth for once, as long as he didn't get carried away. A little truth spread thin enough could help a lie go down. He'd sent Duffy out to avoid the young man showing any surprise as he laid out the tale for his hands.

"Ollie," he said, "you and the rest deserve the truth. The plain fact is, I've stepped in shit and I need all of you to help me out of it."

"What's that mean?" lean Tom Howard asked.

"I went outside Redemption for a man to deal with Matthew Price, is what I mean. You all know what he did to Chad and Perry and the others. We've lost more hands since the shooting, running off for fear I'd ask the rest of you to face his gun. Instead of risking that, I sent for a professional who knows Price, going back a ways."

The room was silent for a moment, Rankin worried that he might've put them off with too much truth. The next to speak was Micah Lauter, a young wrangler in his early twenties. "Who's this shooter, then?" he asked.

"His name's Cole Hardwick," Rankin stated.

"I heard of him," said Jonah French. "He's kilt a couple dozen men."

"I hear it's more'n that," Kurt Dietrich replied.

"The point," said Rankin, interrupting them, "is that he came recommended to me as a shooter who could do the job. From what I understand, he's faced Price once and lived to tell it."

"What's the trouble, then?" Bret Dinsmore asked.

Rankin surveyed his audience, sensing what would appeal to them. A smidgen more of truth, before he piled on the sugar. "Hardwick's a gun for hire," he said. "I knew that going in. We made a deal before he got here, but he's welshing on it now. Aside from jacking up his cost, he wants a piece of everything we've worked and fought for in Redemption all these years. He wants to be on top, and I say no."

"You told him that?" Bill Prentiss asked. He sounded skeptical, some of the others frowning silently.

"I'm standing here before you, so you *know* I didn't say it to his face." He forced a smile, making it a joke at his own expense, giving the others that much of himself but no more. "I'm telling *you* I don't intend to give up everything because some gunslick rides in here and reckons he can write his own ticket. We need to get rid of him, and I'd be a liar if I told you I could do the job alone."

Ed Woodall had been quiet, but he spoke up now. "You want us to go after Price *and* Hardwick?"

"No such thing," Rankin replied. "He's out there taking care of Price right now, supposedly—or Price is taking care of him. Whichever way it goes, there won't be more than one to deal with, and I hope to handle it the way I should've from the start, with men I know and trust."

"How much?" asked Murphy.

"What?"

"How much did Hardwick ask you for?"

Rankin considered fudging it, then changed his mind. "A thousand dollars flat."

"That ain't much, when you split it seven ways," French said.

"It's more than any of you'll have if he comes back here, telling me the deadwood has to go." He heard them muttering and added, "Never mind that, now. I don't forget my friends. I hope you'll trust me far enough to let it go at that."

"The thousand dollars?" Prentiss asked.

"A bonus, free and clear."

"What would we have to do, exactly?" Howard asked.

Rankin put on a solemn face and said, "Here's what I had in mind."

The street was dark when Hardwick left the livery to look for Matthew Price. He wasn't going far. The woman was his bait and there was too much risk in dragging her along if he went hunting. It was better all around if he could make Price come to him.

The woman must've thought she'd wear him down with warnings of what Price would do when he caught up to them. She didn't know that he'd already seen the worst her man could do and it had brought him here, to take her life and turn it upside-down.

The woman talked too much. He could've shut her up for good, but Hardwick thought he might have need of her alive, if Price was slow to take his bait. For now, he'd tied her to an upright beam that stood dead-center in the middle of the stable, using bridle straps. He'd gagged her with a strip of cloth torn from her own nightdress, hurting her a little in the process, for the way her brat had stung him with the jackknife. Truth be told, he'd liked that part the best of anything so far.

But Hardwick knew it couldn't hold a candle to the moment when he pulled a trigger on Matt Price.

Where is he, dammit?

Hardwick imagined it would take some time for word of what he'd done to reach Price in his hotel room. A bit more time for him to shake the cobwebs out, get dressed, strap on his gun and hit the street. A little longer then, before he had to think of finding someone to go down and wake the bastard for him.

Hardwick's leg still hurt a little from the shallow cut, but it was nothing that would slow him down. He could've finished off the boy after he knocked the mother cold, but even in his rage he'd known the brat might be his best bet for alerting Price. A crippled husband damn sure wouldn't do it, and Redemption's marshal didn't worry him.

With that in mind, he hoped he hadn't kicked the boy too hard and put him out. A gunshot in the middle of the night should rally neighbors, but he saw no evidence of anyone around the dry goods store so far. Maybe Redemption was the kind of town where people stayed alive by minding their own business, even when they heard Hell cutting loose next door.

He made another slow sweep of the shadowed street and this time saw a lean form stepping out of the hotel. He didn't need to see the face. There was a certain attitude about the man Hardwick would recognize even if Price tried to disguise himself.

Smiling, he drew his right-hand Colt and fired a single shot into the air.

Jesse was crouching in the alleyway between the hotel and the barbershop, waiting for Price to show himself.

He'd run out through the back and found the darkest place he could to hide, hoping the shadows there would cover him. His feet were bruised from running over rocks and gravel, making Jesse wish he'd put his boots on first, before he left the house. There was no time to think about that now, though, with his mother's life at stake.

A shot rang out from somewhere down the street—the night's second so far, and still there was no hint of any response from the town. Jesse knew in his heart that they weren't all asleep, and he hated the cowards who couldn't be bothered to help. They were worse than Sedge Rankin in his mind, because they had nothing to gain and were only afraid for themselves.

He heard footsteps approaching from the left and huddled closer to the hotel wall, within a few feet of the spot where one of Rankin's men had fallen to his death on Saturday. It didn't bother Jesse now, as he watched Price pass by the alley's mouth and disappear again. The only thing he cared about was learning where the scar-faced man had taken his mother, doing what he could to help.

He gave Price a lead, then crept out of the alley to follow. Bare feet were helpful now, making no noise as Jesse moved along the wooden sidewalk, clinging to the storefronts that he passed. He understood what Price had meant about distractions, but if he was careful now the shooter needn't know that he was being followed. Jesse couldn't be a bother then, and there might still be some way he could help.

Jesse wished Price had let him keep his father's pistol, but it didn't matter that he was unarmed. If it proved necessary, he would find a makeshift weapon on the street and do whatever was required to get his mother safely home. If she'd been hurt or worse—

His mind went blank at that, unable to imagine life without her in Redemption. Part of Jesse's brain knew that if she were killed, the shooters would come back for him and for his father. They were running out of time and Matt Price was their only hope, but Jesse wasn't sure if

Price could do the job. One shooter, maybe—but as long as Rankin lived, there'd be another and another, never letting up until he and his parents were laid out beside the Kelseys in their separate holes.

His head cleared and he saw Price well ahead of him, still unaware that Jesse trailed behind. He felt like running to catch up but couldn't risk the noise. Instead, he started taking longer strides, still careful how his feet came down against the dusty boards.

Beyond Price, farther down and almost hidden in the shadows, Jesse saw a tall man standing by the entrance to the livery. He knew it was the stranger without being close enough to see his scar or the white-handled guns. It must've been him shooting in the air, to help Price find him. Now, as Jesse watched, the stranger turned and walked into the stable, out of sight.

That told him where his mother was, but not how he could get her out. Tingling with dread, he stayed behind Matt Price and hoped for inspiration as they moved along the streets—a tall man and his smaller shadow moving toward a rendezvous with Death.

Price knew he wasn't going in the front door of the livery if there was any other way to handle it. Cole Hardwick had been five years brooding on revenge, and while he might desire to meet Price for a stand-up fight, there was no guarantee he'd play it straight. If he was confident about the outcome of a face-to-face encounter, Price thought Hardwick would've waited for him in the street, instead of ducking back inside the stable.

No front door if he could help it, then.

Another narrow alley opened on his right, when he was still a hundred feet short of the livery, and Price ducked into it, moving along until he found himself behind the Main Street shops. He'd checked the stable out and noted its back door the day he paid to board his horse. How long ago was that? A week? Not quite. So much had happened in the past few days, Price felt like he was losing track of time.

Tonight was all that mattered, though—the next few minutes. If he lived through that, he could begin to think about what happens next. Sedge Rankin was responsible for this. Until that debt was settled, neither Belle nor any member of her family could live in peace.

Another moment brought him to the livery's back door. Price drew his Colt and eased the hammer back. He wasn't playing and this fight wasn't for show. If he could drop Hardwick without a call, so much the better. If the shooter had him covered going in, at least he'd shave a fraction of a second off returning fire.

The back door had a latch-pull on it, but it was also barred from the inside. If it was locked against him now, he'd have to circle back around and go in from the street, regardless of the risk. He tried the latch-pull, heard it click, and toed the door to start it swinging inward. It was halfway open when he lunged inside and heard the first shot, felt the bullet burn past him and out into the night.

Price tumbled through a shoulder roll and lost his hat before he fetched up under cover of some hay bales, stacked two deep and five feet high against the wall. He waited for another shot but heard footsteps instead.

"You think I'm stupid?" Hardwick asked him from the shadows. "Two ways in, and you think I'd forget to watch the back?"

"You never know," Price said. "I thought it might run in the family."

"What's that supposed to mean?" Hardwick demanded, furious.

"Your brother's dead because he was a stupid man who pushed a stranger over nothing," Price replied. "You wear a scar because you backed his stupid play and couldn't make it stick. Tonight you made your last stupid mistake."

"Think so? Maybe I oughta kill your woman then, and get it over with."

"Somebody's pissing in your ear, Hardwick. She's not mine, never was."

"Hear that, bitch?" Hardwick said to someone else. Then, back to Price: "If that's so, why'n hell'd you come to get her back?"

"See what I mean about stupidity?" Price taunted him. "I came for you."

The voice that answered him was stiff with rage. "What's stoppin' you?"

"You'll understand if I don't trust you," Price replied.

"Straight up and face-to-face. You have my word."

For whatever that's worth, Price thought, but he believed that any more delay might cost Belle's life. Rising from cover, he still kept his six-gun cocked and ready, with its muzzle pointed at the ground.

"You want an edge, I guess," Cole Hardwick said. He stood fifteen or twenty feet away and to the left of a support beam, Belle lashed to the upright post with leather straps below her breasts and just above her knees. She whimpered something from behind a gag that kept her jaws apart.

Hardwick stood empty-handed, both guns holstered. Price put his away, leaving the hammer drawn. It only made a heartbeat's difference, but the man in black was right. He wanted any slim advantage he could get.

"That's better," Hardwick said. "This time, we're even."

"Are we?"

"You're a cocksure bastard, aren't you?"

"I've already heard you talk," Price said. "How do you shoot?"

Hardwick was moving when a small shape suddenly appeared behind him in the lamplight, calling out in Jesse's voice, "Hey! Scar-face!"

Startled, guns in hand, Hardwick half-turned to face the boy. He must've known it was a critical mistake, because he tried to take it back.

Too late.

Price fired and saw his bullet strike Hardwick an inch
or two off-center. Staggering, Hardwick still raised both
guns and cocked them, squeezing off two shots as if the
reflex had a chance of saving him. Instead of dodging
right or left to meet the slugs, Price dropped below the
shooter's line of fire and triggered two more rounds.

Hardwick sat down as if a blade had cut his legs from
under him. Numb fingers let his pistols drop to either
side. He stared at Price with eyes already going dim, then
slowly toppled over on his back.

The next thing Price heard was the sound of weeping,
Jesse clinging to his mother's nightgown as Price stood
and moved to set her free.

17

Belle was trembling, weeping silently as Price fumbled with the knotted bridle straps that bound her. After several awkward moments he gave up and cut them with a pocketknife, feeling resistance in the leather even then, as if the straps hated to let her go. As soon as she was free, Belle knelt and folded Jesse in her arms, ruffling his hair with hands that couldn't get enough of him. They cried together, but it didn't sound like aching grief to Price, this time.

He watched them, standing several paces back, until he felt the weight of time across his shoulders like a yoke. "I have to go," he said, "before somebody comes to see what all the shooting was about."

Belle didn't understand him right away. "You're leaving now?" she asked.

Price shook his head. "It isn't finished yet."

That brought Belle to her feet, Jesse still clinging to her nightgown, tugging on it in a way that pulled it tight across her chest. Price focused on her eyes and willed himself to concentrate.

"You're going after Rankin now," she said, not asking him.

"It isn't done till he is," Price replied.

"You've done enough," she said. "Maybe too much. I never should've brought you here."

"It's not your fault," Price said. "I learned something tonight."

"What's that?" There was a tremor in her voice.

He nodded toward the shooter lying on the ground a few feet to his left and said, "He taught me that you can't leave work unfinished, or it comes around and bites you when your back's turned."

"Rankin has too many men. You'll never reach him."

"I have to try."

She reached for him with one hand, while the other clutched their son against her legs. Price might've stepped into her arms, but Jesse stood between them, holding on to Belle as if he'd never let her take another step.

"Please, Matt." She almost whispered it. "For us?"

"That's right," he said. Taking the small gun from his belt, Price placed it in her outstretched hand. "This ought to get you home."

Belle recognized the gun, eyes flaring wide. "Where did you get this, Matt?"

"I must've picked it up somewhere," he said. "It shouldn't be a long walk home from here, but if you meet someone along the way who doesn't look quite right, shoot first and skip the questions."

"Take us back," she said.

Price took for granted that she meant for him to walk them home. "I can't right now," he said. "Someone will be along to check this out. I'd rather go to them."

"We need you, Matt." Tears glistened on her lovely face.

His heart ached like a wound that wouldn't close. Eye-

ing the pistol in her hand and Jesse at her knee, he told
Belle, "You've got everything you need to get back
home. Your husband's waiting for you there."

Her shoulders slumped a bit, or maybe Price imagined
it. "You're right," she said. "Be careful, please."

"Go out the back. When you get home, lock yourself
in and load those guns you've got downstairs. Stay off
the street till sunrise, anyway."

"I will."

"Go now."

She left, leading their son, but Jesse pulled away from
her after a few steps, bending to retrieve Price's hat from
the ground. He brought it back to Price, held gingerly in
both hands like an offering. When Jesse spoke, Price had
to bend closer, straining to hear.

"Watch out for Mr. Rankin," Jesse cautioned. "He's a
cheater."

"I'll keep both eyes open," Price replied, shaking the
small hand that was offered. "Thanks for helping me
back there. You keep your ma safe now."

"I will."

Jesse returned to Belle and took her hand. She led him
to the back door, pausing there for one last look at Price,
then they were gone.

Price spent a moment with his Colt, ejecting and replacing empty cartridges. He loaded all six chambers,
then went through it twice more with Cole Hardwick's
pistols, tucking them under his belt at front and back.
They made a tight fit, but he didn't mind. Cole didn't either, from the blank look on his face.

Price tried the hostler's quarters for a backup piece and
stepped across Señor Dorado's corpse to lift a shotgun
from the corner where it stood. He broke the gun and
checked the load, buckshot, and snapped it shut again. He
could've searched the place for extra cartridges but let it
go.

Price spent a moment with his Appaloosa, topping off
its bin of oats. The horse made welcome noises as he

stroked its neck. "I'll be back soon and we can shake this place," he said. "How's that?"

Sedge Rankin listened to the gunfire, as he sipped whiskey in the Nugget's doorway with a silent room behind him. He'd announced the early closing half an hour ago and sent his customers across the street to the Trail's End, where they were still his customers. A few had been disgruntled, but they didn't argue with his guns and most were mollified when Rankin sent the Nugget's girls along to keep them company.

The last two shots came close together, echoing along Main Street like the sound of giant hands clapping from the general direction of the livery stable. That made four or five shots, all told—he'd lost count—and Rankin waited a few minutes more to be sure it was done. He didn't need to see the shooter coming for him. If the two rough bastards hadn't done the world a favor and killed each other off, Rankin knew one or the other would be along directly.

He drained his whiskey glass and took it back to the bar where his men were lined up, waiting. "I believe we've heard the last of it," he said. "Whoever won the draw, we'll see him soon if he's not hurt too bad."

"Maybe they took each other down," Tom Howard said, a couple of the others nodding in agreement.

"Don't count on it, gentlemen," Rankin replied. "If no one shows up in an hour or so, we can have Marshal Gresham go see."

That got the laugh Rankin was hoping for. He liked to break the ice before hard work began, and poking fun at Gresham in his absence helped distract the hands from what they'd have to do tonight—what might be done to them.

A couple of them were still making snide remarks about the marshal when he cleared his throat and said, "We need to take our places now. Look sharp. You all know Price by sight, and I've described Hardwick. Whichever one walks through that door tonight, make sure he goes out on a plank."

Price didn't hurry on his walk down to the Nugget. Rankin might not be there, but he didn't know where else to start. If he'd run out, someone at the saloon was bound to have an address for the boss. Price trusted his ability to pry the information loose. If Rankin had guns waiting for him at the Nugget, they could get in line.

The place was quiet when he got there, all lit up inside but standing silent, in stark contrast to its twin establishment across the street. Still open but devoid of customers, the Nugget was a trap so obvious he had to smile at Rankin's sheer audacity. What kind of fool would walk in there tonight?

My kind.

It struck him that the trap was indiscriminate. Unless there'd been a spy he missed back at the livery, Rankin had no idea who'd won the night's first contest. That in turn told Price that something had gone sour between Hardwick and his employer. Rankin meant to kill whoever came back from the showdown, trusting blood to clean his slate.

It might, at that, but not the way he'd planned.

Price didn't feel like walking through the bat-wing doors in front. He had no way of counting Rankin's guns until he got inside the place, but reason told him most of them would have the front door covered, ready to cut loose when he or Hardwick crossed the threshold. Rankin wasn't dumb enough to leave the back unguarded—*probably* not dumb enough—but if he had to split his forces, Price was betting on the rear to have less cover than the street.

With that decided, all he had to do was walk around in back and make his way inside. It sounded easy, but he knew the first false step could get him killed.

He'd guessed the back door would be unlocked during business hours, and that proved to be the case. Turning the knob, he heard the well-oiled latch click softly, with no other sound that would betray a trap. Silence meant nothing if the watchers on the other side were steady, but at least they hadn't started blasting at him when he tried the door.

It opened outward to reveal a corridor Price recognized. He'd walked along the other end to Rankin's office . . . when, again? Three nights ago? It seemed longer, the insult and his elbow to the big man's face, the killing that had followed. The events had taken on an almost dreamlike quality, detached from waking life.

Get on with it.

He stepped across the threshold, more than half expecting to be cut down on the spot. Price held the shotgun ready, glad that this end of the hall was dark enough to spare his night vision. He didn't need his eyes, though, when someone on his flank called out, "That's far enough, boy."

Turning toward the voice, Price saw a staircase rising into darkness, with a shooter crouching on it halfway down. The man was slender, with a hat too large for him and scruffy whiskers on his face. He had a pistol aimed at Price but never got to use it, as a shotgun blast tore through his chest and brought him tumbling down.

Belle flinched and pulled away from Jared when she heard the muffled shot. It drew her from the bed where she'd been sitting, toward the windows, Jared wheeling after her. Jesse huddled underneath the covers, trembling, crying silently.

"There's nothing you can do about it," Jared said.

"There ought to be."

"I'd help him if I could."

She knew he meant it—thought so, anyway. What good was that? "You can't," she said.

"Nobody can."

"Somebody ought to try."

"It's suicide."

"He's doing it for us."

"For *you*."

She turned on him. "I'm only here because of him. I'd be dead now, and Jesse with me, if it weren't for Matt."

"I'm sorry I can't kill men for you, Belle."

"Nobody asked you to."

"What is it, then?"

She almost whispered in reply. "He shouldn't have to be alone. It isn't fair."

She'd done as Price had told her on returning home. A shotgun and two Winchesters were loaded, laid out on the bed. The pistol Price had given back to her lay on the vanity beside her comb and hairbrush. If the shooters came for her again, Belle thought she'd have no problem killing them—but how did that help Price?

Another gunshot made her jump. Even expecting it, she wasn't ready for the sound. Jared wheeled forward, reaching for her hand, but she pulled away from him. "They're killing him," she sobbed.

"The marshal—"

"*Marshal?*" Belle surprised herself, laughing in Jared's face while tears streamed down her own. "What did the *marshal* do for us? What does he do for anyone but Rankin?"

Glancing back at Jesse huddled on the bed, Jared lowered his voice until she had to strain to hear him. "Belle, he saved your life and Jesse's. Don't you think I want to thank him for it? Don't you think I'd help him if I could? What can I do?"

"Nothing." Her lips were numb; her own voice sounded flat and dead.

"That's right, nothing." Jared had found a grip on her left hand. Belle didn't pull away from him this time but couldn't bring herself to face him, either. "He sent you and Jesse home to keep you safe. You go back now and put yourself at risk, it's just like spitting in his face."

"Jared—"

"You know I'm right. What can you do for him out there, except distract him from his work and get him killed?"

She recognized the truth in that but didn't have to like it. "If he dies for me—for us—because nobody helped, I don't think I can live with it."

He gave her hand a squeeze that made Belle look at him. "You'd be surprised what you can live with," Jared said.

"Would I?"

"I need you, Belle. *We* need you."

Something broke inside her and the tears came fresh again. "I know," she said, and sat down on the bed between the rifles and her son.

Rankin had gone upstairs after he saw his men in place. His office felt too vulnerable, even with eight guns waiting to kill whichever shooter came to settle up with him. He would've felt better with twenty, but he'd called in all the men he had and they would have to do.

His quarters at the Nugget had been furnished with an eye toward luxury, but with a measure of restraint that stopped short of the garish whorehouse look one might expect upstairs from a saloon. In fact, Rankin had taken his cue from a gentlemen's club in Austin, patronized by the governor himself. Dark wood and leather predominated, accented by touches of silver and gold. At the moment, though, Rankin was more concerned with blue steel—namely, the pistol he'd brought with him from his office, leaving the holster beneath his desk empty.

Rankin didn't know which shooter would be coming to the Nugget—Hardwick for money or Price for revenge—but he wasn't fool enough to think he could take either one of them in a fair fight. He'd never been a gunfighter, although he'd shot a man or two in situations where speed didn't count for much. The men downstairs were his defensive line. Rankin believed there were enough of them to do the job.

He hoped so, anyway.

But while he waited, it felt good to keep a pistol in his hand.

Rankin had poured a double shot of whiskey for his nerves and had it halfway to his lips, when an explosion startled him and made him slop the booze across his knuckles. Rankin took a breathless moment to identify the racket as a shotgun blast and knew the final act had started.

Who among his men was carrying a shotgun? Rankin couldn't think of anyone, but he kept one behind the bar. One of the shooters could've borrowed it. He felt a smile tugging around the corners of his mouth, thinking it might be just that easy, finished with a single shot.

A second blast erased his smile and sent him rushing to the door. He'd locked it coming in, but Rankin double-checked it now, making sure. The door and lock were solid, but he knew they wouldn't stand against a twelve-gauge fired at point-blank range.

Relax, he told himself. Some shooting was expected. Why else had he stationed eight gunmen around the premises? Hardwick or Price, it stood to reason either one of them would take some killing. That's what he was paying for, and if he lost a few men in the process—well, what difference did it make?

The main thing—no, the *only* thing that mattered— was for *him* to stay alive. It didn't matter if the others all laid down their lives to keep him safe. In fact, the more he thought about it, Rankin calculated that a decent body count would make the ambush more believable as self-defense. And if his shooters all had lead for breakfast, he would save a thousand dollars in the bargain.

But they had to keep him safe. Dead or alive, they had to do the job.

Clutching the pistol tight enough to make his knuckles blanch, Rankin took a seat and waited for the noise downstairs to stop.

Gil Gresham checked the street both ways and made sure it was empty as he left his office, moving toward the livery stable. Hurrying past the hotel, he kept an eye out for Heck Fleagle, half expecting the night clerk to call him back and ask what Gresham planned to do about that ruckus down the street.

To which his answer would've been, *Not one damned thing.*

Gresham was clearing out, his main fear being that he'd stalled too long and missed the chance to save himself. It sounded like the men who might've stopped him had their hands full at the Nugget, though, and Gresham meant to have a decent lead before the winners stopped and looked around for someone else to kill.

The whole damned town could go to hell, for all he cared. Some might've said that it already had.

He'd left his badge back in the office, with a ring of keys to fit the front door and the holding cells in back. The office gun rack was a rifle short, but Gresham loved that Winchester and didn't feel like leaving it behind. His saddlebags held clothing and supplies, along with seven hundred dollars' worth of fines and taxes he'd collected in the past six months. As far as Gresham knew, nobody else in town had ever known the combination to his office safe—and if they did, to hell with them.

To hell with everybody in Redemption, from the top on down.

Sedge Rankin wouldn't waste time looking for him, that was certain. He could pin a marshal's badge on any fool who wanted it and get the same results. Gresham was tired of being at the big man's beck and call, doing his dirty work while Rankin claimed the lion's share of the rewards.

As far as Gresham knew, he made it to the livery stable unobserved. The Nugget sounded like July fourth with the fireworks going off, and still no one was on the street. It said something about the town, but Gresham didn't mind. The fewer folks who saw him leave, the better he liked it.

The stable smelled of gun smoke when he stepped inside. At first he thought it was a trick of his imagination, something wafted on a night breeze from the far end of the street, but then he saw old man Dorado stretched out in a small room to his right, looking as if someone had used a hammer on his skull. It was too bad, he thought. The beaner never hurt a soul, as far as Gresham knew.

There was a second body farther in, a tall man lying on his back in blood. Gresham stood over him and recognized the stranger he'd seen crossing from the Nugget to the Trail's End ninety minutes earlier. He took the man for one of Rankin's guns who obviously hadn't cut the mustard when he got his turn with Matthew Price. Speaking of guns, the stranger wore twin holsters but his shooting irons were gone.

Won't need 'em where he's going, Gresham thought, moving along the line of stalls to where his roan stood waiting. He got the mare saddled in under five minutes, leading her out past the bodies and into the street. Mounting up, Gresham turned his back on the saloon where the gunfire still echoed.

A flicker of motion surprised him, passing by the dry goods store, and Gresham glanced up toward the second-story window. Annabelle Mercer stood watching him, something beyond mere contempt in her eyes.

Gresham lowered his head and dug in with his heels, spurring the roan into a gallop toward the west end of Redemption and the vast, dark night beyond.

The second shooter didn't give himself away by calling out to Price, but he was evidently shaken by the shotgun

blast and sight of his friend spilling down the stairs. He
came from the office where Price had spent time with
Sedge Rankin on Saturday night, pistol naked and cocked
in his hand. He was hasty to fire, with a jerk on the trigger instead of a squeeze and no effort to aim.

It was close, even so, the slug whistling past Price with
six inches to spare as he turned. Price went down on one
knee and let go with the shotgun's left barrel from six or
eight paces, a shot that a blind man could make. Buckshot plucked the young man off his feet like a pup-
peteer's hand yanking strings, and he slid on his back
after dropping, red streaks on the floor in his wake.

Price discarded the shotgun and palmed Hardwick's
Colts as he rose. No one else in the office, he made sure
of that, but he heard voices muttering from the saloon.
They were spooked by the shooting, too nervous to keep
their mouths shut, but he couldn't make out what they
said or count heads from the sounds.

Get it done.

They'd be waiting for Price when he came through the
door, cutting loose all at once, but he didn't know how
long they'd wait. If he didn't show soon, they might wise
up enough to send someone around back and cover the
alley, cut off his retreat or come in from behind him and
make it a cross fire.

Price had a sudden inspiration. He went back to
Rankin's office and picked up the big man's chair, walking it back in his arms so the rollers were quiet and clear
of the floor. In the hallway, he set the chair down, then
hoisted the young shooter into it, letting him slump to a
settled position, head back, with his hands in his lap.
Price retrieved the dead man's hat and wedged it on his
head, shading his face. He braced his empty shotgun on
the stout arms of the chair, held firm between the
corpse's elbows and his chest.

Not bad.

All that remained now was to give the chair a running
start and send it rolling through the open doorway into

the saloon. Price shoved it hard and waited for the nervous shooters on the other side to spot their target. Suddenly, half a dozen guns unloaded as the dead man wobbled into view.

Price followed close behind him, with the ivory-handled six-guns blazing in his fists.

18

The dead man in the roller chair was taking hits as Price came through the doorway after him. He saw the body jerking, bullets ripping through the chair and lifeless flesh it held, until the whole thing toppled over sideways and the shooter sprawled before his friends.

Price caught the first of them aiming a handgun from behind the bar, immediately to his left. The range was ten or twelve feet, tops. He saw the shooter notice him, starting to turn, before Price shot him in the chest with one of Hardwick's guns and knocked him down behind the bar. It might not be a kill, but it would do until he had the time to check.

Off to his right, a stout man with a gray mustache and bushy eyebrows spun to face Price, fast-handing the lever action on his Winchester. He got the shot off, but it was a hasty one, tugging at Price's sleeve instead of drilling him dead-center. Price had barely a second while his adversary pumped the rifle's lever, but he used it well. The right-hand Colt spoke once and blew a rat hole in the shooter's groin.

Squealing, the rifleman went down and took a table with him, scattering the cards and glasses someone else had left behind when Rankin chased them out. He wasn't dead, but in his pain he'd dropped the Winchester, and that was good enough for now.

At least four guns remained in the saloon and all of them were throwing lead at Price. He triggered two quick shots with no targets in mind, to shake them up and spoil their aim, before he threw himself across the bar and belly-wallowed out of sight.

It was a painful drop, but the young pistolero Price had shot behind the bar helped break his fall. If there was any life left in the youngster, that appeared to finish it. His blood was smeared on Price's shirt and vest as Price rolled off and kicked his way into a crouch.

His enemies beyond the bar kept firing, even when they didn't have a target. The activity and noise helped them regain a bit of confidence, although they must've known they couldn't blast him out with the artillery they had. One thing they *could* do, though, was heap his sanctuary full of broken glass, their bullets smashing into rows of bottles and a giant mirror set behind the bar. In seconds, Price was splashed with half a dozen brands of whiskey, blinking at the alky fumes.

Security was fleeting in a barroom fight, unless a shooter put his adversaries down without delay. Defending a position had inherent risks. The same bar that protected Price from bullets blinded him to movement by his enemies. There was a little swinging gate at each end of the bar, for easy passage in and out. A shooter could approach from either side, or simply roll across the bar as Price had done.

He spied a sawed-off shotgun braced on hooks beneath the cash register and duck-walked over to claim it. Price checked the load and cocked it, easing Hardwick's pistols under his belt at the back, barrels warm against his backside. The scattergun was best for close-range killing, which was what he had in mind.

The roar of guns slacked off, and Price could hear a couple of the opposition whispering, although he didn't catch the message. It was obvious a moment later, though, when he heard footsteps closing in on the bar, both ends at once.

The hell of hiding out, Sedge Rankin thought, was that he couldn't make out what was happening downstairs. It gnawed at him, flurries of gunfire echoing up through the floor, Rankin hoping each shot in turn would be the last. Eight guns to one, and still they couldn't do the job. How difficult could killing Price or Hardwick be?

Rankin wondered which one it was and caught himself drifting in the direction of the door. He could sneak down, make sure nobody saw him, and find out who it was—or keep going, right on out the back and gone, if he didn't like what he saw.

Forget it.

Rankin wasn't running out on everything he'd worked and fought for in the past five years. It wasn't in his nature to retreat without a backup plan, and at the moment Rankin's mind was blank. He was aware of fear and anger grappling for control inside him, without knowing which would win, but either way he meant to stand his ground.

Redemption was *his* town. Its people owed him more than they could ever hope to pay back in a lifetime. He would stay because it was his right, and because running out would make him look ridiculous. Dead or alive, Sedge Rankin wouldn't let himself become a laughing-stock.

More shooting, and a scream cut through the floor-boards to find Rankin's ears. Someone was begging for mercy down there and not getting any. Rankin thought about the shambles he'd have downstairs when they finished, then decided anyone who lived to mop the mess would be a lucky man. Rankin might even pitch in himself, if the crew was shorthanded.

A shot snuffed out the screams and silence followed. Was it over, finally? How many of his men were still alive? The suspense gnawed at Rankin with tiny rat's teeth, working relentlessly on his nerves. Waiting was torture. Worse, if everyone downstairs was dead or wounded he could wait all night and never know he'd won.

Rankin poured three fingers of courage at his private bar and drank it in one scalding swallow. Short of breath and teary-eyed, he crossed the sitting room, unlocked his door and stepped outside. Still nothing from below as he moved slowly, cautiously toward the stairs. Each step was perilous; a squeaker was all he needed to betray him and bring Death upstairs to hunt him down.

The booze kicked in and told him not to worry. Death had all the action it could handle down in the saloon. As if to emphasize the point, another ragged burst of gunshots echoed in the stairwell, followed by the sound of what he took to be a body dropping.

One more down. How many left to go?

He reached the stairs and hesitated, pistol clutched in one hand while his other gripped the banister. Rankin inhaled a trembling breath and started down the stairs.

The shotgun saved him when they rushed the bar, both ends at once. The shooter on his left was quicker, firing one shot through the swinging gate down there and bursting through it in a haze of gun smoke. Price triggered one barrel from a range of twenty feet or less and watched a storm of buckshot rip through wood and glass, as well as flesh. The lanky gunman seemed to leap backward, as if he'd been lassoed and yanked away.

Someone across the room cried out, "Jonah!" but Price had no time to consider it. Another enemy was at the sec-

ond swinging gate, behind him, as he spun around to face
the threat.

This one was older and more cautious, but his hesi-
tancy worked against him. Shoving through the gate, he
paused to aim his shot at Price when fanning his Peacemaker might've served him better. Even so, their guns
went off together and the stranger's bullet bit a chunk
from Price's thigh. It toppled him, but not before he saw
his adversary flattened in a spray of crimson mist.

Damn it!

He straightened out his leg, clenching his teeth around
the pain, and saw it was a flesh wound. It would scar, but
he wasn't disabled and he wouldn't bleed to death. Rising to walk would hurt like hell, but he'd survived worse
injuries without losing his edge. Right now, he had shooters to deal with, and their boss man afterward. First aid
could wait until Price saw whether his case was better
suited to a sawbones or an undertaker.

Bracing both hands against the bar and grinding his
teeth, Price made it to a crouch without squealing. When
he was fairly balanced, he drew Hardwick's guns and
tried to figure where the next attack would come from.
There was no question of *whether* it would happen—he
still heard at least one man shuffling around out there—
but rather when and where his enemies would strike.

The crouch made Price's wounded thigh feel like the
muscle was on fire. Fresh blood was soaking through his
pants around the bullet hole. It was a deep graze, with the
slug long gone, but if he didn't change positions soon,
Price knew he'd lose the feeling in his leg. He was already light-headed enough to wobble on his heels where
he was hunkered down behind the bar.

Cursing, Price slumped a little to his right and let grav-
ity take him the rest of the way. He felt better, stretched
out on his side, but didn't take time to savor the relief.
Pushing with elbows and his good leg, he began to crawl
through broken glass and pools of liquor toward the west
end of the bar. The last few feet, blood mixed with booze

where he'd blown up one of the shooters added fresh stains to his clothes.

Price wriggled underneath the swinging gate, not touching it, and crept around the corner for a clear view of the room. He was in time to see a shooter stand up from behind a table lying on its side, gun hand atremble as he left cover behind.

Price shot him with the right-hand Colt before the man knew what was happening. It staggered him, lurching around to find a target, and Price met him halfway with a second shot, the left-hand gun this time. The shooter's legs folded and he dropped to his knees with jarring force. It would've hurt if he'd been capable of feeling it, but he was gone, a mannequin collapsing facedown on the floor.

Price waited, heard somebody whimpering, and was relieved to find it wasn't him. Gritting his teeth, he pushed off from the floor and struggled to his feet.

Rankin was halfway down the stairs when the last shots rang out. He heard another body drop and wondered who it was this time. A few more steps and he would have a fair view of the barroom from the east end, facing west. A velvet rope was hung across the bottom of the stairwell, barring customers from access to his private quarters. It provided an illusion of security, enforced by hirelings packing iron, but it was all that stood between Rankin and death tonight.

Or maybe he'd already won.

The silence didn't have to mean bad news. Hardwick or Price had put up one hellacious fight—the kind that would draw business to the Nugget, once the bodies and debris were cleared away—but there was no sign of a shooter coming up the stairs to look for Rankin. Maybe it was finished, and he simply had to go on down and claim his rightful victory.

Another step down toward the velvet rope, and he

heard someone moving, footsteps shuffling on the floor—or were they dragging something? Curiosity and fear were grappling for the reins in Rankin's mind, and cautious curiosity won out at last. He tried tiptoeing down the stairs but it was awkward in his boots. He almost fell, and only saved himself from tumbling down because his left hand had a death grip on the banister.

After the stumble, Rankin froze and waited for the sound of footsteps rushing toward him. Surely someone must've heard him? Counting off the seconds in his mind, he started to relax after a minute passed with no gunman appearing at the bottom of the stairs. He still heard scuffling noises, but they didn't sound like someone walking now—more like an aimless scraping sound with muffled whimpering behind it.

Rankin eased down to the velvet rope and risked a peek around the corner into the saloon. Some of the tables had been tipped, chairs scattered. There were bodies, but he wasted no time counting them. The one that mattered was emerging from behind the bar, limping, a bloodstain showing on the left leg of his pants above the knee.

Matt Price was still alive, but he'd been wounded. All that shooting, Rankin thought, and he'd stopped one round in the leg. As for the shooters Rankin had arrayed against him, only Eddie Woodall seemed to be alive—and he was scrabbling on the floor, clutching his bloody groin.

Price didn't seem to know Rankin had come downstairs. He limped across to Woodall, standing over him. The shooter held two guns and wore a third one on his hip. The two he carried naked looked familiar, but Rankin couldn't place them at the moment.

Woodall wriggled on the floor, trying to scoot away from Price. Price said, "You're hurt."

"Ah'll be alright," Eddie replied.

"I don't think so." The shooter raised one of his guns and cocked it. "Where's Rankin?"

Right here.

Woodall reached down for something at his waist and Price shot him. The noise made Rankin jump, firing his own shot in reflexive action. Blinking through the gun smoke toward his target, he saw Price was down, a long shape stretched out on the barroom floor.

Price didn't know who'd shot him but he heard the sneaky bastard coming up to check his handiwork, not rushing it, hanging well back to make sure he was safe. Price couldn't hold his breath—the pain was too intense for that, but he remained as still as possible, gritting his teeth against the fire that burned beneath his ribs.

Gut shot, he thought. *That can't be good.*

Price had dropped one of Cole Hardwick's guns when he fell, the right-hander, but he still clutched the other in his left. It wasn't cocked, and he'd lost track of how many live cartridges it held, but he would take those problems as they came. Reaching for his Colt in its holster would betray him to the shooter who was drawing closer, step by cautious step. Price couldn't risk it yet, until he had a chance to make the move count.

He waited, taking shallow breaths and feeling blood pulse from his wounds with each heartbeat. His shirt was soaking through. Price willed the shooter to pick up his pace and make whatever move he had in mind, while Price still had the strength to fight.

Another step closer. One more. He had a picture of the shooter in his mind, faceless but solid, standing ten or fifteen feet back toward the stairs. He must've come from there, Price thought. He would've seen a gunman in the barroom or emerging from the hall that led to the backdoor. And if the shooter came downstairs, could it be—?

Rankin's voice told him, "I see you breathing, Mr. Price."

Answer or not? It was a gamble, either way. Price bit his tongue and kept quiet.

Rankin moved closer. "You can't fool me, shooter."

Keep him guessing. Breathing didn't mean a man was conscious. Price guessed it was fifty-fifty that the big man wanted eye contact before he fired the killing shot.

He felt Rankin beside him, kneeling, rolling Price to face him with a rough hand on his shoulder. It was hurtful, but he clenched his teeth and cocked the pistol in his left hand as he wedged it under Rankin's ribs.

The shot pitched Rankin backward, long arms flailing. Price sat up in time to see the last life shiver out of him. His vest was smoldering, ignited by the muzzle-blast, but blood would quench it soon. One of his boot heels tap-tap-tapped the floor until his leg went slack.

It was a struggle this time, standing up. Price threw the borrowed Colt away and gripped a chair with both hands, pulling through the pain. It seemed to take forever, but he knew it had been only seconds. He was awkward on his feet but managed somehow, shuffling past Sedge Rankin and the other corpses, down the hall and out the way he'd come.

The lamplight spilling out from Rankin's office made him hesitate. He found a small lamp on the filing cabinet and brought it back, pitching it underhand toward the barroom. It hit the floor and rolled instead of shattering, the chimney falling off. He missed the first shot with his Colt but got it on the second try, watching the pool of fire spread lazily across the hall.

Price wondered whether he could make it to the stable, much less put his saddle on the Appaloosa. The numbness spreading through his midsection might help, but it wasn't a hopeful sign. He concentrated on the simple act of walking, putting one foot down before the other. Taking one step at a time.

The waiting had become impossible. Belle had been trembling since the gunfire stopped, uncertain what it meant, afraid to speculate. She'd used up her supply of tears for this day, but her eyes still burned. She wasn't cold but couldn't stop the trembling in her arms and shoulders.

In her heart, she felt ashamed to be alive.

My fault, she thought. *It's all my fault.* Belle knew it wasn't true, but she was burdened with a weight of guilt beyond logic or common sense. Her telegram to Price had brought them here, endangered Jesse's life and sent God knows how many others to untimely graves. She didn't know if Matthew was alive or dead, but she'd been no help to him either way.

She stood and grabbed the nearest Winchester. Jared wheeled after her. "What are you doing, Belle?"

"The thing I should've done at first." She ran to make the stairs before he caught her, knowing that he couldn't follow in his chair.

"Belle, wait!" he shouted after her. "Don't go!"

"Keep Jesse home!" she called back to him, racing through the shop, past scattered stock. She didn't stop to shut the front door as she ran into the middle of the street and faced eastward.

The Nugget was on fire. Belle couldn't see the flames from where she stood, but they were flickering behind the windows and she saw smoke drifting out around the batwing doors. A crowd had formed outside the Trail's End, gawkers edging closer to the Nugget for a better view, but no one made a move to douse the fire. They would've heard the shooting, maybe watched some of it from across the street, and now they were afraid to go inside.

Belle didn't care if Rankin's place burned down. She wished the flames could leap across Main Street and take the Trail's End, too. If Rankin was inside it would be perfect, but she had to look for Matt.

She'd covered half the distance from her doorstep to the Nugget when a mounted rider came out of the livery stable, moving toward her at a steady trot.

Saddling the Appaloosa hadn't been as tough as Price had feared. He'd only fallen once, slumping to one knee in the stall, and even then it didn't hurt. He was surprised and gratified at how the pain had given up on him so easily, chewing around inside him for awhile before deciding that it didn't like his taste.

Mounting was harder, with the gunshot to his left leg and no strength to speak of in his arms, but Price succeeded on his third attempt. The Appaloosa shied and might have dumped him, but he leaned across the pommel, stroking it and whispering encouragement. When they were friends again, he flicked the reins and rode out past Cole Hardwick, past the hostler's office, to the street.

The fire had caught a fair hold on the Nugget since he'd left it. Drunks from the Trail's End stood gawking in the street, some of them pointing, others whooping rebel yells. They didn't seem to mind the loss of one saloon, as long as there was still another left in town. There seemed to be no volunteer firefighters in the crowd.

So much the better.

Tugging on the reins, he nosed the Appaloosa west and urged it to a gentle trot. The horse was barely moving when his eyes picked out a woman standing in the middle of the street, a rifle in her hands.

Price wished she hadn't come, but there was no way to avoid her now. He reined his mount in next to Belle, wishing his weary eyes would focus properly.

"You should go back inside," he said.

"I had to know." There was a tremor in her voice.

"It's done. Go home, Belle."

"Home? This isn't *home*."

"Then find it, while you can. For Jesse's sake and yours."

"Matthew—"

"We had our time," he said. "I thank you for it, for our son."

"Please wait!" She stepped in closer to him, lowering the rifle, reaching for him with her right hand. Price was too slow pulling back from her. She touched his hip, his side, and drew her hand back crimson-slick. "Oh, God!"

"It's nothing, Belle." It felt like nothing, anyway.

"I'll get the doctor, Matt. You can't go off like this!"

He gave the horse another stroke and said, "We've overstayed our welcome as it is."

"You haven't."

"Belle."

"Please, stay. At least until you're well."

"There's a right time to go."

"But Jesse—"

"Needs his folks around him now," he finished for her. "I expect he's wondering where you've gone."

Again, "Please stay."

"You know I can't. Be strong for Jesse now," he said, and spurred the Appaloosa to a trot, then to a gallop. Belle called out once more behind him. Price lifted a hand, not looking back. He let the horse take over, closed his eyes against the night and held on for dear life.

Turn the page for a special preview of Lyle Brandt's

JUSTICE GUN

Coming from Berkley Books in August 2003!

The gunman woke to pain and wondered, *Is this Hell?*

It didn't seem to hurt enough for what he'd have expected, but it wouldn't have surprised him greatly if the preachers had it wrong. He hadn't trusted them to speak of when he was alive, so why start now?

The place was hot and stuffy, but he wasn't burning. In the place of smoke and sulfur he smelled something more like trail dust, mixed with scents of leather, canvas, and the sweat of horses.

Jesus wept.

What would he do if the Hereafter was a godforsaken cattle drive?

Punch cows, what else? he thought. And hope the trail led to a friendly town, with a saloon and someone warm to wrap his arms around.

The last town had been anything but friendly, he recalled, and felt another flare of pain beneath his rib cage at the memory. He would've loved to meet the fool who

named the place Redemption. A committee could have la-
bored long and hard without arriving at a name less fitting.

Desolation, maybe. Or *Helltown.*

There was no end of names they could've chosen, but
Redemption wasn't even close.

Still, Belle had been there. And their boy. . . .

The gunman's name was Matthew Price. He knew that
much without having to think about it, even if the rest
was jumbled in his mind like swirls of campfire smoke.
He could recall the final hours in Redemption, Texas,
facing down the men who meant to kill him. Killing them
instead; so many of them that he'd given up counting and
simply concentrated on the placement of his shots.

There'd been too many of them, finally, for him to
walk away unscathed. He'd known that going in, but
there'd been no way he could turn his back on Belle,
much less the boy.

Price had left Redemption in flames, riding out of
there hell-bent for nowhere. He'd been gut-shot and
dying, no two ways about it. His one thought, after seeing Belle that last time on the street, watching her flinch
away from him with bloody hands, had been to ride as far
as possible before he toppled from the saddle or his horse
collapsed. Nobody would come looking for him in the
badlands. There'd be no pathetic ceremony, with a
preacher trying to make Price out to be something that
he'd never been. Belle and the boy in tears—or maybe
not.

And which would have been worse?

No matter, Price decided. It was over now, and all he
had to do was work out in his mind what waited for him
on the other side.

He wished the world, or whatever they called it, would
hold still and let him think a minute, though. Its slow, un-
even rocking made Price feel as if he'd lose his breakfast
any time now, but the tightness in his stomach told him
there was nothing much to lose.

Perfect, he thought. *I'm sick and sore and hungry, eating trail dust on a nag that has a hard time of it, putting one foot down behind the other.*

Now that he thought about it, though, he couldn't feel the animal between his legs. The saddle wasn't chafing his behind, and when he flexed his toes there was no pressure from the stirrups.

Where's my boots?

He shifted, stretching, and the pain came at him like a knife blade grating on his ribs. It stole his breath away and made him whimper like a child, no helping it.

And afterward, the voices.

"He's awake, I told you."

"No he's not. He made noises before."

"Not *that* noise."

"You don't know."

"Bet you a dollar."

"You don't have a dollar."

"How do you know?"

"I go through your pockets when you're sleeping."

"Do not!"

Cruel laughter. "There might be a snake in there right now, curled up and waiting from last night."

Price let his right had creep toward where the holster and his Colt Peacemaker ought to be. He wasn't sure what good the gun would do against demons, but old habits die hard.

"There's no snake in my pocket!" said one of the imps.

"Stick your hand in there and see," the other challenged.

"I'm not scared to do it."

"I don't see you moving."

"I *like* snakes. I keeps them in my pocket *all* the time."

"Pull that one out and show us, then."

A third voice, smaller—*younger?*—than the first two said, "You both talk foolish."

"Who asked you?"

Price found his hip and noted two things almost simultaneously. First, he wore no gun belt. Second, and more troubling still, he wore no pants. His fingers pinched the woolen fabric of a union suit and caught the short hair of his thigh. No pain to speak of, in comparison to that tucked underneath his ribs.

"Nobody has to ask me," said the small voice, somewhere to his right. "I see things for myself."

"'See things,' is right," one of the others answered back. "I recollect you saw a ghost the other night."

"There *could* be ghosts." Stubborn, but less assertive now.

"And if there were, you'd wet your drawers."

Laughter, seasoned with spite. Two of the imps had found a common cause against the third and left their quarrel behind.

Price turned his head, careful to take it slow and easy. Every movement cost him, but this wasn't bad. He made it slow because he didn't want them catching him and prodding him with pitchforks, or whatever imps did to the damned. If he could see them first, at least he'd know what to expect.

Price cracked one eye and saw . . . children.

They sat no more than three feet to his right, lined up like stair steps. Farthest from him was a boy of twelve or thirteen years. Beside him, closer, was a second boy, say eight or nine. The nearest of them was a girl dressed up in calico, no more than six years old. The boys wore matching denim overalls, with homespun shirts beneath.

It took a moment more for him to register that they were black.

Distracted by their argument, they didn't notice Price at first. He had a chance to look around, discovering that Hell appeared to be a covered wagon, canvas patched and sagging on the metal ribs that arched above the bed. He lay beneath a blanket, covered from his bare feet almost to his chin. Wherever his eyes settled, there were trunks or wooden crates or burlap sacks, filled up with who-knows-what. A wedge of pale sky showed out back, beyond the canvas, with the barest trace of cloud.

It was the sky that told Price he was still alive. He wasn't sure, off-hand, if that should be a disappointment or relief.

But if he wasn't dead . . .

A hiss beside him made Price wonder if they'd found the pocket snake. He turned again and found the children staring at him, silent now. The older boy looked sour, just this side of angry. Next to him, the younger boy seemed simply curious. The girl waited for Price's eyes to fall on her, then squealed and bolted from her seat.

"Momma! Daddy! White man's awake!"

Price lay and watched the two boys watching him until the wagon rumbled to a halt. He missed the Peacemaker but reckoned if these people meant him harm, they could've done most anything they wanted to while he was out. For that matter, they could've left him to the ants and buzzards wherever it was they'd picked him up.

He had no cause to fear them yet.

And anyway, it wasn't like he had much left to lose.

The little girl was coming back when someone stopped her, saying, "Essie, get on back here."

"Yessir," she replied, no argument, before a soothing older female's voice said, "It's all right, child. Just be still a minute."

Price tried sitting up to meet the man who loomed above him, but his muscles didn't seem to understand the signals coming from his brain. It wasn't pain this time, so much as weakness that defeated him. He felt as if he hadn't moved for days, joints stiff and sore. His backside felt as if the wagon bed had pressed it flat.

"Best not exert yourself too much," the stranger said, kneeling beside him so the two boys had to shift away on either side. "My missus stitched your wounds, but that one in your side is serious. The first I saw of you, I thought you might cross over. Still might, if you start to jump around."

"I don't feel much like jumping," Price replied.

"That's wise." The dark man's face was solemn, shaded by a wide-brimmed hat. His deep-set eyes were brown, a perfect complement to his complexion. Price couldn't decide if he was working on a beard without much luck, or if he simply had one of those faces that could never seem to hold a shave. "My name is Lucius Carver," he declared.

"Matt Price."

There was no blink of recognition, nothing to suggest Carver had heard the name before. So far, so good. Price tried to work his right hand out from underneath the blanket, but a big hand on his shoulder stopped him.

"We can shake another time," said Carver. "You just try and rest now, while we make some time."

"My things—"

"Are safe and sound," Carver assured him. Lowering his voice a notch, the man said, "You won't be needing guns right now, nor any of the rest, I'd say."

"I had a horse," Price said.

"Still do. Fine Appaloosa, hitched up to the tailgate right this minute. He's not going anywhere without you."

"Both need to be going," said the older of the boys.

"Hush now, Ardell. That's not a Christian way to talk."

"When did you ever see a white man act like he's a Christian, Daddy?"

Carver swiveled on his knee to face the boy. "Don't make me tell you twice."

Ardell stared past his father, eyeing Price with animosity he hadn't learned to hide. Some didn't get the knack of covering until they had more years behind them, and a handful never picked it up at all. Price guessed the boy would learn to hide his feelings or else suffer for it in the long run, since the West was by and large a white man's world.

"I need to ask you something," Carver said. "There wasn't time or opportunity before, you being on the shady side of dead and all."

"Ask it," Price said.

"This country being what it is, you find a man shot up along the trail, it raises possibilities. You still have all your hair. That makes me guess it wasn't Indians that put you down."

"It wasn't," Price agreed.

"And since you still had all your gear, along with that fine animal, I'm thinking you weren't robbed by outlaws, either."

"No."

Carver held eye contact with Price. His face was solemn, just a whisper short of grim. "That means I need to ask if you'd be running from the law yourself."

Price thought about that for a moment. There'd been no real law to speak of in Redemption when he got there, nothing but a coward with a bought-and-paid-for badge. When he rode out, even that mockery was gone. As for the townsfolk who survived, he couldn't see them forming up a posse to pursue him. They'd be occupied with funerals and the business of reordering their lives.

"Mr. Price?"

"I'm not on any posters that I know of," Price replied at last.

Carver considered that, frowning. "You strike me as a man who's made some enemies," he said, "but I guess most of them have gone to their reward."

"Such as it was," Price said.

"That's not for me to judge. I have my family to think of, though. I need your word you mean no harm to me or mine."

"A *white* man's word," Ardell protested.

"Boy!"

"He's wise to keep a wary eye on strangers, white or otherwise," Price said. He locked eyes with Ardell until the boy blinked once and turned away. "I'm in your debt. You have my promise."

"Fair enough."

Carver was on his feet. Price held him with a look and

told him, "Still and all, best thing for all concerned might be to drop me off in the next town we come across."

"That's what I had in mind," Carver replied. "I calculate a few days yet. Last town before we hit the border ought to be New Harmony. That's what we came to find."

Price knew his Texas well enough, or thought he did. He drew a blank on that one, though. The name meant nothing in the least to him.

"New Harmony?" he asked. "What's that?"

"End of the rainbow, Mr. Price," Carver replied. "That's what they're saying, anyway. I've got my fingers crossed."

He went back to the wagon seat, and in another moment they were rocking on their way. Price closed his eyes, letting the children watch him if they wanted to. He guessed they'd tire of it before much longer, with the possible exception of Ardell.

New Harmony.

Price wondered if it was another town misnamed by wishful thinking, wondered where it was and what he'd find there.

Wondered why he wasn't dead.

Short moments later, he could feel the wagon's motion and his bone-deep weariness combine to bring the darkness on again. Price gave himself up to it, with a silent hope that he be spared from dreams.